THE ALCHEMIST'S TOUCH

A BOOK OF UNDERREALM

GARRETT ROBINSON

THE ALCHEMIST'S TOUCH
Garrett Robinson

The author greatly appreciates you taking the time to read his work. Please leave a review wherever you bought the book or on Goodreads.com.

Interior Design: Legacy Books, Inc.
Publisher: Legacy Books, Inc.
Editors: Karen Conlin, Cassie Dean
Cover Artist: Miguel Mercado

1. Fantasy - Epic 2. Fantasy - Dark 3. Fantasy - New Adult

Second Edition

Published by Legacy Books

To my family
Who make everything I do better

To Johnny, Sean and Dave
Who told me to write

To Amy
Who is endlessly patient (though I don't deserve it)

And to everyone who followed me
from the Birchwood to the Academy

You have made my life epic.

I hope I can enrich yours.

GET MORE

Legacy Books is home to the very best that fantasy has to offer.

Join our email alerts list, and we'll send word whenever we release a new book. You'll receive exclusive updates and see behind the scenes as we create them.

(You'll also learn the secrets that make great fantasy books, *great.*)

Interested? Visit this link:

Underrealm.net/Join

For maps of the locations in this book, visit:

Underrealm.net/maps

THE BOOKS OF UNDERREALM

THE NIGHTBLADE EPIC
NIGHTBLADE
MYSTIC
DARKFIRE
SHADEBORN
WEREMAGE
YERRIN

THE ACADEMY JOURNALS
THE ALCHEMIST'S TOUCH
THE MINDMAGE'S WRATH
THE FIREMAGE'S VENGEANCE

CHRONOLOGICAL ORDER
NIGHTBLADE
MYSTIC
DARKFIRE
SHADEBORN
THE ALCHEMIST'S TOUCH
THE MINDMAGE'S WRATH
WEREMAGE
THE FIREMAGE'S VENGEANCE
YERRIN

THE ALCHEMIST'S TOUCH

A BOOK OF UNDERREALM

GARRETT ROBINSON

ONE

THERE WAS A BLUE DOOR ACROSS THE STREET FROM the tavern, and no matter how hard he tried, Ebon could not stop himself from looking back to it every few moments.

To an unknowing observer, there was little to mark the door as special. Unadorned wood, painted blue, with a simple iron latch and no ornamentation. But everyone knew what lay behind it. Ebon did, certainly, and so his attention returned there, his gaze passing across it as if by chance before returning to the cup of wine in his hand.

It was easier to look at the blue door than around

the common room of the inn where no customer would sit at his table. Indeed, they even avoided the tables next to his. Often Ebon felt the weight of a curious gaze upon him, yet when he tried to meet it the observer would turn away quickly, as though afraid of being caught. Only Tamen, sitting opposite, would look at him openly. But Tamen had nothing to fear from Ebon. Rather, it was the reverse.

It struck Ebon as a cruel joke. At home, he often had only a single wish: to be left alone. The wish was rarely granted. But now he would have given much for any companionship aside from Tamen's—and mayhap one type of companionship in particular.

His eyes darted away from the blue door again.

"The High King's Seat," he said, and drank from his cup. It was his third, or fourth, and a tightness had begun to form behind his eyes. "Long have I wished to see it, and yet now I wish they had never brought me."

Tamen did not answer. He only took a sip from his own drink, though it was much gentler than Ebon's swig.

"Mayhap I am greedy," said Ebon. "I wish for too much. Father has made it plain that I shall never attend the Academy. Yet still, when he told me I would accompany him to the Seat . . . still I held out hope."

The tavern was a bit quieter for a moment. Tamen's eyes flicked to one side, and then the other. "Mayhap it would be wise for you to speak more softly."

Ebon sighed and leaned back. "Wise. Who has ever called me wise, Tamen? If I were wise, I would be in the Academy. Or mayhap if I were in the Academy, they would call me wise. I feel it sitting there. Do you remember? We passed it in our carriage when we arrived. Straight past its wide front doors we drove, and then it was gone. Yet the place where it stands is forever burned in my memory. I feel that even after Father takes me home, I will be able to point to it."

"A sorrowful state of affairs indeed." But Tamen's words were accompanied by a rolling of the eyes, and Ebon knew the man grew weary of complaints.

Tamen was his retainer in name, but certainly not his friend. Not truly. Ebon knew the man's real purpose: a guard. If ever Ebon strayed from his father's wishes, thought to defy the will of his parents, Tamen would carry word of his misdeeds straight to them. He had done so often in the past. And then again, other times he had held his tongue. Ebon never knew which would happen on a given day.

His eyes strayed across the blue door before returning to his cup. He drank again. Did he wish to be left alone or not? Just now, he could not decide.

"What would my father say, were I to go to him and ask to see the Academy? Not to attend, but only to see it for myself. It would allow me to return home with some glimmer of a dream, some memory of the place I have longed for since I was a child. Would he deny me so small a thing?"

"Yes," said Tamen. It sounded as though there might be more to follow, but he left it at that.

Ebon nodded. "Of course he would. My father is not one to grant trivial boons. No doubt even my presence at this tavern would strike him as trivial. 'Stand your lazy self, whelp,' he might say, as he likes to do, before commanding me to return home."

Again Tamen looked about the room, and this time his eyes flashed anxiously. "Keep your voice down."

Ebon sagged back in his chair. A spark of defiance flared in him, but he quickly extinguished it. What could he do? Make Tamen uncomfortable? Then the retainer would only speak to Ebon's father, and then Ebon might not be allowed to leave his room for a month. Mayhap longer. The vindictive will of Shay Drayden knew little of restraint.

He realized he was staring at the blue door and quickly turned away.

"I thought the Seat would be different," he muttered. "Not—not better, I suppose. But different. I thought that upon its streets, or in such a place as this, I might meet some chance stranger who would speak to me in ignorance of where I come from. Yet everyone here fears to sit beside me. They fear to sit within arm's reach. It is as though they can smell my family name upon me. Who here will even look towards our table? Even now, when I speak too loud because I have drunk too much wine?"

Several heads turned away from him, as though their owners knew they had been caught staring.

This time Tamen smirked. "At last you speak the

truth. You *have* had too much wine. Mayhap it is time to think of turning our steps towards the manor . . . unless you have some other reason to remain."

This time it was Tamen who glanced towards the blue door.

Ebon's heart skipped a beat. But he would not let himself dwell on the thought that sprang to mind. Mayhap Tamen was hinting towards something, and mayhap not. Hope could be a cruel thing once taken away. Instead he leaned forwards, cupping his wine tighter and taking still another pull from it. Tamen leaned in to hear his murmur.

"Will my life always be this way, Tamen? Tell me true."

"You have asked me this before. How would you like me to answer this time?"

"Never does he turn his wrath on Albi. He looks at her as though her eyes are the moons. Yet we are almost of an age."

"Almost of an age. But not quite. And she is not the eldest child."

"Nor was I, once. Yet my life was the same even then. Shall I never be free of his scorn?"

Tamen pursed his lips and took a small sip of wine. "This may be of small comfort to you, but no one lives forever."

Ebon's jaw clenched, and he leaned away while draining the last of his cup. "That is a dark thought. You should not have said it."

Tamen shrugged and finished his own drink. "I mean no ill intent, and you know it. It is a truth none can ignore—neither the High King upon her throne, nor the wealthiest of merchants, nor the poorest beggar upon the Seat. Now, I would ask if you wish for more wine, but I think that would be very unwise."

"I would give anything not to be my father's son," whispered Ebon. He had not meant to say the words aloud, and he caught Tamen's eyes widening. But he would not shy away now. He pressed his fingers into the rough wood of the tabletop. "It is the truth. You know you would not trade places with me. Who would? Anyone who would desire my place thinks only of our family's riches. They spare no thought for the family itself."

Tamen stood abruptly. "We have been here too long, and you have drunk far too much. We must leave at once. Speak no more, or I will repeat your words."

Ebon grasped his hand, holding him in place. "Tamen, stop. Stop, I beg of you. I am sorry. My tongue runs too freely, it is true. Only . . . only this is unbearable. I know I cannot go to the Academy. But I . . . I only wish, for just a little while, that I could pretend I am not of the family Drayden. Can you find no pity in your heart for that?"

Tamen paused, and though his lips were pressed tightly together, Ebon thought he saw something soften in the man's eyes. He peeled Ebon's fingers away from his wrist.

"Mayhap I can find pity. But do not speak of it out loud. If you do, pity will not be enough to stay my tongue—and your father will not judge such talk lightly."

"Thank you," whispered Ebon.

Tamen leaned forwards over the table and fixed Ebon's gaze with his own. "Do you wish it in truth? To pretend you are not a Drayden?"

Ebon drew back, confused. "You know I do."

"Then follow your wandering eyes. They have rested often enough upon the blue door. Go there for a little while."

Ebon found his throat was suddenly dry. He wiped sweaty palms on the golden silk of his tunic. "You mock me. I tell you this trip is more pain than pleasure, and you mock me by dangling a wish before my eyes."

"Why would I mock you?"

"You would tell them. You would have to."

Tamen shrugged. "Why should I? There is no harm in such a thing. You may not believe me, Ebon, but I take no pleasure in the service I provide your parents. I am paid well, and so I do my duty. But I think this might be good for you. And for at least a moment, it might give pause to your endless whining. So I shall turn the other way—but just this once, do you understand?"

Ebon saw no hint of a lie in Tamen's eyes. He wanted to believe it. But how could he? How often had Tamen carried tales of his misdeeds straight to the ears of his father?

Yet never before had Tamen promised to keep such a thing secret.

His stomach did a turn. Darkness take them all. Even if Tamen did spread the tale afterwards, what could Ebon's father do? Lock Ebon up in his room—again? He might do that for any perceived offense. And yet Ebon would still have one happy memory of the Seat. No punishment could take that away.

He rose from his table and reached for his purse.

"Keep it," said Tamen, waving him off. "My coin is enough for these drinks, and you will need yours."

Ebon swallowed hard as he took the man's meaning. He turned to go, and the tavern's denizens turned their faces away as he passed into the night.

TWO

THE DOOR'S LATCH LIFTED LIKE A FEATHER, AND IT swung inward on well-oiled hinges that gave no sound. A heady fragrance rushed out to greet Ebon, nearly stopping him in his tracks. He could pick out fine, exotic perfumes from Calentin as well more familiar ones from his homeland of Idris; the unmistakable scent of Wadeland tea together with the cinnamon wine of Hedgemond. And under it all there was something sweeter, pungent but light, something that stirred his heart within his breast.

His knees had begun to shake. He forced them to

move again and stepped across the threshold before his nerves ran out.

Here the lights were dim, even dimmer than they had been in the tavern. But the darkness seemed warm and comforting, inviting rather than ominous. Partly that was thanks to the fine music that floated on the air, the steady plucking of a harp that teased his ears like a whisper at midnight.

He turned to find the source of the sound and saw a harpist in the corner. One of the room's few lamps sat just beside her on a table, so that it looked as if it had been placed just to illuminate her. As he saw her clothes and the shape of her face, he realized with a start that she was a woman of Idris. But the light brown of her braided hair was rare in his homeland, as were her hazel eyes that glowed from the lantern.

Those eyes captured him for a moment as she met his gaze, though her fingers never faltered where they plucked at the strings. Ebon gulped and looked away before she thought he was staring, but he could not entirely turn from her. Instead he looked down, taking in her clothing. It was of a familiar cut, but he did not think he had seen anyone at home wear it quite so well. Her feet were bare upon the floor, resting against the harp's wooden base. He looked upon them for a moment and blushed before he could finally tear his gaze from her.

It was not until then that he realized there were many other figures in the room, men and women, all of them draped across chairs and couches that ran along the walls. Some studied him with curious little smiles, while others let their attention wander. Ebon gripped his trouser legs tightly as he realized that many of them were only half-clothed, and some less than that. Suddenly he did not know where to look, and his eyes darted wildly back and forth. But he was rescued as the house's matron arrived, smiling as she came to him.

"Good evening, young sir. How may the house ease you this evening?"

Ebon found that his tongue suddenly refused to work. As he tried to force the words out, he fumbled at his purse before finally producing a gold weight. "I have coin."

The matron's smile widened in amusement, but she was quick to take the coin from his trembling fingers. "Thank you. Is there any sort of girl you would prefer?"

He knew his face was the color of a beet. He looked down at his fine shoes and then around the room. He could scarcely see any of the figures in the dimness, a fact not helped by the fact that spots of light now danced before his eyes. He thought he might faint. From the corner of his eye he saw the harpist grinning, though she tried to hide it.

The matron seemed to misunderstand. "My apologies if I have made an assumption. Of course we have many fine men as well. I only meant to ask if you preferred a certain type of companion."

Ebon nearly choked. He shook his head quickly, but words would not come.

Her head tilted back slightly, and her eyes softened. "Ah. I may understand. Is this your first time, young sir?" At his shaky nod, she went on. "Your first time at a house of lovers, or . . .?"

"I have not—that is, I have never—"

She stilled him with a hand on his arm. "Forgive me for not realizing it at once. Worry not. We have some experience with such things, after all. But it is important that you know there are rules—very strict rules indeed, and behind them lies the weight of the High King's harshest law."

"I have heard something of them," mumbled Ebon.

She patted his hand. "Somehow I do not worry that you will break them. But I will tell you the most important one regardless: always you must obey the words of your lover. Only if you gainsay them, or act against their command, will you have anything to fear. Now, then. Would you prefer a recommendation? Sometimes that makes it easier."

Ebon hesitated, for in truth he had no idea how to answer her. His gaze wandered again and fell upon the harpist. She now looked demurely at the floor. But the matron seemed to catch his mind.

"Adara," she called out.

The girl's fingers ceased on the harp at once, and she rose from her chair. One of the men in the shadows took her place, and soon the chords rang out once more—though Ebon thought they were not quite as sweet, and he wondered if that was only his imagination.

As Adara approached him, it seemed that her beauty was magnified many times over. The sway of her walk stirred him in ways he was not overly familiar with, and she did not break his gaze, so that he found he could not look away. She said nothing when she reached him, but only took his hand and drew him towards the back of the room, where a blue silk curtain hung across a small doorway.

Beyond was a hallway that stretched in both directions. She took him left, and then around a bend that turned right, finally coming to a halt before a wide door. Ebon was thankful it was wooden, and looked thick—he had feared it might be open, or covered only by a sheer curtain. Adara lifted the latch and drew him inside, and then closed it behind them both with a soft *click*.

The room was well-lit, far better than the entry had been. Fine crafts sat upon shelves and chests of drawers, pots and urns worked in fine clay with handles wrapped in gold. But of course, Ebon's eyes were drawn to the bed that dominated the space. Its coverings looked even finer than those in his own room back home, though his came from all the considerable coin of his family. And this bed's legs looked far, far sturdier.

"You may sit," said Adara, waving a hand towards

the bed. Ebon blinked for a moment before hastening to do as she said. He perched upon the edge of the bed and tried to find something sensible to do with his hands.

She smiled and shook her head. It made her braid sway back and forth, and he found himself captivated by her hair again. "That was no command. You will know a command if you hear it, though I do not suspect I shall have that need."

"Ah. Yes, I . . . thank you," said Ebon, immediately thinking that that was a stupid thing to say.

"Would you like some wine? It can bolster the nerves."

"Sky above, yes," said Ebon, never wanting anything so badly.

A fine golden pitcher sat next to goblets of silver, and Adara filled them both—though Ebon noted she filled one almost to the brim, and that was the one she placed in his hand. He drank greedily, recognizing the taste of cinnamon. He did not often care for cinnamon wine, but just now it seemed the finest thing he had ever drank.

Soon his cup was empty, and Adara took it gently to put on one of the tables beside the bed. Then she sat next to him, making the bed shift gently. He fought a sudden urge to edge away from her, wondering where it came from—especially since the greater part of him wanted nothing more than to move closer.

He realized she had not taken her eyes from his

face, and he forced himself to meet her gaze again. She was not smiling, but neither did she look displeased. She looked only curious, as though she longed to know what he was thinking. Sure enough, she spoke at last. "Why have you come here tonight?"

Ebon gave a quick chuckle. "I should think that would be obvious. Why do most step within the blue door?"

"You know I mean more than that."

He looked at her askance, as his mind went to his words with Tamen. Yet she could not possibly know of that, or where he came from, or what drove him here.

To distract himself as well as her, he changed the subject. "Would you not you like to know my name first, at least?"

"If you wish me to know it."

"It would not displease me."

"Then?"

"I am Ebon."

"Ebon. And have you a family, Ebon? Or are you a bastard?"

His nostrils flared for a moment. "I am a trueborn son."

Adara arched an eyebrow. "You speak as if it were some great shame to be a bastard. I take It you are from Idris, then?"

"And are you from elsewhere? You have the look of the women from my kingdom."

"My parents left there when I was very young. I

was raised in Dorsea, where it is nothing special to be a trueborn child. Indeed, I think only Idris clings to the ancient tradition which shames bastards."

Ebon blew out a slow breath through his nose. "I am sorry. I did not mean to seem so . . . prickly."

That made her smile, and his heart warmed to see it. "Worry not. But also answer my question. You seem to think I shall forget it, but I will not. What drove you to open the blue door tonight, Ebon?"

You came here to forget you were a Drayden, at least for a while. He bit back the words on his tongue, though he wanted to tell her the truth. Yet what if she told others? It would not do for word to reach his father that he had visited a house of lovers. His wrath would be terrible.

Darkness take my father.

"I am here because I do not wish to be anywhere else. Wherever I go, I am my father's son, and none will let me forget it—him least of all. He has brought me here to the Seat, where I have long wished to go, and yet what can I do here? I remain in my room all day, only slipping out into the city when my mother tells me to do so and tells my retainer not to breathe a word of it to Father. Yet I cannot visit the Academy as I wish, for then he would hear of it, and I cannot even go to a tavern without its patrons refusing to sit with me, or speak with me, or even be within arm's reach. It is as though I walk draped in the curse of being a Drayden—"

He stopped short, looking at her in fear. But Adara shook her head gently and took his hand.

"I had guessed it already. Anyone in the front room would have known it at a glance. You need not trouble yourself. There are laws that you must follow while you are here, but we have our own code that we shall not break. No one will speak of your presence."

A great breath rushed from him, and in his relief it took him a long moment to realize that she still held his hand. Now she turned it over, its palm facing up, and she traced one nail across the lines of it. It sent a prickling feeling up his arm and into his chest, where it stayed and mingled with the comfortable warmth of the wine.

"You said you wish to visit the Academy," she said softly. "Why?"

"I have wished to go to the Academy since I was a child, and they discovered I have the gift."

Her eyes turned sharply towards his, and he saw a spark of excitement within them. "Are you a wizard?"

"An alchemist," he mumbled, blushing now for an entirely new reason. She looked at him as though he were some great champion of war. "But only by virtue of my gift. I have no training. I can do nothing."

She pouted. "You cannot show me even some simple spell? I should greatly love to see it."

He looked around. "Have you any water? I know only one spell—the one with which they test children, to see if they have the gift in the first place."

"I have no water. Only wine."

"I can do nothing with wine. I am sorry."

She smiled. "Then the next time you come, I will be certain to have water ready for you."

He looked down at his lap. "I shall not come here again. My family returns to Idris soon, and they will take me with them. But I would come if I could."

Her hand met his cheek, and she lifted his head until he looked into her eyes once again. Time seemed to slow for a moment, and he could hear his heartbeat thundering in his chest.

"Nothing is certain. If you have come here to forget your life outside these walls, then let us have a dream together: you, that you can stay upon the Seat; and I, that you will visit me again."

He forced himself to laugh. "Those are pretty words indeed. I thank you for them, though I know you must be bound to say what I wish to hear."

She caught his meaning, and her eyes took on a wry twist. "You think I mean to flatter you? I do not. Some lovers would do anything to please their partners. I am not one such. If I tell you something, for good or for ill, I mean it. That is one promise I will make now, and keep always."

A voice at the back of his mind told him that even those words were a lie, and yet Ebon believed her. And now she was so close that her breath washed sweetly across his face, and he drank it in, even as his hands rose of their own accord, and she pulled him closer to kiss him.

A short time later, they lay together beneath the satin sheets as Ebon fought to reclaim his breath. Adara was curled up beneath his arm, her head laying on his shoulder, her braid now undone to let her hair spill across his meager chest.

"You must tell me," he said between heaving breaths. "Was I any good?"

"Not at all," she said, stretching up to kiss him. "But that is all right, for we have our dream. And in it, you will keep coming to see me—and mayhap, one day, practice will see you perfect."

THREE

HE WOKE WITH A TERRIBLE HEADACHE AND THE URGE to vomit. Soon it grew too strong to ignore, and he fell from his bed to crawl for the chamber pot. Twice he retched, his face growing red. Then at last it poured out, thick and purple, full of the wine from the night before.

When it was over he rested for a moment, leaning his forehead on the chamber pot's chilly rim. At last he raised his head and looked around. The sight of his own room in the Drayden manor somewhat surprised him.

He remembered Adara—remembered her in vivid, lurid detail that even now made his stomach turn in knots—and he vaguely recalled leaving the house of lovers. He remembered returning to the tavern and ordering another flagon of wine. And there the memory faded.

The door opened without a knock, and Tamen came in with a warm, wet towel. He began to scrub flecks of vomit from Ebon's lips.

"I am fine, Tamen," said Ebon. But he put the lie to his words by clutching his forehead, where an iron spike seemed to be trying to burst from his skull.

"Of course you are," said Tamen, raising an eyebrow. He helped Ebon up and back to his bed, covering him with a sheet for decency. "I shall fetch some tea and empty your chamber pot before the whole manor smells of your insides."

He closed the door just a little too hard. Ebon winced at the sharp sound. Then he could do nothing but wait, until the door reopened at last and Tamen came to sit by his bedside.

"Here." With small brass tongs he held out a lump of sugar, which Ebon put on his tongue. Then from a saucer he served the green tea, not too hot, and Ebon groaned as its warmth filled him.

"Thank you," Ebon croaked, relaxing back into his pillows.

"You are only halfway to a cure. Now you must eat."

"Food is the last thing my stomach desires just now."

"And the first thing it needs."

"Leave me be, just a moment, I beg you." Ebon threw his head under the pillow to shield it from the sunlight coming through the window.

"I will not leave while you might still retch again. But I suppose I can guess from your current state that you enjoyed your evening?"

Beneath his pillow, Ebon could not keep a small smile from playing across his lips. "You cannot tell me I said nothing of it when I returned to the tavern."

He peeked out from his covers. A smirk tugged at Tamen's lips, and the man's eyes held a knowing glint. "You could barely speak. I have seen you drunk often enough, but not like that. It was all I could do to get you home."

Ebon's heart froze. "Tell me that my parents were not awake to witness it."

"Do you think I would have let them? Then their wrath would have fallen on me, not you. But they stayed at the palace late last night, and have returned there already this morning. You slept through their entire presence here."

That made him shoot up from beneath the pillow. He regretted the sudden motion at once. His hand went to his forehead with a sharp groan. "How long did you say they have been waiting? They must have risen early."

"Hardly. It is nearly time for midday's meal. You have slept long."

Ebon slumped back upon his pillows with a groan. He still did not know why his parents had brought him here. He hardly saw them, even to eat together. Why bring him just so that he could stay in the manor all day? If they had left him in Idris, at least he would have been free from Father for a time, with Albi for company.

He knew better than to voice these complaints to Tamen, of course. But at the thought of his sister, he lifted a weak hand. "Fetch me a quill and parchment. I should write to Albi."

But the retainer only folded his arms. "For what purpose? You will return soon, and then she will be alone no longer."

"We are to leave the Seat?"

Tamen rolled his eyes, as though it were Ebon's fault that his parents never informed him of such things. "As soon as they have concluded their business at the palace, which, sky willing, should be today."

Ebon's hand closed in a fist, scrunching his bed sheets. He forced himself to relax. "Then this trip was truly a waste. More than a week holed up in the manor, and for no purpose. My father—"

He bit the words off at once. *My father's cruel joke is complete,* he had almost said. But that would pass from Tamen's ears straight to his parents.

The retainer tilted his head as if curious, though he

must have known that Ebon's next words would not have been courteous. "Do not regret your journey here too strongly. Just think: if you had been left home, a certain . . . opportunity would never have presented itself."

Ebon flushed. When he returned home and told Albi of the High King's Seat, last night would be one part of the story he would certainly leave out. But then a thought struck him. Had Tamen's leniency been at the command of Ebon's parents?

He dismissed the notion at once. They could have had no purpose for doing so. His father would never be so generous. Ebon's mother would sometimes grant him little boons, when she thought his father might not see it, but a visit to a house of lovers seemed a step quite too far.

Out loud, he said only, "I wish I were not going to be dragged off home again."

This time Tamen could not stop a wide grin, though he quickly hid it. "Still thinking of the blue door? Goodness. You must have had quite the time."

Ebon felt a mighty need to steer the conversation in another direction. "I should get dressed. Fetch me some clothes."

"Very well." Tamen rose, and from a cabinet by the window he produced a suit of fine yellow silk, tailored like all of Ebon's clothes to hug his thin frame. "But do not fret overmuch. One day, when you are head of the household, you can return to the Seat. The blue door will still be there."

"As will the Academy," said Ebon. "Mayhap I shall even enroll in studies."

Tamen snorted. "Forgive me if I am blunt, but that is a ridiculous thought. Children are expected to begin in their tenth year. If fate is kind to your father, you will not be head of the household until you have nearly reached your fortieth."

Ebon glared as the retainer laid his outfit at the foot of the bed. "I shall have no one to gainsay me. I could do whatever I wished."

Tamen turned sharply, throwing down the trousers in his hand. They fell in a rumpled heap atop the rest of the clothes. "No, Ebon, you could not. Even you are not so foolish. You will have responsibilities then, to your sister and to the rest of the family. Would you abandon that responsibility? I know you have no great love for our kin, but you should think at least of Albi."

"She could take charge in my stead. Indeed, I would welcome the shedding of that burden."

"Albi is not being groomed for the position."

Ebon spread his hands in a helpless gesture. "What grooming has my father given me, Tamen? I am forbidden from our trade meetings. I am forbidden from speaking to any members of the other merchant families. I have never even seen a member of the royal family. How does he expect me to step full-formed into his shoes, when I do not have the faintest knowledge of the leagues they have walked already?"

"And Albi? Could she manage better than you? I imagine she could do a fine job of directing a caravan, if pressed to it, and if she were surrounded by a staff of those who knew most of her business for her. But she has received no instruction in such matters. You at least know something of the family's trade routes, our goods and services, and the relationships your aunt has worked hard to build across the nine kingdoms."

Ebon turned away. He wanted to shout, but Tamen was only an instrument, not the object of his wrath. The retainer's words were not his own, but came from Ebon's parents. Ebon wondered if Tamen believed them himself, or if he even cared.

In any case, the man's words were carefully chosen, for they reminded Ebon of his aunt Halab. Where Ebon's father was cruel at every opportunity, Halab had always treated Ebon with courtesy and respect, and mayhap even affection. In her presence, even Ebon's father seemed less harsh, less cruel, as though he did not wish to shame himself with ill conduct before his sister.

Yet still Ebon shied away at the thought of one day replacing his father. "Never do I wish to be involved in our family's trade," he muttered.

"Sky above," said Tamen, eyes widening in false shock. "Does the world exist to grant our wishes? If I had known that, I would have asked to be born a royal son."

There was a knock at the door. Ebon cocked his

head at Tamen, but the man only shrugged. "Come," said Ebon.

It opened to reveal Mako. Ebon tensed, and Tamen grew very still.

Tall and very broad, but wiry, Mako was clad in a tunic of light grey, with sleeves to the elbows that revealed the designs tattooed on his forearms. Over that he wore a short jerkin of black leather. His trousers, too, were black, clasped at the waist by a belt with a silver buckle, and upon that belt hung a long and wicked dagger. His hair was cut so short it was almost stubble, and his hairline on both sides swooped up and away from his brows. Though his eyes often twinkled as though at some hidden joke, they were hard as steel, and couched in a face painted by many scars. Mako was in the service of the family, and though Ebon was not certain, he thought the man reported directly to Halab herself. He seemed to go from household to household, bringing messages and doing whatever might be required of him. But the simplicity of his duties did not hide the danger he wore about him like a cloak.

Now he strode into Ebon's room with a smile, and the smile widened as he hooked both thumbs through his belt. Though Ebon was still covered by a sheet, he felt utterly naked before Mako's keen gaze, and he had to fight the urge to cover himself. Then Mako took a deep sniff.

"A good morrow—or midday, as it were. And how fares the family Drayden's newest full-grown man?"

Ebon's eyes widened, panic seizing his throat. He shot a fearful look at Tamen, but the retainer shook his head.

"I said nothing."

Mako burst into laughter, a deep, ringing peal that surely thundered through all the halls of the manor. He bent partway over to lock gazes as though Ebon were a child, and then he slapped a hand against the leather pants that tightly gripped his legs. The sound of it made Ebon flinch.

"Sky above, the looks upon both of your faces are priceless. Fear not, little Ebon. I did not need any words from Tamen to smell the scent of your lovemaking. "Sky above, the looks upon both of your faces are priceless. Fear not, little Ebon. I did not need any words from Tamen to smell the scent of your lovemaking. It is so strong that I imagine I could find the woman herself if I visited enough lovers upon the Seat."

"I . . . you are wrong," said Ebon, aware of just how weak his voice sounded.

Mako's chuckles died away, but they left behind his wide, toothy grin. "Save your terrified looks, little goldbag. If you fear I will tell your father of your—shall we call it an indiscretion?—then worry not. I have no interest in petty scandals."

"I say again, you are—"

Mako chopped a hand through the air, and Ebon's words died upon his lips. "I told you I will say nothing.

And I did not come to sniff between your legs. Your mother and father require you for midday's meal."

"They sent you to summon me for a meal?"

Mako shrugged, his smile never leaving him. "And why not? I was to hand. I do not hold so high an opinion of myself that I cannot deliver a message."

So saying, he turned and left as quickly as he had come. Tamen went to the door and closed it, throwing the latch in place.

"Come, Ebon. You must ready yourself for the meal. And whatever else you can say about that man, he is right—we must wash that smell off you before you get within ten paces of your parents."

FOUR

TAMEN HAD A STEWARD FILL A BATH, THOUGH THEY had no time to heat it. Ebon shivered in the water, cold and brackish, drawn from the Great Bay. He spit it out quickly whenever it touched his tongue, despising the salty taste of it.

"Hurry, Ebon," said Tamen. "You know better than to keep your father waiting."

"I can scarcely move faster than I am." Ebon's voice came harsher than he intended, and thick with fear.

"Then this will have to do."

He leaped from the tub and began to dry himself.

Tamen fetched some perfume and splashed it at his neck, his underarms, and his wrists.

"That is too much!" said Ebon. "I smell like a chemist!"

"Sky above, stop your bleating," said Tamen. He made a halfhearted attempt to swipe some of it off with a washcloth.

"Forget it. I must go anyway. My clothes!"

Tamen helped him dress in haste, shaking his head at Ebon's anxiety. But Tamen did not have to fear whatever capricious punishment Father would inflict if Ebon was late.

Soon he was running through the manor towards the dining hall. Fine tapestries fluttered on the walls in the wind of his passing, and he nearly bowled over the servants Liya and Ruba, who were dusting fine suits of armor mounted on stands. They cried out after him, but Ebon barely managed to call out "I am sorry!" as he fled.

He burst into the dining hall much faster than he had meant to, and the door flew around to slam into the stone wall behind it. Ebon froze on the threshold. His parents, Hesta and Shay, looked up sharply from the table, where they had already begun to eat.

"Did you have to run across all the nine lands to get here?" Though Ebon's father did not raise his voice, disdain dripped from each word, like rainwater sliding down the tiled roofs of home.

"I am sorry, Father," said Ebon, breathing hard. "I was in the garden when—"

But his father had already turned away to resume conversing with his mother. Ebon lowered his head, cheeks burning, and approached the table. A servant pulled out a chair. As he sat and scooted closer to the table, Ebon tried to edge away from where his father sat. But both his parents turned to him, eyes wide, and his father's lips curled with scorn.

"You smell like every courtesan on the Seat took a shit on you at once. Sit at the other end of the table before your stench makes me retch."

"Shay," said Hesta gently. Ebon's father shut his mouth with a sharp *click* of teeth and turned away.

Ebon rose hastily to follow the command. He did not sit opposite his father—that would no doubt be seen as a great slight, trying to claim the other end of the table. Instead he took the chair just to the left. A servant ran to put a plate of food before him, with seared pork and some strange vegetables he did not recognize. Ebon ignored the vegetables and tore into the meat, his stomach growling loudly. Almost from the moment the greasy meat touched his lips, he could feel his headache subsiding, and he sighed gratefully.

He glanced up towards the other end of the table, where his father was now complaining about some perceived slight he had suffered at the High King's palace. But Hesta very nearly ignored him, and instead looked at Ebon curiously. As her eyes played across his face, her brows raised slightly. Ebon ducked his gaze to focus on the meal.

Did she know? Could she see it somehow, or sense it in him? He dismissed the thought as ridiculous. Yet from the corner of his eye he could still see her studying him, only turning away to give his father cursory nods and sympathetic sounds at the most appropriate times. But then Shay's complaints grew in volume and energy, and Hesta finally turned to give him her full attention. Ebon vented a long sigh of relief.

His anxiety at his mother's lingering look turned his thoughts back to Adara. When he thought of the night before, he flushed. He could still see the light hazel of her eyes, feel her nails scraping his skin. He could almost sense the way she had—

Ebon had to shift in his seat. He found his attention dragged back to the conversation with his father as Shay raised his voice.

"The audacity she has, to keep us waiting for four days now, without *deigning* to grant us so much as a firm appointment."

"She is the High King, and we must serve at her pleasure," said Hesta, but her tone spoke only of full agreement with her husband.

"She is an arrogant sow."

Ebon's gaze jerked up at that, and even the servants standing at the edges of the room tensed. Shay ignored them all, while Hesta patted his hand reassuringly. He tore into his meal again, as though he had run out of fuel for the bitter fire that burned in his gut. The peace lasted only a moment, and then he slammed his cup on the table. "Wine!"

A servant scurried to obey. Ebon shook his head—slightly, so that his father could not see—and let his mind wander. His gaze fell upon the room's eastern wall, which was comprised entirely of glass doors that were now open. Through them he looked out across the Great Bay and its far reaches that vanished beyond the horizon. He had sailed those waters to get here, and would sail them again to return. It would be any day now, he imagined, unless his father extended the trip until they could meet with the High King.

Ebon would return to Idris, never having set foot inside the Academy. One day even the Seat would fade to a distant memory, until he could scarcely remember the manor where he now sat. Once again he found himself wondering why they had brought him in the first place.

Was the suspicion of his innermost heart right? Was this all some cruel new torture by his father? To dangle the Seat before Ebon, only to rip him away just as he began to love it? Then, for years to come, he could torment Ebon with the memory. *Do as you are told, boy, if you ever wish to return to the Seat,* he might say. *Speaking to a royal, were you? I had thought to take you to the Seat with me the next time I went, but you seem determined to prove yourself unworthy of that honor.* No doubt his father could come up with a thousand ways to phrase the same threat.

And though Ebon knew it was foolish, the most painful thought of all was that he might never again see the blue door. Or that if he did, in some far future year, he would not find a pair of hazel eyes behind it, waiting for him.

His mind was drawn back to the present as the hall's door clicked and swung open. Ebon looked curiously over his shoulder—and then he shoved back his chair, leaping to his feet with a cry of surprise. His aunt Halab strode through the doors, long golden dress sweeping behind her across the floor. Her hair, intricately braided and wrapped about her head like a crown, bobbed with each step, and she took them all in with sharp, dark eyes. Ebon's parents rose quickly in respect.

"Sister," grumbled Shay, stepping away from the table.

Halab went to him, and he kissed her cheeks before bending for her to kiss his forehead. Hesta came forwards more eagerly and wrapped Halab in a warm embrace.

"Sister," said Halab. Then she released Hesta and came straight to Ebon. He straightened with a smile as Halab stopped less than a pace away. "And look at you, darling nephew. You are a man now, and no mistake."

For a moment he quailed, for in his mind the words held another meaning. But he shook the thought away quickly—Halab had not seen him in more than half a year, and he had grown taller since then. He stepped forwards to kiss her cheeks, but she pulled him into a hug instead.

"None of that formality. My heart sings to see you."

"And you, Aunt." Then, just for courtesy's sake, he kissed her cheeks all the same.

"You are never lacking in charm. May I join you all for your meal?"

"Of course," said Shay brusquely. Quickly he went to scoop up his plate and move it to the next seat, and Halab sat at the head of the table. Ebon returned to his seat at the other end, but Halab stopped him with a sharp word.

"Nephew. What are you doing all the long way down there? Surely you were not banished for anything so trivial as the perfume you doused yourself in?"

Ebon froze, unsure of how to answer. He knew better than to speak ill of his father, especially with the man right there to hear it. But Shay spoke first, saving him from the dilemma. "He stinks worse than the palace."

"Yet family is family," said Halab. "Come, sit beside your mother, so that you may be as far from your father's delicate nose as may be."

Still uncertain, Ebon went to do as she asked, keeping a careful eye on his father. But Shay said nothing to gainsay his sister, though Ebon noticed his knuckles whitened where they gripped his silverware.

Meanwhile, a servant ran to fetch a new plate of food for Halab. The man's hands shook when he set the plate before her, and Ebon scoffed. The servants were too used to serving his father, and seemed not to know of his aunt's more genial nature.

Halab spoke around a tiny morsel of food. "How did you fare at the palace this morning?"

"The same as always," growled Shay. "She keeps us waiting in her halls, and will not even give us a time to return when we might actually speak with her. They claim it is because of the brewing trouble between Selvan and Dorsea, but I think that is an excuse. She thinks herself too high and mighty for us."

"She is the High King," said Halab, shrugging. One of her thin braids came loose and swung down towards her ear, and she lifted it carefully back into place. "We serve at her pleasure."

Shay snorted loudly. But Ebon noticed that he did not again slur the High King as he had done before.

"In any case, I had already heard something of your troubles," Halab went on. "I spoke with a friend at the palace—a very highly placed friend indeed. He has se-cured an audience on your behalf. Visit the palace at midday tomorrow, and you will find the doors of the throne room are open to you."

"Do you see, my love?" said Hesta. She smiled gratefully at Halab. "I told you that this would work out."

Shay kept his eyes firmly fixed on his plate. "Thank you for your help, Sister. That is most kind of you."

"Think nothing of it. I am confident the High

King will speak on our behalf and secure our new trade route through Dorsea. Their border squabble is nothing of import, and certainly not to us."

His father's hands clenched harder. "Certainly."

Ebon smiled inwardly, but was careful to keep his expression impassive. He did not like to think what his father would do if he was seen snickering. But then Halab turned to Ebon, and he straightened somewhat in his chair.

"And what of you, Nephew? How have you enjoyed your time upon the Seat? I hope you have been able to experience all of the island's . . . oh, what word am I searching for . . . pleasures?"

Ebon blanched, but again he kept his mask of tranquility. "I have—that is, I have spent most of my time here, at the manor. But I have walked the streets once or twice, and found them to my liking. It is a grand city, to be sure." He knew he must not even hint that Shay had largely kept him confined to the manor.

Halab's brows drew close. "You have not wandered much? I thought you would eagerly poke your nose into every corner of the city. Surely you have visited the Academy?"

Ebon tried not to gulp, though his throat had gone dry. "No, I have not. It holds little interest for me." Those words nearly stuck in his throat, yet somehow he managed to make them sound earnest.

Halab glanced at Shay, but his eyes were fixed on his food. "That is unacceptable," she said lightly. "You must venture out upon the Seat. You are a Drayden, after all, and should know as much as you can of this place of power. I suppose I could show you one or two of my own favorite haunts . . ." She seemed to think for a moment, and then snapped her fingers at an idea. "I know. I will take you on a tour of the Academy myself."

The world stopped for a moment. Ebon could not move. His head, already aching, became light, and he thought he heard a high, thin whine at the edge of his awareness.

"Yes, that will do nicely," said Halab, and now it was as though she was talking to herself. "The dean is Cyrus, my cousin—and your cousin, too, Ebon, though more distant. Surely he would be only too happy to show his school to us. You may think it holds little interest for you, but I know you will love it. There you can find wizards of all four branches practicing their spells. Oh, flame and wind and weremagic and— yes, and alchemy. It is a sight to behold."

Ebon could not speak; he could barely breathe. He looked fearfully at Shay. Surely his father would not allow this. But his father still stared down at his hands. When the silence in the room stretched a moment too long, his gaze snapped up to Ebon, and he growled through his dark beard.

"Your aunt has asked you a question. Answer her."

Still Ebon could not force any words to come. In his heart he wanted nothing more than to go. But then he thought ahead. In a matter of days he would be leaving the High King's Seat, likely forever. Already he knew he would miss it, and would waste away days in Idris thinking of its clean streets and the high, pristine spires of its buildings. That pain would only magnify if he saw the Academy itself, for that was where his heart truly lay.

But then he thought further still. In Idris, his sister Albi would be waiting for him—Albi, in whom he had confided all his deepest wishes about his magic. He had spoken of it for so long, and in such warm terms, that she herself had come to dream of seeing it. If he went, he could return and tell her all about it. If he did not, Albi would not only be disappointed for herself. She would berate Ebon for years, telling him how he should have gone with Halab.

His hands steadied on the tabletop. "Thank you, dearest Aunt. It would be my pleasure to accompany you."

"Then it is settled," said Halab.

The dining hall fell silent. Ebon's father stabbed his knife savagely into his meat, and his mother dabbed gingerly at her lips with a napkin.

FIVE

EBON HAD ASSUMED THEY WOULD TAKE A CARRIAGE, but Halab surprised him by proposing a walk instead. "It is not so great a distance, and I would find it most invigorating," she told him.

As though he did not already know how far away it was. Ebon had memorized the streets between the manor and the Academy, though Tamen had never let him draw too close to the place.

Speaking of Tamen, Halab ordered him to stay at the manor, to give her some special time with her nephew. But she did bring Mako, and the man followed close behind them, almost within arm's reach, so that Ebon felt his presence no matter how hard he tried to forget it.

Just past midday, the streets were busy with all manner of folk going to and fro. There were no open markets in this part of the city, and so no vendors screamed their wares at passersby, but there were shop-keepers, and deliveries of food and drink passing by on wagons. Among the crowds, Ebon often caught flash-es of red—either the red leather armor of constables, or the red cloaks of Mystics. These last he noted with some keen interest, for the order's strength had less-ened in his homeland of Idris, and they did not often present themselves to his family. At least, not in any meetings that Ebon was privy to.

Halab soon noticed his wandering eye. "You find the Mystics intriguing, do you?"

"I suppose. It is only that they are very rare back home."

"That is just as well. They are a meddlesome lot. And they have no love for wizards, except those who wear the red cloak as well. That means they would have a particular dislike for you."

Ebon glanced at her with concern, but she laughed and gripped his shoulder before taking his arm.

"Sometimes I worry that you are too serious, though I think I may know the cause of that. It has not escaped me that your father puts great strain on you. You must forgive him for that."

He did not have the faintest idea how to answer. Even with Tamen gone, he had no wish to speak ill of his father, for Mako walked close behind them both.

She patted his arm gently. "I know it must be difficult to speak of. You need say nothing. And I take back my words—you need not forgive him. He has not forgiven you for some things in which you were blameless."

Ebon ducked his head, for suddenly his eyes stung. He spoke very carefully. "Momen's loss was a great pain to us all."

"It was," she said, patting his arm once more. "Come. It is far too pretty a day for such thoughts. And we are nearly there."

He looked up. There they were: the spires of the Academy's four wings, and in the center of them all, the great tower. High and mighty the place stood, nearly as tall as the High King's palace. But where the palace was laid all in stone of white and grey, with windows and bracings of gold, the Academy was of a stone so dark it was almost black, and its trimmings were in silver. Silver too were the banners that streamed from its many flagpoles, and all of them bore the simple white cross that stood for the four branches of magic, inside a white circle that was itself nested in an orb of black. Ebon had heard of the banner, but had never seen it until the day he had arrived on the Seat. Since then, it had remained ever in his thoughts.

Its size made it appear much nearer than it was,

and still they had some distance to go. As they drew closer, Halab explained something of the place's construction. Many of the details Ebon already knew, knowledge gleaned from whispered conversations with servants who should have known better. Still he drank them all in, for he felt he would never tire of hearing tales of the Academy.

"Four wings it has, for the four branches, of course. But that is only a symbol, and the students are not kept to each wing according to their gifts. Rather, they are arranged by their age—or, I should say, their year of study. Now, do you see how high the walls are? They were built a good distance from the central building, the citadel, and there they have the training areas where more advanced students learn their arts. Though the walls are tall, they are never guarded. They are not meant to protect the Academy from attack, but to safeguard the city from the students. It would not do to have a young firemage blow himself up and take half a dozen nearby buildings with him."

Ebon laughed aloud at that, but Halab did not join him. He looked over to her, and saw that one of her eyebrows was arched.

"I am afraid that is no jest, nephew."

He blanched and looked away.

At last they drew near to the wide front door, set straight into the wall itself. The door was made of iron, dark and unpolished, as though crafted by a smith of little skill. But as he drew closer, Ebon saw that in fact the door was carved with innumerable small characters in some tongue that he did not know. Ten of them were as wide as his smallest finger, and they covered the door from top to bottom and from one side to the other, except on the trim, which was made of burnished brass. He tried studying the symbols for a moment, but they made his eyes hurt, and he had to look away.

Halab glanced back, and Mako stepped forwards to swing the huge iron knocker twice. It was wrought in the shape of a wolf that gripped a brass ring in fierce jaws.

For a short while, no one came to answer. Ebon shifted back and forth on his feet, though Halab seemed unperturbed. He was just about to suggest they knock again, when finally he heard a hideous iron screeching on the other side of the door. But it did not open; instead, a tiny metal hatch slid open at chest height. Ebon had not noticed the hatch before. Through the hole appeared a tiny, wizened old woman, who must have been standing on tiptoes and yet could barely see through the opening. Both of her eyes were wide and crazed, and one was completely white.

"What do you want?" the woman screeched.

Ebon's mouth fell open. Halab blinked and answered lightly. "Well met. I am here to visit my cousin, Dean Cyrus Drayden. He will be happy to receive me."

The woman studied them for a moment of uncomfortable silence. Then she vanished, and a moment later the hatch slid shut with another rending shriek of iron.

They stepped back, expecting the door to swing open. But nothing happened. Ebon looked uncertainly to Halab, and then to Mako. The bodyguard seemed faintly amused, and he kept his eyes fixed on the door. But Halab looked up and down the street in both directions, blowing a long sigh out her nose.

Just as Ebon thought she might knock again, they heard the heavy *snap* of a latch being thrown on the other side. With a bone-deep groan, the door swung in. On the other side was a short, portly man, thin dark hair clinging determinedly to a balding pate. He wore black robes of unremarkable fabric, but they were trimmed with golden brocade of fine make that caught both the sun and the eye as he moved his arms, which was often.

"Cousin Cyrus," said Halab, smiling graciously. "What a pleasure to see you."

"Halab, Halab," said Cyrus, stepping out to greet her. He took her hands in his and ushered her inside. "Come in, please. I offer my deepest apologies for the delay."

"Think nothing of it," said Halab. Then she turned to Mako. "Wait here for us."

Mako nodded and stepped to the side, facing out towards the street with his hands clasped before him. Ebon hurried after Halab as Cyrus drew her inside, and an attendant swung the door shut behind them with a *clang*.

Ebon froze, dumbfounded by the sight before him. The Academy's entrance hall stood at least ten paces high, its floor all black marble, thin white veins glinting with light from the many chandeliers hanging high above. A staircase with bronze railings swept up before them, seeming to promise the sky itself at the top, though Ebon could see it ended at a landing that went both left and right to vanish into hallways on the second floor. Other passages led off on either side of the stairway, while two doors stood closed at both ends of the great chamber. All the doors were wooden, but polished until they shone like metal, and everywhere were tapestries of glorious make. Ebon thought he recognized Calentin craftsmanship in their weave.

Students and instructors bustled about in all directions, like ants swarming through a hive, and none of them spared even a glance for Ebon and the others standing in the entryway. The illumination from the chandeliers was joined and strengthened by the sunlight from great windows set high in each wall, and they were made of colored glass that depicted many tall figures Ebon did not recognize. But they were beautiful, and clearly ancient, and he felt that the figures stared down on him in judgement as he stood beneath them.

"How do they light them?" he breathed, not meaning to speak aloud.

Cyrus snapped a glance at him and frowned. "Eh? What is that?"

"The chandeliers," said Ebon. "They are so high."

"Ah," said Cyrus. "The candles are placed and replaced by mentalists, and lit by elementalists, of course."

Of course. Ebon knew he might have thought of that on his own, were his father not so adamant about refusing to allow Ebon any knowledge of magic and other wizards. He gawked up at the chandeliers, his mouth open, and tried to imagine the wizards lifting and lighting the candles with their spells.

With a start he realized that Cyrus and Halab had almost vanished from sight, making for the passage to the right of the staircase. He scurried after them, barely able to tear his eyes from the windows high above. Quickly Cyrus took them down the hallway, past many doors on either side, until it branched right and he turned. At last he reached his destination: a door of iron not unlike the one in the front, and Ebon saw that it was worked all over with the same small symbols. It swung open easily at his touch, and they followed him inside.

They were in an office now—the dean's, Ebon guessed, for it was wide and well-lit and had a second half-floor reached by a narrow staircase to the right. All sorts of artifacts sat on shelves along the walls, and many were strange to Ebon: crystal globes and metal orbs and rods of strange materials, beside and sometimes on top of many books that stood in great stacks in every corner. On the second floor were more bookshelves, and windows that let light come pouring in from outside. But Ebon noted that the books and the artifacts all seemed unused, for they were covered in a fine layer of dust.

"My heart sings to see you, Cousin," said Cyrus, going to Halab and kissing her on both cheeks before she kissed him on his forehead. "Again I must apologize for your treatment at the front door. Despite my years here, I have never succeeded in ridding this place of Mellie, daft old bat that she is."

"I hope you do not trouble yourself about it," said Halab graciously. "Allow me to present my nephew, and your second cousin once removed: Ebon, Shay's son."

Cyrus regarded Ebon with a cool tolerance. "Indeed. Welcome, Ebon. You travel in mighty company."

He held forth a hand, and on it Ebon saw a ring bearing the cross-and-circle sigil of the Academy. For a moment Ebon was not sure how he was supposed to respond. After a moment that was just too long, he realized his mistake, and quickly leaned forwards to kiss the ring. Cyrus gave him a thin smile and turned away immediately.

"What purpose brings you here today, honored cousin? Is there any service you require of me, or anyone here at the Academy? Only name it, and it is yours."

"In fact, I am here for Ebon," said Halab. "Long has he dreamed of seeing the Academy, and as his family is busy in the palace, I thought to show him. Who better to introduce us to its labyrinthine halls than the dean himself?"

It looked to Ebon as though Cyrus tried to hide some slight displeasure. "Indeed. Certainly I would be happy to—ah!" He turned to Ebon again, and now his eyes lit with recognition. "You are the transmuter. Your father would not let you attend for schooling."

Ebon felt his cheeks burning, and he lowered his gaze to the floor. "Yes."

"A pity. And now you are . . . how old? Fourteen? Fifteen?"

"I have seen sixteen summers," mumbled Ebon.

"Sixteen!" The dean shook his head and pursed his lips. "Such a waste. Such a waste. But then, it is only transmutation. And better a glimpse of opportunity lost than to never know it at all. It will be my pleasure to show you my school."

He took Ebon's hand in his own, smaller, clammy one, and patted it. Ebon felt an urge to withdraw, but he did not wish to appear rude. The dean was looking at him like he was some boy whose legs had been cut off in a farming accident.

Cyrus opened the study door again and motioned them out. He made his way through the hallways, his steps sure, though Ebon was already lost in the massive place. Soon they stood in the entrance hall again, and once more Ebon was left to marvel at its craftsmanship.

"The student dormitories are near the top of the central citadel," he said, pointing up to where the staircase turned into hallways far above. "No need to visit them, of course, unless you like beds dressed in plain grey wool." He tittered.

"No, indeed," said Halab.

"Most of the classes are taught on the bottom floor, and here also are the kitchens and the dining halls. Come, let me show you where the students learn their spells."

He took them to the hallway left of the staircase. Doors lined the walls to either side, but Cyrus passed them by. "Instructor's studies," he said, waving at them dismissively. Soon they reached a set of double doors on the left, and Cyrus threw them open with a flourish.

Inside were many students sitting at long tables, and at the front of the room, a podium. Behind it stood a thin wisp of a man, clutching the wooden stand as though for support. He had wide eyes like an owl's, which blinked as fast as a heartbeat. His blinking sped still more at the sight of the dean.

"Dean Cyrus!" the instructor wheedled, leaping away from his podium as though from a coiled snake. He came forwards, wringing his hands together, mouth working as though chewing a tough bit of gristle. "What an unexpected visit."

"This is Instructor Credell," said Cyrus, putting a hand on Credell's shoulder, from which the poor man shrank witheringly. "He is the beginner's transmutation instructor—the man you would learn from, Ebon, if you were attending the Academy."

"Well met," said Ebon, holding forth a hand.

Credell stared at the hand with suspicion, then jerked his gaze up and tried to smile, but failed. "Are you a transmuter then? Fascinating! Where have you studied?"

"I am unlearned," said Ebon, feeling a familiar blush creeping across his face.

Credell blink-blinked rapidly with his owl eyes. "Oh, I . . . oh." Behind him, Ebon could see several of the students—all of them children far younger than he was—leaning to try and get a look at him.

"Mayhap we could leave these students to their studies," said Halab, giving the room a smile. "After all, they have much to learn."

"Of course, of course," said Cyrus, clapping Credell on the back until Ebon thought the instructor might fall over. "Carry on."

He stepped out and swung the doors shut again, whisking them a bit farther down the hallway to another set of double doors. Inside was a class of mind-mages listening attentively to their instructor. The man's eyes glowed as he made a small iron ball dance in the air. Ebon stared in wonder, but to his disappointment the instructor lowered the ball the moment he saw the dean.

Then Ebon noticed something else intriguing: though there were surely more than a score of students inside, they all wore the same simple black robes. At first he did not know why that caught his eye, until he realized that he could not tell which students came from wealthy families, and which from poor. In his own household, even if he did not know all the servants by name, he knew them by their dress, just as he knew a member of his own family the moment he saw their bearing. Here, all the students were equal. He marveled at it, though only for a moment before Cyrus began to speak again, and Ebon had to pay attention to the name of the instructor as they were introduced to each other.

After a hurried explanation of the class, Cyrus pushed on to another room with another lesson, though Ebon could see no magic at play, and Cyrus did not say which branch the students were studying. They passed another room, and then another, as though Cyrus was in a hurry now and only wanted the tour to be over as quickly as possible.

Evidently Halab noticed Cyrus' haste, as well as Ebon's dissatisfaction, for she stopped the dean after he closed yet another set of classroom doors. "Good cousin, mayhap we could see the training grounds? I think my nephew tires of seeing so many classrooms that look the same." Then, before Ebon could claim in politeness that he was fascinated by the tour, she smiled at him and said, "And I think I agree with him."

Cyrus grew flustered and produced a silk handkerchief, with which he dabbed at his forehead. "Ah, of course, good cousin. The training grounds indeed—though be careful! They are not without peril."

"I trust your ability to protect us, dear cousin."

"Ah, I . . . ah, yes, of course. This way."

He set off down the hallway now, faster than before, until Ebon nearly had to jog to keep up with him, although Halab's long strides kept the pace with ease. After three turns that left Ebon utterly bewildered, he stopped at another set of double doors, these made of white wood. Cyrus hesitated only a moment before throwing them open.

Ebon's eyes burned at the sudden daylight, and he had to raise a hand to shield his vision. Once he could see, he found himself in a stone courtyard that extended many paces from the Academy until it ended at a grassy lawn that might have been trimmed with a barber's shears, it was so precise. And there, for the first time, he saw wizards using the full strength of their magic.

They had come upon a class of firemages, who bent flame and lightning in their hands before flinging them at iron figures set in the ground many paces away. One sent an infernal ball flying through the air to engulf one of these targets in flame. A short distance away, a girl Ebon's age drew water from a bowl, twisting it into swirls in the air before sending it shooting into the ground. Ebon thought that was the end of it, until a moment later the water burst from the soil again, erupting with a stream of earth to slam into an iron dummy's stomach.

"This is where the elementalists practice," said Cyrus, as though they needed the explanation. Ebon found himself rooted to the spot and scarcely able to hear the dean's words. "Let us move on to the mentalists—my branch, as it happens."

Halab had to prod Ebon's elbow before he moved, and then he quickly followed Cyrus. He saw now that they walked between two of the great wings of the Academy, and were moving from one to the other. As they went, Ebon could not take his eyes from the elementalists casting their spells. Each seemed more wondrous than the last.

There was another white wooden door set in the wall before them. Cyrus opened it to a short passage that cut straight through the wing and out the other side. Ebon stepped into the passage with a final, regretful look at the wizards behind him. But when they came out the other side, he found himself dumbfounded again—for here were mentalists, and if their magic was not so wondrous at first sight, when he looked closer he was even more overawed. For they raised plates of metal and heavy chairs with only their magic, so that it looked like some spirit caused the objects to move. Then the mentalists would drag them back and forth through the air, or make them spin. As Cyrus hurried them along, Ebon saw some students engaged in what looked like simple duels. They would throw things at each other—soft, straw-filled balls of cloth, not the iron weights he had seen at first—and the other student would try to halt the attack with their own magic. Sometimes it worked, and sometimes not; Ebon saw one student struck in the midriff by an attack, and she doubled over. It seemed the missiles were somewhat weightier than they looked.

They passed through another wing into another training area, and there he saw weremages. Some changed only the color of their skin, or the shapes of their faces, but Ebon saw some who turned into animals and back, as quickly and as naturally as he could change his own clothing. But Cyrus was moving faster now, and they stepped through one final passage into the last training area.

This one was smaller than all the rest, and looking up, Ebon saw that they were tucked in between the Academy's northwestern wing, the citadel's main entrance, and the wall. But Cyrus turned to them with a smile and gestured at the students gathered there, giving Halab a little half-bow.

"Here, I think, you will find something to hold your nephew's attention. Here is where the transmuters practice their craft."

Ebon looked at them in wonder. Some students sat cross-legged upon the ground, their palms pressed into the earth. Beneath them the grass roiled and shifted, turning now to wood, now to stone, and then back to turf, so smoothly that he could barely tell it was changing before it finished. There were iron dummies in rows, just like before, only now the students took the dummies into their hands and turned the metal soft, malleable, twisting them into different shapes, or posing them so that they looked like warriors in combat. Still other students dueled, like he had seen the mindmages doing before. Only these students would throw the cloth balls at each other with their hands, and the other student met the missile with palms open. The balls would turn to water at a touch, splashing harmlessly across the student's skin, or mayhap vanish in a puff of smoke.

Then Ebon saw one instructor standing far off to the side, with a student standing several paces away. The instructor held a bow and arrow in her hand, and the student watched intently.

Slowly the instructor raised the bow and drew, until the fletching rested against her ear, and then released the shaft.

Ebon cried out in alarm—but the student raised a hand as if to catch the arrow. When it struck her palm, it vanished in a puff of smoke, just like the cloth balls the other students used for their practice.

Ebon glanced at Halab. Even her brows had raised at that. Cyrus' smile widened. "A powerful bit of transmutation, that. Not one in a hundred transmuters can achieve such skill."

"Powerful indeed," said Halab. She turned to Ebon

with a small smile. "So, my nephew? Are you glad to have seen this place?"

Ebon swallowed hard, forcing a smile. "Of course, dear Aunt. It is a wonderful sight. Thank you for bringing me here."

But in truth, his heart quailed. His steps came heavy and hard as he followed Cyrus back inside the Academy. He had seen the place he had always dreamed of, and he knew he would never forget it. Yet his dreams did not matter, for he would travel home all the same, back with his parents to Idris, likely never to see the High King's Seat again for decades, if ever.

Something of his mood must have shown in his face, for Halab stopped and turned to him. "Why, what is the matter, Ebon? You do not seem happy at all. Are you not glad to have come?"

"Oh, I am," said Ebon. He had no wish to seem ungrateful when Halab had done so much. "Only . . ."

She pursed her lips and patted his arm. "I think I understand your mind, dear nephew. Do not let yourself fall into despair. Not all paths are laid clear before us, and our fate is never set in stone."

"Of course not," he mumbled. But her words gave him little comfort.

SIX

WHEN HE RETURNED TO THE FAMILY MANOR, EBON learned from Tamen that his parents had at last gained their audience with the High King, and thus the purpose for their visit was fulfilled. So it was that the next morning he was in his room, despondent, while Tamen packed his things in preparation for the journey home.

"I wish you would cheer up," said Tamen. "You make for horrible company."

"Do you think it is that simple?" said Ebon. He picked at a loose thread in his pant leg, refusing to look up. "The place was glorious. I did not know that half the things I saw there were possible."

"No one forced you to go."

Ebon snorted. "Do you think I could have refused? I suspect this was all an elaborate torture. He has brought me here only to show me that from which he has kept me all my life. And my dear aunt—she thought to help me, to cheer me, but she has only increased my pain tenfold."

Tamen frowned and shook his head. "Mayhap it is for the best. Not even the very wise can see all ends."

"I see only one end before me, and it is one I do not wish to face."

Outside the window, the sky was bright blue with a few wispy clouds. They passed in and out of sight, moving quickly with the wind. Soon that wind would carry Ebon away on a ship, across the Great Bay towards home.

He had a thought and sat up, eyeing the door to his chamber nervously.

What if he fled? He could vanish into the Seat. Surely Father would not waste much time looking for him. Mayhap the Academy would take him, and he could begin his training, late in his life though it was.

But it was a flight of fancy. The Academy charged a tuition, and though he had some coin, he could not pay his way for long. Besides, if Shay did think to look for him, the Academy would be the first place to search. Ebon could well imagine his father's cruel sneer as he was dragged from his classes, not to mention the punishment he would face at home.

Soon all his things were packed, and Tamen summoned servants to carry them downstairs. Ebon forced himself to his feet and followed, moving slowly as though his shoes were made of iron. Many crates and bundles were stacked in the manor's front room, ready to be loaded onto carriages and driven to the docks. It seemed to Ebon that they were leaving with even more possessions than they had arrived with, though he had not seen his parents buy anything new.

He made his way out the front door and into the courtyard, and there he found a surprise: Halab had come to see them off. Beside her stood Mako, and in the middle of the courtyard was the main carriage, in which he would ride with his parents to the docks. They were present already, Shay engaged in some conversation with Halab, while Hesta stood quietly nearby. Ebon could not hear the words, but his father looked angry, and made many sharp gestures with his hands. But as soon as he saw Ebon he stopped, his face going stony, and he turned away from his sister.

Halab greeted Ebon with a smile. "Good morrow, my dear nephew. Did you rest well?"

"I did, Aunt," said Ebon. "I shall miss you dearly. The days will seem like years until you grace Idris with your presence again."

"Such manners," said Halab, going to him and taking his kisses on her cheeks.

"A silver tongue he has indeed," said Mako, grinning at Ebon over Halab's shoulder. Ebon tried to still a shiver of unease that ran down his spine. His aunt he would miss, but he was glad to be leaving Mako's presence, at least.

Then Halab drew back and looked past Ebon, to where Tamen held a satchel with some of his clothing in it. Her eyes widened, and her full lips parted slightly as she looked at Ebon again. "But Nephew, why does your retainer bring your possessions? You look as if you are making ready to leave."

Ebon stopped short, brow furrowing. "I am. Is our trip here not finished?"

"You cannot tell me you thought you were going back to Idris. Surely your parents told you that you are staying here?"

At first, Ebon could not put meaning to the words. He looked over Halab's shoulder. Father's face had darkened, his eyes drawn together in a squint while a vein throbbed in his forehead. But Mother had turned her face away from Shay, and upon her lips Ebon thought he saw a tiny smile trying to burst free.

"I . . . I do not understand," he said lamely.

Halab gripped his wrists tighter. "My dear nephew. How plainly must I state it? You will be staying upon the High King's Seat to attend the Academy."

His knees did not seem capable of holding him up, and he grasped for something to steady him. Tears sprang to his eyes, and his other hand tightened its grip on Halab's arm until he loosened it, fearing he might hurt her. He opened his mouth to speak, but a lump in the back of his throat prevented him.

It seemed Father had kept his peace as long as he could. He stepped forth angrily, spittle springing from his lips as he spoke. "If you think the Academy to be some lark, then you are an idiot. You are six years too late. You will look like an infant in a king's finery there. And never will you be a great wizard, no matter your foolish dreams."

Ebon choked back furious words, biting his lip to keep them from spilling forth. Halab looked back at her brother, and a cool anger smoldered in her eyes. But when she turned back to him, her expression was kind, and she squeezed his arm in reassurance.

"The choice is yours, of course. I would never dream of forcing you into such studies, if they are not what your heart truly desires."

"Show some wisdom for once in your life, and think ahead," snarled Shay. "What do you think you can still learn, now that you are nearly full-grown?"

Ebon looked at him and then back to Halab. His first instinct was to shout, with all his joy and fervor, that of course he would stay and attend the Academy. And yet, as they so often did, his father's words wormed their way into his mind.

What *would* it be like at the Academy? One thing was certain: he was here six years later than he should have been, and that would be plain to everyone if he attended.

If?

He had dreamed of nothing more for many years. Now that the gift was presented to him, would he shrink back from it? He had seen the Academy now and all that lay within its granite walls. And he knew he had never longed for anything so keenly.

"I wish to attend the Academy," he said, almost shouting it. Then he leaped forwards, forgetting all his courtesy, and squeezed Halab in so tight an embrace that he heard the air *whoosh* from her lungs. "Thank you, Aunt. Thank you. This is a gift greater than I could have dreamed."

"You are welcome, my dearest nephew," she said, gently patting his back. At last he released her, and she stood back from him. "Now you are under one obligation only: to make your family proud to have sent you. Can you do this for me?"

He refused to look at his father, and so kept his eyes on hers. "Yes. I give you my oath."

"I will remember it. Now quickly—say your farewells, for you should make your way to the Academy right away. I have sent word to Cyrus already, and they are waiting for you."

Ebon turned to look at Tamen. His retainer wore a befuddled look, as though he did not fully understand what had happened. He raised the satchel in his hand and lowered it again. But then a curious light shone in his eyes. He dropped the satchel and reached for Ebon's hand.

"I did not expect this."

Ebon clasped his wrist. "Nor did I. Are you happy for me?"

"I find that I am." His other hand came up to grip Ebon's shoulder. "Fare well. I shall tell Albi."

"Please do. And thank you." Ebon tilted his head, hoping the retainer heard the words he could not say. "For your years of service, and all you have done here on the Seat."

Tamen answered with a smile—and then they both jumped as a door slammed. Ebon turned to find the carriage door was shut, and his father was inside. But his mother waited for him by the carriage, arms wide, a pleased smile upon her face. He went and took her in his arms, breathing in the familiar smell of the perfumes she favored.

"Go and make me proud, my son," she said, scarcely speaking above a whisper. "I do not weep to see you go, for I know you are ready."

"Then you know more than I, Mother," said Ebon. "But Father . . ."

"Do not concern yourself over him," she said quickly. "I know you cannot see it, but he, too, knows this is best. And mayhap the distance between you will mend what time never could."

Ebon doubted that very much, but he forced himself to smile as he gave her a final kiss on the cheek. At last he turned to Halab, who stood there beaming at him. Mako stood just behind her, but Ebon tried to ignore him.

"Well, what are you waiting for?" said Halab. "Go, or they shall mark you tardy on your first day."

"Do well, little goldbag," said Mako. Ebon's skin crawled at his crooked grin. "I know you will be of great service to the family."

Ebon tried to keep his smile up for his aunt. But at the last moment he turned towards the carriage. Its door had a window, and though a curtain was drawn across it, the sunlight showed his father's silhouette inside. The shadow did not move, even as it grew silent outside the carriage, and the others looked at Ebon expectantly.

Darkness take him, then, said Ebon.

"Fare well," he said, and though he spoke to Halab, he knew his words would carry inside the carriage. "The next time you see me, I shall be a wizard."

Then he turned and strode from the manor's courtyard. He kept his pace measured until he was out of sight, but the moment he turned the first corner, he burst into a run.

SEVEN

By the time Ebon reached the Academy he was panting, and he had to double over to catch his breath. Sweat made his tunic stick to his back, and immediately he regretted his flight through the streets. He did not wish to appear for his first day a stinking slob. But it was too late for such worries now. He stepped forwards and rapped sharply on the front door.

Unlike the day before, the response was immediate, and he cringed at the sharp cry of the door's hatch sliding open. There was the old woman Mellie, ghostlike eyes glaring out at him. Before he could so much as open his mouth she screamed "The Drayden!" and slammed the hatch shut.

Ebon cast a quick look over his shoulder. He had no wish for people to know his family name if there was any way he could help it.

The door clanged open, and Mellie waved him in with sharp, almost frantic gestures. She seized his wrist as he crossed the threshold. Her fingers were bony and frigid, but surprisingly gentle as she drew him up the great staircase that dominated the hall. Behind him he heard the door slam shut with a heavy boom. When he turned, there was no one there who could have closed it. A shiver ran through his limbs.

I am in the Academy now, he thought. It was a giddy prospect, and he fought the urge to burst out laughing.

Mellie took the stairs quickly, despite her age. Once they reached the top she whisked him off to the right, stopping at the first room they came to. Within were many shelves, running from floor to ceiling and covering the walls, and all of them filled with folded black robes. Mellie ran along the shelves, brushing each one with her fingers as though she could see them by touch, glancing back often at Ebon.

"How tall do you stand?" she snapped.

"I—just under ten hands," he said, squaring his shoulders.

"Hah! I will give my good eye if you are more than half past nine." Ebon barely kept himself from pointing out that if she already had an answer, there seemed little purpose in asking him the question.

Mellie went to a shelf and took one of the robes from it, and then shoes from another shelf. Without ceremony she threw them into Ebon's arms. He tried to catch them, but they came unfolded anyway, and one fell to the ground. He barely had a chance to scoop it up before Mellie had snatched his arm and drawn him out of the room again, screaming at him to *Hurry! Hurry!*

They did not have far to go; she took him across the hall, where he found a simple brick room and a large bronze tub. It was filled with water, and steam rose languidly from its surface.

"Clean yourself," said Mellie, thrusting a gnarled finger at the tub.

"I bathed just last night."

Mellie glowered and said nothing, only thrusting her finger at the tub again.

He sighed. There was a bench at one end of the room, and he carefully laid his new student robes upon it. Then he turned to Mellie, raising his brows.

"Be quick!" she snapped. "I do not have all day to deal with new arrivals, you know."

Ebon thought to himself that he did *not* know, since he had no idea what Mellie actually did here. But he did not wish to sound rude. "Are you going to leave?"

"Humph!" she said, placing her hands to her hips. "Do you fear an old lady leering at you? I will not leave the room only to have you take an hour to bathe yourself."

His cheeks burned. "I—I do not often disrobe before others."

She rolled her eyes. "Merchant children," she muttered. "If I turn my back, will that preserve enough modesty that you will get in the tub?"

"Yes—and thank you."

Mellie turned, and he hurried to throw off his clothes. The moment she heard the splash of water, she came and took the golden clothing he had worn from the manor.

"Wait! Where are you taking those?"

"To be burned, of course. No one told you? The clothes you bring here are destroyed. While you study here at the Academy, you will wear only your student robes."

"But those are expensive!"

Mellie held them up, appraising them with narrowed eyes. "I have burned far better. The king of Wadeland's second cousin came here wearing clothes worth enough coin to feed an army for a month." Then she vanished through the door.

After his surprise faded, Ebon found himself somewhat liking the idea of the fine tunic and trousers curling in the tongues of a fireplace. If nothing else, the unnecessary expense would no doubt rankle Father, if he knew. Ebon laughed at the thought and gave the bathwater a little splash.

When Mellie came back a short time later, her hands were empty. Ebon had finished bathing and had just dressed again by the time she appeared. Scarcely waiting for him to put on his shoes, she seized his wrist and drew him from the room.

Now they ran back down the main staircase into the great entryway, and then around to the right side, where he entered the hallway opposite the one Cyrus had taken the day before. He remembered the dean saying these were where the instructors had their chambers. Mellie stopped at the first door on the right and threw it open.

"New student!" she shrieked, and then scampered off towards the front hall again.

Beyond the door was a study. But this was no elaborate room filled with gilded ornaments like the dean's office. It was warmly lit by candles placed in the corners, and a soft green rug covered the floor. Bookshelves lined the side and back walls, and they were filled with books in perfect, neat rows. In the center of the room was a modest desk with a single leather tome on one side, and a stack of parchments in the center, just beside a pot of ink with a quill stuck in.

Behind the desk sat a woman of middle years. Her short, prim hair had once been flame-red, like a performer from Hedgemond that Ebon had seen in his youth, but now it was half grey. Light blue eyes fixed on Ebon's face with calm assessment. He noted that she wore dark grey robes, like the dean, but hers had none of the gold brocade that Cyrus had worn.

"Come in, please," said the woman. "And shut the door behind you, if you would be so kind."

Ebon stepped in, chiding himself for feeling so timid, and closed the door with a soft *clink*.

The woman sat back in her chair, sinking into its soft, stuffed leather. She studied him a moment more before gesturing with an open hand to one of the two wooden chairs opposite her. "You are welcome to sit."

He did, looking around the room with interest. Though he knew she was an instructor, he felt none of the discomfort he had felt in Cyrus' office. This place seemed warm and gentle, if not entirely comfortable. She let his gaze wander, her fingers steepled under her chin. When he at last turned back to her, she said no word, and only kept looking him over.

She must recognize me for a Drayden, he thought. Surely that explained her reluctance to speak. Ebon knew well how his family was regarded across the nine lands. Would that legacy follow him here? He had hoped to escape it at last, but now that hope seemed unlikely, or even foolish.

But when the woman spoke, it was not of his family at all. "How many years have you seen?" she said. "Fourteen? Fifteen?"

Ebon breathed a sigh of relief. But the question presented another problem, and he answered reluctantly. "Sixteen."

An eyebrow raised briefly. "Indeed? Well, no doubt you think that is a terrible burden to bear. Do not worry yourself overmuch. I had seen fourteen when I came here. Mayhap not so grievous a situation as yours, but an annoyance all the same. You will find it difficult at first, but not forever."

He sat a little straighter, surprised. "I am relieved to hear that."

"And your branch?"

Ebon blinked. "I am sorry. I do not understand."

"Of magic. What is your gift?"

"Oh!" said Ebon, clearing his throat. "I am an alchemist."

Her brows rose again, and this time they stayed there. "Indeed? I daresay we could use more of them."

His brow furrowed. "I am sorry?"

"Never mind. It is of little consequence. You should know, though, that your branch's proper name is transmutation, and you would do well to start using that name immediately. The same applies to the other four branches. We do not speak with the commoner's casual indifference in these halls."

He nodded thoughtfully, finding himself growing curious about her. "And you? What branch are you gifted with?"

She smiled at that. Then Ebon nearly jumped out of his chair, for her shape changed before him. First her eyes glowed, and then her hair grew grey and stringy as she shrank in her seat. In a moment Mellie

sat before him, still regarding him from behind steepled fingers.

Frantically he looked over his shoulder to the door
where Mellie had just left him. But the woman laughed
and swiftly changed back. "I am not Mellie, boy. That
was an answer to your question."

At last he understood. "You are a weremage."

"A therianthrope, but yes. Very good. And I have
forgotten my manners entirely, or you have. Either
way, my name is Jia."

He noted carefully that she did not give a family
name. Mayhap she was a bastard, but mayhap that was
custom here. He hoped so. "I am named Ebon."

"Ebon. A strong name. Well, Ebon, let us show
you to your quarters."

He scooped his spare robes back up from where he
had thrown them in the other chair, and Jia stood to
lead him from the room. Ebon remembered that the
dormitories were on the second floor, and he expected
her to bring him back out to the main hall to climb the
wide staircase. But Jia led him farther into the citadel
instead, where he soon saw another staircase leading
up. This one was a spiral, and very narrow, so much so
that he could easily touch both sides of it with his arms
stretched out. Jia led him up, passing one landing but
stopping at the second. They emerged into the hallway
to find a door facing them just on the other side, and
Jia led him within.

They entered a room with many chairs and couches set in small circles all about its edge, with a large open space in the center. But Ebon scarcely had time to study it before Jia took him to a door at the back. Through that door was a long, low room with many beds, along with cabinets and chests of drawers. She led him to a bed almost at the back and waved a hand at the cabinet beside it.

"Here you may store your spare robes," she said. "This bed is yours now."

Ebon looked around the room at all the other beds, wondering how many were occupied. "Is this where all the alchemists sleep?"

"No alchemists sleep here at all."

His cheeks burned. "I am sorry. Is this where all the transmuters sleep?"

She smiled warmly. "A quick student, then. The answer is no. The branches study together, but here in the dormitories you are arranged with the other students according to your ages."

That was a relief. Ebon had no wish to spend his days sleeping in a room full of children. But Jia must have seen the pleasure on his face as something else, for she fixed him with a stern glare.

"Do not look so excited. You should know that it is strictly forbidden for students to philander upon Academy grounds. This is a place of learning." Ebon's face grew beet red as he realized what she thought she had seen in his mind, but she pressed on before he could speak. "There are many places upon the Seat where you and the others may see to your needs. This is not one of them. Instructors walk the halls at night, and often inspect the dormitories. Keep yourself restrained while you are here, and if you require silphium, you will see to procuring it yourself. Is that very clear?"

"Yes," he said, voice strangled with embarrassment. "I assure you, I understand completely."

Jia lifted her chin, eyes softening slightly. "Good. Know also that fighting is forbidden, whether magical or otherwise. And *that* rule extends beyond the Academy's walls. Take some private duel out upon the Seat, and we will hear about it. If that happens, you will be expelled. Now then. You know where you will be sleeping, so allow me to show you where you will be studying."

She led him downstairs again, this time to the entrance hall and then down the hallway on the left. Soon they reached a door with iron bands that Ebon thought looked familiar. Sure enough, when she opened it he recognized the room where Instructor Credell taught beginning alchemy. But the room was empty now, and neither Credell nor his students were anywhere to be seen.

"This is your classroom," said Jia. "Your instructor is a man named Credell."

"I met him," said Ebon. He realized he had interrupted her, and lowered his gaze, blushing.

Jia did not seem annoyed, and only nodded. "That is good, since as you can see he is not here for an introduction. His students are dismissed just now, though they will return soon. In the beginning, your days of learning will be divided into two periods of three hours—one period before the midday meal, and one after. This is where you will study for the first period."

Ebon remembered the classroom full of young children with some despair, but he nodded at her words. "And my second period?"

"That is general study, and it takes place in the library. There, I shall be your instructor. Come."

She led him away, and Ebon thrilled at the thought that she would be teaching him. He had not liked the look of Credell, or the way the man seemed to flinch away from any word spoken above a whisper. Though Jia was a weremage, mayhap she could help him fill in the gaps in his alchemy, for he strongly suspected Credell would not.

The gaps in my transmutation, I mean. Ebon smiled to himself.

Jia turned this way and that, and soon Ebon was utterly lost again within the halls. When she saw him looking around, desperate for a landmark to locate himself, she said, "You will get lost often in your first days, and little will help to prevent it. Therefore we will not waste time teaching you where to find your classrooms, but rather how to recognize them. You can ask your fellow students if you have trouble placing yourself."

"Thank you," he mumbled, and abandoned trying to find some way to determine where he was.

"There are a some things you may try to keep in mind," she went on. "For example, the beginner's classes are located near the front of the citadel, while the advanced classes are towards the rear. Therefore you will move deeper and deeper as you advance in learning—except for your general studies, which are always in the library, and therefore always at the very back of the citadel."

Already his head swam. But it was clear she was trying to help. "I will try to remember."

She pursed her lips as though hiding a smile. "Mayhap that is not as helpful to a student newly arrived as I think. But here we are."

They had come to double doors of dark wood. Jia opened them, and he stepped inside—and then he froze, looking around in wonder.

Never before had Ebon beheld a sight like the library of the Academy. Never before had he imagined that so many books existed in all the world. He stepped just over the threshold to look up, for he could see at once that there was a second floor—yet as he craned his neck, he could see that in fact there were three, each one reached by a narrow iron staircase. Far, far above, the library's roof was a great yellow dome, worked of some substance like glass, but which cast a golden glow on the whole place. The glow was strengthened by glass lanterns set in many fixtures on the walls—no open flames were permitted, he guessed, for the safety of the books.

And books there were. He thought that there must be tens of thousands of them. The bottom floor where he stood had many tables laid out, and at each one sat one or more students with books laid open before them. Above, he could see more tables set against the railings, with more students reading more books. And yet the shelves seemed full to bursting with still more, and he could not see an empty space anywhere.

"Where . . ." he stopped, trying to collect his thoughts. "Where did they all come from?"

"All across the nine lands, and all throughout the long centuries of history," said Jia, and he heard the reverence in her voice.

"What knowledge do they hold?"

"All of it, I should not be surprised to learn. But you could spend five lifetimes here and not read them all, even if you did nothing else, and then you could never put such knowledge to use. I must admit to some small pleasure at the wonder I see in your eyes. Are you fond of reading, then?"

Ebon shrugged slowly. "I certainly enjoy it. And this . . . how could anyone see this place and not be struck by wonder? The dean took me through the Academy yesterday, but he never showed me the library. If he had, I would have called this the greatest wonder of the citadel."

Jia's lips drew into a thin line. "That does not greatly surprise me. Cyrus is not the most avid reader, nor was he even when he was a student here himself."

Ebon blinked. "You were here when he was a student? How can that be? You cannot have seen enough years."

It looked as though she was trying very hard to fight back a smile. "You will find that flattery has very little effect on me, Ebon."

He ducked his head at once. "I did not . . . I meant only that . . ."

She patted him on the arm. "I am mostly joking. Come. That is all you need to see today, and we should return you to your dormitory. You can return tomorrow, your first true day as an Academy student."

Quickly she brought him back through the halls to another spiral staircase leading up. This time Ebon recognized the staircase, and thought he might even be able to find it again, if pressed. That boded well. Once they reached the third floor she brought him to his dormitory and stopped at last before his bed.

"There is one more thing you should know. If you wish to send a letter to your family, you may bring it to me. I will see to its safe transport. The fee for a letter is a silver penny. But if you should wish to send a letter and do not have the coin, come speak with me, and I will see if there is anything that can be arranged."

Ebon blushed, for he had a thick coin purse in his robes—transferred from the clothes he had worn when he arrived, and always kept upon him in case of emergency. "I thank you for your consideration, but I do not think I shall have a problem with coin."

"I imagine that is true, for a son of the family Drayden."

A sudden chill flooded his bones, and he blanched as he looked at her. Wordlessly his mouth worked, trying to form some explanation. Jia smiled sadly at him, and then, to his surprise, she took his hand.

"You thought I did not know your family? It is written plain on your face, and your bearing, and your manner of speech. But if you think that matters here, you are mistaken. No one worth their salt cares for the name you and your kin bear. And the Draydens have produced many good wizards—sky above, one of them is the dean."

Ebon found words hard to muster. "But . . . but on the Seat, they . . ."

"I do not doubt that many on the street looked at you askance. But you will find—or you *should* find—that being a wizard is different. Many worries you have struggled with during your life will fade away during your time here. If they do not, then you are not learning all that you should. Do you understand me?"

He swallowed hard. "I am afraid not."

"Of course not. But you will. Your first class is tomorrow morning, two hours after the rising of the sun."

Then she left him, and Ebon stared after her, dumbfounded, as the dormitory faded to silence around him.

EIGHT

AFTER JIA HAD GONE, EBON WENT TO HIS CABINET and ensured his robes were neatly stacked. He doubted anyone would care how his cabinet looked, but he liked his things well ordered, and he no longer had Tamen to take care of them for him.

Tamen. Thinking of his retainer sent his mind spinning. Only a few hours ago he had left Tamen standing in the courtyard of the Drayden manor, and now he was in the Academy. He might see Tamen again someday, and then again he might not. Certainly it would be a long time, unless his parents returned to the Seat for some reason Ebon could not predict.

But when he thought of his parents, he thought of the closed carriage door and the shadow behind the curtain. That thought did not bear dwelling upon, and so he looked about the dormitory for something else to do. It seemed no duties were required of him, at least not until the next day. Mayhap he could inspect the common room, for he had only seen it twice, and both times in haste. He left his bed and walked the long aisle to the door leading out.

The common room was wide and tall, but somehow it maintained an air of coziness and comfort. He inspected again the plush chairs set all about the room and the fireplaces in either wall. Though it was late autumn, the day was warm, and so no fires were lit, but he did not doubt that they would give great warmth when winter's shroud descended upon the Seat. The walls were the same granite as the rest of the citadel, but they were hung with many tapestries of red and green and gold, and everywhere he saw the cross-and-circle of the Academy worked into the designs.

To his surprise, he noticed another student sitting in the common room. He did not remember seeing her when he had passed through with Jia. Mayhap she had come in only a moment ago—but then, mayhap he had missed her, for she sat quietly in the corner of the room and made no noise. Indeed, she did not even look up or appear to see him. Her hair was lank and black, her skin sallow, and dark bags hung beneath her eyes.

Slowly Ebon drew closer to her. Still she did not see him. She was holding something in her hands, and now he could see that it was a goblet of silver. Then, to Ebon's amazement, her eyes glowed with an inner light, and she pulled her hands away—but the cup stayed there, floating in midair.

She is a mindmage, he thought.

As the girl twisted her hands, the goblet began to spin. First it turned end over end, in line with the girl's nose. Then she concentrated, her nose twitching, and it began to twist in another direction at the same time. Her hands clenched, wiry muscles taut beneath the skin, and it spun in another direction entirely. It turned faster and faster, becoming a blur, and moving so fast now that Ebon thought it looked like a spinning silver globe, and not a cup at all.

Entrancement made him forget his fear, and now he walked eagerly over to her. He stopped just next to the arm of her chair, yet still she did not look at him. He waited a moment in silence, out of manners, and then gently cleared his throat.

"That is astonishing," he said, fearing his voice was far too loud in the stillness of the room.

The girl said nothing. Now he felt sweat beading on the back of his neck, and he pulled at the collar of his robe.

"I . . . I am Ebon. I am only arrived to the Academy today. How long have you attended?"

At last she looked up, meeting his brown eyes with her own, darker ones, though they still glowed from the use of her magic. Then her hands constricted, like an eagle's claws sinking into a rabbit's neck. The goblet abruptly stopped spinning, and it crumpled into a tiny ball of metal with a terrible rending noise.

Ebon jumped and turned to scurry hastily away. He found a chair at the other end of the room, blocked from sight by the furniture in between, and tried to sink into the plush cushions.

It was a little while before his heart slowed and his breath came easier. As the fright finally died in his breast, his fingers began to tap on the armchair. He looked about the room but could see no one else, nor could he hear the sound of anyone passing in the hallway. He could only feel the presence of the girl, as though her eyes were boring into his soul, despite the fact she could not see him.

Mayhap he had better practice his own magic. Soon he would be expected to perform it, after all, and he had not tried to use it in many years. Whenever Tamen caught him playing at spells, his father heard of it immediately. And he had never been allowed to meet another wizard, much less an alchemist.

His only knowledge of his gift was the spell he had done as a boy, when the Academy's examiner had come to see if he had the gift. Now he looked around and saw cups and a pitcher of water on a table nearby. Hastily he went and filled one, his movements quick, careful to keep his eyes from the corner of the room where the girl sat.

In his chair once more, he gently swished the water around in the cup before placing a forefinger into it. He stirred gently. It was neither cool nor warm, but the exact heat of the room itself. He closed his eyes and concentrated.

Hazy across the long years since he first heard them, the old wizard's words returned to his mind: *Feel the water. See it the way it truly is. And then change it.*

Ebon concentrated with all his might. His eyes squeezed shut so tightly that they began to pain him. But nothing happened. He opened one eye, just a crack, to be sure. But the water still sat lukewarm against his finger. The back of his neck prickled, and his forehead beaded with sweat. He thought he could feel something . . . something within him, yearning to break free. He reached for it, but the harder he grasped, the more quickly it slipped away.

A long, slow breath escaped him. He stopped reaching, stopped trying to know the unknowable power that danced at the edge of his awareness. Instead he thought only of the water. It grew before his vision, the goblet swelling until it took up all the world. Now even his finger was forgotten, except as the bridge that connected him to the liquid.

His vision brightened.

Ebon felt his heart hammer in his chest, but he forced himself to concentrate. Slowly his finger stirred, swirling in little circles and causing the water to splash against the cup's rim. But wherever he touched the water, it turned thick and soupy, until soon the cup was filled with an oil that resisted the turning of his finger.

With a gasp he sat back, leaning into the couch. His hand trembled as he lifted the cup again. Within, the water was a thick, oily soup.

He wanted to burst into laughter. It had worked. Years had passed since he had last dared to slip away from Tamen for long enough to try it. He thanked the sky above that he could still do it. What a bitter irony it would be to reach the Academy at last, only to find that he had lost his gift.

The door to the common room slammed open, and three students came storming in.

Ebon shot to his feet. Across the room, he saw the sallow-faced girl had gone. With a sinking feeling in his stomach, he realized he still held the cup before him. Swiftly he turned to place it on the table beside his chair, and then he straightened and wiped his finger against his robe to rid it of the oil.

A girl led the other students who had entered, and her gaze fixed on Ebon. She paused for just a moment, brows drawing close, and then she came to him. Her skin was dark, and her thick hair was cut just below her ears and intricately braided to frame her face, making her light eyes all the more captivating. She stopped before Ebon and put her hands to her hips, sizing him up. Though Ebon stood half a head taller than she, he felt himself quail in her presence—an effect greatly enhanced by the girl and boy who stood behind her, both of them several fingers taller than Ebon was. Though the girl wore the same plain black robes as any other student, her stance and the look on her face spoke plainly: here was a girl from wealth and power.

"Who are you?" she said. "I have not seen you before."

Ebon tried to speak, but coughed instead as spit caught in his gullet. He cleared his throat hard. "I—I am Ebon," he croaked. "I have only just arrived at the Academy today."

"Where did you train before? You cannot be sponsored by some lord. You are far too old. Did your family hire you some tutor?"

Ebon felt a burning all along his skin and knew his face must be dark as a well-cooked roast. "I have never trained before."

She stared at him for a moment, eyes wide, mouth open slightly. He could see in her face that she did not believe him. Behind her, the other students looked at each other askance. But then the girl's eyes darted past Ebon, to the wooden cup that sat on the side table. He tried to shift to the side, to block her view with his body. But her lips twisted in a cruel smirk, and she pushed past him to grasp the cup. Lifting it before her face, she dipped a finger into the crude oil.

"The trial spell?" she laughed. "That cannot be the only magic you know."

"It is," said Ebon, still flushed with shame. But now annoyance was blossoming to anger in his breast, and he spoke without thinking. "My father never wanted me to train, and if he caught me trying magic—"

The girl stopped him with a loud laugh, the others behind her snickering along. Then her eyes glowed white, and she snapped her fingers. A spark sprang from her hand and landed on Ebon's sleeve. He felt the heat of it immediately, and with a cry of dismay he tried to beat it out.

"Oh, does my flame bother you?" said the girl, laughing harder. "Here, mayhap this will help."

She threw the cup of oil on his sleeve. It doused the spark, but it also splashed across his whole body, soaking through until the cloth clung to his skin, cold and clammy.

"I have not seen a greater waste in all my years here," she said. "But I suppose I am grateful. We have a jester back home, and I have missed having someone to amuse me. I am Lilith of the family Yerrin, jester, and I am most pleased to make your acquaintance."

Lilith dropped the cup and strode off through one of the dormitory doors—not the one that led to Ebon's room, he noted with relief. Ebon sat back down in the chair, not caring that his wet robe would soak into the cushions, and hung his head. No matter how hard he squeezed his eyes shut, he could not stop a tear of shame from escaping to run down his cheek.

NINE

When he had composed himself, Ebon retreated to his own dormitory and changed into a clean robe. Then he thought better of it and removed the robe, and once in his underclothes he climbed beneath the covers of his bed. He had no wish to meet any other students, especially not now. He had imagined the Academy would be better than his home. Here he thought to free himself from family obligation, from the infighting and politics that had surrounded him since he was old enough to understand them. But it seemed instead that he would face a whole new host of problems—or mayhap just Lilith, but she seemed trouble enough to last a lifetime.

Mayhap she will forget about me soon—especially once I begin to learn my magic, he thought.

You are a fool, came another thought. And for that, he had no retort.

Classes must have just ended, for soon other students came in from the common room, bustling with noise and conversation. Ebon ignored them all, and when they drew too close he pretended to be asleep. It was late in the afternoon, but still hours from nightfall, and Ebon spent them all in bed, curled up and pretending not to exist. It was a long time before he finally drifted off into a restless slumber.

When he woke, the dim grey shining through the window told him that dawn had not yet broken. He rose quietly, thankful that no one else had risen yet, and donned his robes. Then he made his way out of the dormitory, through the common room, where fires burned in both hearths, and down the stairs to the first floor.

The Academy was quiet and empty. Ebon felt as though everything around him had taken on a magical quality, otherworldly and not quiet real. It was easy to imagine, at least for the moment, that all the world had gone, and he alone was left to explore it. It made his feet itch to run about, his eyes seeking for cracks and corners.

Silently he padded down the passage to the entrance hall, afraid to make any noise too loud and break the spell. Though torches burned in sconces, and must have been lit by attendants, the place was empty so far as he could see. When he reached the hall he stood and, for the first time, looked freely upon the place.

The windows far above were just beginning to glow with dawn, and the staircase shone in the colored sunlight that came floating down. The bronze banisters glinted in his eyes, and he reached out for them. The metal was warm, though the rest of the air clung to night's chill. The stone steps were worn smooth from centuries of students' passing shoes.

He stepped away and went to the iron front door. It was still too dim to see well, so he pressed his nose quite close to the small symbols inscribed all over it. Now he saw that they were similar to regular letters, and yet somehow different. They were harsher, more angular, with no curves to be seen anywhere. Yet he could not read them, for the words were strange and ancient, and the more he studied them the more his head began to hurt.

"What are you doing?"

Ebon leaped half a pace in the air and came crashing down hard upon the marble floor. He scrambled backwards on all fours—and then stopped as he saw Mellie quivering above him. Her white eye was thrice its normal size, and the other one was squinted, a scowl warping her lips.

"Sky above," he muttered. "You frightened me."

"Next time do not bury your nose in an iron door," she screeched. "What in the nine lands were you looking at?"

Ebon shook his head and got to his feet, brushing dust from the seat of his robes. "The symbols on the door. Why? What does it matter?"

Mellie turned and put her own eye up to the door, looking for all the world as though she was noticing the symbols for the first time. Then she looked back to Ebon, blinked once, and stalked away. He sighed.

The entry hall was much brighter now. Soon the other students would come down from the dormitories to break their fast. Ebon had no great wish to be there when they did—especially since Lilith would be among their number. He thought he remembered where Jia had showed him the dining hall, but he went the other direction towards the classrooms. *Your morning classes will be in the first room on the left with an iron band on the door,* Jia had told him.

He found the door and opened it. The room was empty, and he paused on the threshold. A sigh escaped him as he thought of his frightened little mouse of a teacher, Credell.

Mayhap it will not be so bad as it seems, he thought hopefully. But he did not believe it.

Shutting the door behind him, he went to one of the benches at the rear. They were arranged in rows, all facing the front of the classroom, and each had a long table in front of it. He slid down the bench until he was in the farthest corner, where he could lean against the wall. There he sat, waiting for the start of the day, and his first class as a wizard of the Academy.

Somehow, it no longer excited him as much as he once thought it would.

Thankfully he did not have to wait as long as he feared. It was mayhap half an hour until the first other student arrived. She was a small, sharp girl with wild hair that stuck out all about her head like a halo. When she entered the room, she saw Ebon and stopped. For a moment she studied him, face pale, eyes darting about every so often. Then she leaned out the door and looked up and down the hallway before stepping back inside once more. Back and forth she rocked on her feet, from tiptoes to heels, mouth working as she tried to summon the courage to speak.

"I . . . I think you have come to the wrong room," she squeaked.

"I do not blame you for thinking so," said Ebon. "But this is where I am meant to be, though it pains me to say so."

The girl did not seem to have a ready answer for that. Once more she looked out into the hall, as though making sure she was not the one in the wrong place. Finally she came in and closed the door behind her, going to the opposite corner of the room from Ebon and sliding all the way down the bench, until she was as far from him as she could be. Ebon slouched against the wall. With every passing moment, it was harder to resist an urge to flee the Academy forever and catch the first ship back home to Idris.

Slowly the room filled up, students arriving one by one and filling the benches. Most of them looked to be eleven or twelve years old at the most—Ebon saw one who he thought might have been thirteen, but mayhap the boy was just tall. Each one stopped for a moment when they spotted Ebon. Many of them looked about the classroom as the first girl had, ensuring that they were in the right place. Soon most of the other benches in the room had been filled—but no one came to Ebon's table, or even to the other bench in his row, though it was across an aisle.

The time passed with intolerable slowness until Ebon felt that half the day must be gone. At last the door creaked timidly open and Instructor Credell entered. Once he had stepped inside he stopped, looking around the room with wide eyes as though he was surprised to find himself there. He did not seem to notice Ebon. After a moment's awkward pause, he gave a little jerk and scuttled to his lectern, gripping it for support. Again he stopped, this time looking across the students before him.

His eyes fell upon Ebon. He gave a little jump and a yelp, and his knuckles went white. His throat wobbled a bit, and a weak smile crawled across his lips as though it had been dragged there screaming.

"Ah!" he said. "Ah, yes. Er. Class, we have a new

student. Greet our Ebon, of the family Drayden, will you?"

He waved a hand generally in Ebon's direction. Slowly the other students turned to look at him. Ebon withered, though he felt ridiculous at his embarrassment. These were only children. But in many of their eyes he saw fear, and knew it was fear of his family's name. He tried to smile, but was sure he summoned only a grimace.

"Ah," said Credell. "Yes. Well, we shall . . . ahem. We shall begin the day's lessons, then. Yes. You may all resume practice of your spells. I shall be around presently to instruct you. If you require help, raise your hand for assistance."

Awkward silence hung on the air for a moment, and no student moved. Then Credell flapped his hands, as though shooing a cat from the room, and the students broke into muted activity. Some went to retrieve wooden rods from a cabinet in the corner of the room, while others took hold of cups of water that already waited on the tables before them. Credell left his lectern and began to putter about the room, going from table to table and asking the students questions in hushed voices. Ebon could not help but feel that the instructor was very deliberately avoiding his gaze.

He shifted on his bench, unsure of what to do. All the other students seemed to know their business already. Ebon saw some of the children stirring the water in their cups and thought they must be practicing the testing spell. Others gripped their wooden rods, faces twisting as they concentrated. But he had no cup nearby to practice with, and he did not know what spell to cast upon the wooden rod, and so he stayed in his seat.

Credell moved through the room slowly, and seemed to move still slower the closer he drew to the back of the room where Ebon waited. Still Ebon forced himself to sit still; he had no wish to make a nuisance of himself on his first day. But when Credell finished with the table across the aisle, he spun and made for the front of the room. Ebon sat forwards in surprise. Quickly he leaned out into the aisle and thrust his hand in the air.

"Instructor Credell?"

The man leaped half a pace in the air and looked over his shoulder, face twisted as though in pain. "Ah. Er. Yes. Quite right."

He turned reluctantly and came back, each step as slow as though he was moving through water. But when he reached Ebon's table, a wide smile was plastered upon his face, looking as unnatural there as a mouse in a suit of armor. Ebon scooted aside to make room for him as he took the bench.

"Ebon," he said, voice quivering. "It is Ebon, is it not? I have such a terrible mind for names."

"It is," said Ebon. "What should I do?"

"Ah, yes, well," said Credell, fingers drumming on the table. "I was told you were never trained in transmutation, though I know that cannot be true, eh? A smart young boy like you." He chuckled and patted Ebon's shoulder. Ebon thought he could feel the sweat on the man's palms through the cloth.

"You were told the truth," said Ebon. "I know only the testing spell to turn a cup of water into oil."

"Oh, I am certain that is what you told everyone, eh?" said Credell, tapping his nose with a wink. "But I know what a curious mind can do. Worry not, for I will spread no tales of any spell I see you cast in this room."

Ebon blinked. "I think you misunderstand me. I could not practice any spells, even if I knew any, even in secret. My father kept a careful watch over me, and if I were to try . . ."

"Ah, well then," said Credell, shaking his head with a soft smile. "If you wish to keep up the pretense, I shall do the same. Anything for your honorable family."

"Instructor, I am *not* telling a tale. I want to learn. What must I do?"

Ebon felt his hackles rising as Credell gave him yet another broad wink. "Well, if you say you know nothing but the testing spell, then you had best practice it, eh? I will fetch you a cup of water."

He leaped from the bench as though stung by a bee and ran for the front of the room, soon returning with a wooden cup of water. This he placed before Ebon, and then stood hesitantly for a moment, looking down at him.

"Go on, then. I am sure you will make short work of it."

Ebon sighed and took the cup. He placed his finger within the water, trying to focus. Nothing happened. He frowned and concentrated, trying to reach for his gift as he had tried in the common room the day before. But now he could feel Credell's eyes upon him, as well as the eyes of every student in the room. They were all watching him, and he could feel their wonder at seeing this older boy try to perform the simplest of spells. He tried to force such thoughts from his mind, but they crowded back in until he could think of nothing else.

He slammed the cup down in frustration. Some of the water splashed out and onto his hand, and he shook it away angrily. "I told you, I never learned any spells. I was not even permitted to practice this one."

Credell shook his head with a kindly smile. But just as he opened his mouth to speak, the classroom door flew open. In strode the dean. He waddled in briskly and came down the aisle towards them, twisting to keep his belly from knocking over the students' cups upon the tables to either side. The other students froze the moment they saw him and drew away in fright as he passed by. Credell seemed to wilt like a flower thrown into a flame, shrinking into himself until he was as small and insignificant as possible. His watery eyes trembled until Ebon thought he might burst into tears. But the dean seemed to ignore the instructor utterly, his eyes fixed on Ebon.

"Ebon, my dear cousin!" he said, puffing mightily as he came to a stop before the desk. "How are you settling in here on your first day? My apologies—your second, I suppose." He chortled, thick jowls bouncing up and down as though he had made the wittiest of jokes. Beside Ebon, Credell tittered uncertainly.

Ebon tried to look anywhere else but at the dean. "I am well. Thank you for your concern."

"Of course, of course," said the dean, waving a hand magnanimously. From his tone, Ebon thought that in truth he could care less how Ebon fared. Most likely he was there only as a favor to Halab, but Ebon feared his presence would only make Credell behave even worse.

As though to put proof to the thought, the dean leaned over to look with interest at the cup that sat before Ebon on the table. His eyes narrowed, face twisting in a scowl.

"The testing spell?" he snapped. "Surely your time is not being wasted on so insignificant a thing. What is the meaning of this, Instructor Credell?"

He rounded on the poor man. Despite his frustration, Ebon felt only pity for the instructor. Credell retreated even further into himself, backing up until he stood against the wall, and his hands flew together to clutch each other at his breast.

"He—he said—he only knows the testing—" Credell tried to stammer.

"Only knows the testing spell? How preposterous!"

blustered the dean. "I will not have you wasting my cousin's time on such tripe!"

Ebon spoke up quickly. "He tells the truth. I never learned anything but the testing spell. My father—"

The dean cut him off with a wave of his hand. "You need not trouble yourself to defend him, Ebon. Now listen here, whelp." He pressed forwards, and though he and Credell were of a height, the instructor had cowered so completely that he stood a head shorter than the dean. "I will not have you wasting Ebon's time. You will see to it that he learns his studies as quickly as he can, not squander his hours here endlessly repeating a spell that can be done by any child aged six summers!"

He turned on his heel and stalked to the front of the room, where he flew through the door in a rush and slammed it behind him. The *crash* of the door made Credell collapse at last, and he sank to the bench with a whimper. There he rested for only a moment before he seemed to realize that Ebon was still there. Then he leaped to his feet with a cry and rushed to the front of the room, where he cowered behind his lectern, refusing to meet the eyes of any of his students.

Every child in the room had turned their gazes upon Ebon, and he could nearly feel the terror radiating from them. It seemed the dean was not well-liked within the Academy walls, at least not by the students—and, if his behavior toward Credell was any indication, not by the instructors, either. Vaguely he remembered Jia's snide words about the dean the day before.

Even here, with his father halfway across the nine lands and drawing farther away each day, Ebon could not escape his family's name. He let his head sink until it rested on the desk and, closing his eyes, he wished he were back in his bed.

TEN

It seemed an eternity before a bell pealed and Credell called out that the students were excused for their midday meal. Almost before he finished speaking the words, the instructor was out the door like an arrow. The other students moved to flee just as quickly, but not faster than Ebon. In mere moments he was out the door and into the hallway. But the place was soon filled with bodies, students emerging from their classes all in a mass until he could hardly move through the press.

He spotted a door of white wood and remembered

that those were the doors leading outside. The thought of open air, free from the crowd and the crushing weight of his embarrassment, suddenly seemed the greatest of luxuries. He shoved past several students to reach the door. Soon he was alone on the grassy lawn outside. Neither students nor instructors were there to disturb him, all having gone inside for their meal, and for a while Ebon simply walked through the gardens, closing his eyes and trying to forget the morning's disappointment.

He wished he had not come. For years he had thought the Academy would be a place of magic and wonder, where he could finally learn to harness the gifts that some fate had seen fit to bestow upon him. Yet thus far, if anything, the place seemed worse than Idris. At least in his family's manor he had Albi to visit and commiserate with. Here he had no one. And while the Academy itself was a beautiful place, and the High King's Seat rich in splendor and history, he found himself, for the first time, feeling a homesickness for the arid deserts of home. Were the sand dunes and the dry air really so bad? At least they were familiar. And at least there, though he was beneath his father's notice, still he was a child of wealth and power. Here he was nothing—or mayhap less than even that.

There was a stone bench nearby, and he slumped down onto it with a sigh. He hung his head so low that it nearly touched his knees, elbows grating against the rough fabric of his robes.

Could he still leave? Mayhap it was not too late. His parents would have left the island already, and mayhap Halab would have done the same by now. But he had some coin, mayhap enough to secure passage back home.

He thought of returning. In his mind's eye he saw himself walking through the broad front doors of his family's home, into the entry hall where Tamen would be waiting, no doubt wide-eyed with shock at seeing his master's return. And he thought of Albi's delight to see him, and his mother's warm embrace.

But the thought ran further, and he saw his father at the head of the dinner table, looking at him across a meal of meat pies and figs, silently gloating at his son's failure.

Ebon's hands balled to fists in his lap, shaking for a moment before he managed to still them. He felt the muscles in his jaw jerking as he ground his teeth together.

He would not return. That would mean that Father had won, and he could not bear such a thought. And he saw, too, the disappointment in his aunt's eyes when she found out. She had arranged all of this; certainly she had been the one to persuade his father to change his judgement. Always she had shown him nothing but kindness and compassion. He would not repay her by spurning her gift, by fleeing from his studies before they had truly begun.

Without meaning to, he shot to his feet. Mayhap

he would fail in his training. Mayhap the Academy would throw him out on his ear, there to find passage home however he could. But he would not leave until then. Darkness take Credell, and darkness take the dean. Here, at least, he could practice his spells without rancor, at least if he kept himself from Lilith's sight. If the Academy could not teach him, then he would teach himself—or find someone else to do it. His heart burned at the thought, and it seemed for a moment as if he could cast a spell right then.

But his stomach rumbled loud in his belly, until he thought they might hear it inside the Academy's granite walls.

Ebon smirked to himself. He had skipped the morning's meal, and had not even had dinner the night before. If he wished to become a great alchemist, he would first have to eat.

He made his way back to the white door. Inside, the passageway was now empty. But Ebon could hear voices, drifting to him along the stone hallway, and he followed the sound. Soon he found the wide doors that led into the dining hall. The room was large, larger than he had anticipated, with a low ceiling and many benches laid out in rows. At the back was the food, served by attendants into simple dishes made of wood. Ebon did not see any sense of order to how the other students sat, except that students of the same age seemed to sit together. But there were many empty tables spread about the place. Quickly he made his way between the benches, thankful that everyone ignored him as he went. An attendant filled a bowl with stew and gave him the end of a bread loaf, and he made his way to one of the empty tables.

He ate voraciously, stomach gurgling in appreciation with every bite. Though it lacked the fine spices of the food he was used to, still after his long fast it seemed one of the better meals he had had in a long time.

When his bowl was empty he leaned back, sighing with relief. Idly he tore a piece of bread away and scraped at the leavings. His eyes fell upon his cup of water.

Mayhap he could practice. He looked around quickly. Though he saw no students using magic anywhere, he had heard no rule that it was forbidden. And he would need all the practice he could get, since Credell seemed too frightened of his family name to be of much help.

He took the cup and dipped his finger within. Slowly he stilled his mind, closing his eyes and trying to envision the water for what it truly was. He opened his eyes again and focused. Something tickled at the back of his mind. But the water remained water. Ebon stirred it with its finger, but nothing happened.

Ebon slammed the cup down, and it *clacked* against the table. Even the testing spell seemed out of his reach.

It is fine, he told himself. *You only need practice. Ten years you have been kept from your magic. You cannot expect to learn it in a day.*

"How go the spells, jester?"

His gut curdled at the sound of Lilith's voice. He turned to see her standing behind him, still accompanied by the two students he had seen in the common room next to the dormitories. The three of them held their meals in their hands, but the bowls were half-empty; they had been eating already, and had stopped to come torment him.

"Leave me alone," said Ebon. "I am in no mood for games."

"Oh, but what else are jesters for?" Lilith stepped forwards to sit beside him on the bench. The boy with her sat on her other side, while the other girl sat on Ebon's left. They shuffled slightly, pressing up against him, Lilith leaning close. "Are you finding your lessons difficult? How do you enjoy the other infants in your class? They must be keeping you good company, for I think you are of a mind with them."

Ebon ground his teeth together. Well he remembered Jia's warning that fighting among students was not tolerated. No doubt Lilith was thinking of this as well, and sought to anger him in order to get him in trouble. He would not give her the satisfaction.

Seeing his restraint, she leaned closer still, and her voice became silky smooth. "You know, do you not, that in truth your ignorance is no great loss? You would only be a transmuter, and what value are they?

All know that elementalism is the strongest of the four branches. Mentalism is a close second, and therianthropy at least has some uses. But transmutation? What will you do, if you learn your magic? Will you become some nobleman's plaything in the outland kingdoms, turning water into wine for his court?"

The other two snickered loudly, drawing gazes from students at the tables nearby. Ebon felt his skin darkening as they looked at him, looked at Lilith, and then quickly looked away. He knew that look from too many years spent in his father's company: he was a mouse, and the favorite plaything of a tomcat, and they would keep their distance lest they get scratched.

I will show them who is a mouse, he thought wildly. His hands balled into fists on the table. Rules be damned, he would knock Lilith to the floor. Let her jeer at him then.

"What is going on here, Lilith?"

Ebon looked up to see Jia standing at the table. Her eyes were sharp and narrow, but they were looking at Lilith, not at him. Lilith and her friend shuffled slightly away from Ebon on the bench.

"Nothing, Jia," said Lilith, her voice light, unconcerned. "We are only welcoming the Academy's newest student."

Jia's voice took a quality Ebon had not heard from her before, and it bit like sharpened steel. "That is Instructor Jia to you, student. And I have no doubt how welcoming you can be. Take your greetings and yourselves and move them elsewhere, or I will see you scrubbing the dormitory floors."

Lilith ducked her head in acquiescence and made to rise. Her lackeys did the same. But as she made to stand, still bent over and facing away from Jia, she leaned close one last time to hiss at Ebon. "Keep your eyes open, little jester. You and I shall have such fun together."

Ebon swallowed hard as they left. Jia stayed put for a moment, watching them go. When she was satisfied, she looked back at Ebon. Still his fists were clenched on the tabletop, and now they were quivering. Shaking her head, Jia made to sit down—but Ebon leaped up in a rush, leaving his bowl and cup behind him as he fled the dining hall.

ELEVEN

EBON RAN THROUGH PASSAGEWAY AFTER PASSAGEWAY,
and soon he was hopelessly lost. He saw white doors
and brown, rooms he thought were instructors' offices
and rooms he was sure were classrooms. But he feared
to pass through any of them, for he knew he would
look like a fool. He had had quite enough of that for
one day.

It was a long while yet before he must go to the
library for his afternoon lessons. He slowed to a walk
and let his steps wander, trying to get some sort of
bearing on the halls and the manner in which they

were laid out. Slowly he came to realize that the doors themselves were a sort of code. White wooden doors led outside to the training grounds and gardens. Doors with iron bands were classrooms. Double doors led to large rooms of special significance such as the dining hall or the library. When he saw some instructors disappearing into their studies, he paused and searched the doors for some identifying marks. Then he realized that their lack of ornamentation was their marker: a door of plain brown wood, undecorated, led to a study. All but the dean's door, of course, which had been made of iron. Ebon wondered why that was.

He found a staircase and took it up, looking for similar signals in the upper floors. But it seemed to him that the dormitory doors looked just like the doors to the studies, unless there was some other identifying mark he could not see. And every so often he came upon a door of ebony, or some other black wood. But all of the black doors were locked, and he had no faintest idea what might lie behind them.

Ebon froze in the hallway. He had entirely lost track of time, and now it seemed to him more than an hour must have passed. The afternoon classes had surely already begun.

He ran down the first stairwell he found and pounded through the hallways on the first floor. Now that he knew which doors led where, he was not quite so hopelessly lost as he had been. But still he did not know how to make his way deeper into the Academy, for he had no sense of direction. The halls were empty, so there were no students to follow or instructors to ask for direction.

At last he found a short hallway ending at two doors that looked very familiar. The library, or so he hoped. When he ran and threw the doors open, he nearly dropped to the floor in relief. Before him and above him the library stretched, vast and dusty and filled with the orange glow of the amber-colored glass in the ceiling far above.

Then he realized that he had come storming through in a rush, and much louder than he had meant to. The gaze of every student for thirty paces was fixed on him, all of them frozen in shock. And in the center of them all was Jia, one brow raised as she regarded him.

Ebon gulped and closed the doors behind him, as slowly and as quietly as he could manage. Only then did the students at last turn back to their books, though a few glanced up at him once or twice. Jia never turned her gaze. He made his way between the tables towards her, keenly aware that now he had sweated through the underarms of his robes. And he had not bathed that day, and had no perfume to wear.

"Well met, Ebon," said Jia. "I see you have found your way to the library at last."

He was grateful she did not bring up the incident at the midday meal. If she was content to forget all about it, Ebon was more than willing to do the same.

"Yes, Instructor. I am sorry for being late. Still I have not learned my way about this place."

"I told you that I expected as much. Think nothing of it—though the citadel is large, soon you will walk these halls like one born to them."

He flushed, suppressing a smile, and looked about. Once more he was struck by the size and grandeur of the place. Though its three levels loomed over him, grave and solemn, still he found himself more curious than intimidated. "What . . . that is, what am I meant to do now?"

"Well, that depends. In the strictest sense, you are not *meant* to do anything, other than to enhance your knowledge in whatever way you and I deem best."

He blinked. "I do not understand."

"Come, sit with me." She waved him over to a table at the edge of the room, and moved to sit in a chair beside it. He took the one opposite her as she shifted the books between them so they could see each other.

"Do you know what you mean to do when you have completed your training here, Ebon?"

Ebon considered it for a moment, and then he shook his head. "I have never thought of it. Until two days ago, I never thought to set foot in the Academy at all. My father had long forbid it. Now it seems that all I can do is try to keep up."

"And you should. I have no doubt that that will consume much of your effort, especially at first. But you must begin to think upon this question at once, for its answer is the entire purpose of your study within the library." Jia leaned forwards, her gaze holding his. "Except for a very few, who stay to become instructors in turn, every wizard who studies here will go on to do something else in Underrealm. Some will serve as advisors in the courts of royalty or merchants. This is especially true of the commoners whose training is sponsored by a noble. Others will wander the countryside, using their spells for the benefit of the common folk. In either case, a wizard's purpose is to serve the nine lands. And therefore, the greater their knowledge, the better for all the kingdoms."

Ebon had never thought of this—not that he had had much cause to, never having been allowed to meet another wizard. "You make it sound like a great burden."

"It is a high responsibility—and one that not every wizard takes seriously. I hope that you will, Ebon."

"But I still do not understand, Instructor. What shall I study here?"

She leaned back in her chair, spreading her hands. "Whatever you think will serve you best, in whatever capacity you think you will find yourself after the Academy."

Ebon shook his head. "I have told you, I do not know what I shall do then."

"Well then, mayhap that should be your first goal: to decide. Do you have any interests already?"

Ebon looked away, studying his fingernails. He cleared his throat quietly. "Not any in particular."

Jia gave him a wry smile. "Your eyes give lie to your words, transmuter. Come now. What do you enjoy reading about? Many here enjoy herbs and healing. Others are interested in husbandry and the growing of crops. All are excellent areas of study, if you mean to travel about the nine lands and help others. So?"

Still he felt embarrassed. Throughout his life, a great many things had brought the sharp words and sneers of his father. But the sharpest and the cruelest were often in response to this love of Ebon's, which he had long since learned to keep well-hidden.

He spoke quietly, still uncertain. "I have often . . . that is, I would sometimes find myself reading a book of history. I enjoy tales of the past, of kings and the like who have long since died. Sometimes I would read of armies and battles, the rise and fall of kingdoms. I do not know why, but such tales always—they seemed to call to me."

At first Jia did not answer him. He felt sure she must be smirking at him. But when at last he raised his eyes to look at her, he saw a small but warm smile tugging at the corners of her mouth.

"That is a fine pursuit," she said. "The wisdom of the past can be of great help to us in the present, and lets us create better times to come."

Ebon smiled despite himself and turned away bashfully. "My father called it stupid. He said only fools spent their days living in the past."

"Your father sounds like the greater fool to me," she said snippily.

Though he had not spoken the words himself, still Ebon felt a little thrill, as though he and Jia had done some petty misdeed together. They shared a brief smile before Jia went on.

"I think you will find many helpful volumes here. After all, every book is history, if only it manages to survive the ravages of time for long enough. The older books are kept on the third level, as are the histories compiled by more modern scholars. Take that staircase just there, and then follow the walkway around to the southern wall. I will give you the name of a few volumes you may find helpful. Some are good to read all on their own. But you should start with one that may point you in the right direction. Read it first, and I think you will find yourself drawn towards others that may interest you."

She took a small scrap of parchment and scribbled at it with a quill from the table. After a moment she handed the scrap over to Ebon. The first title was underlined, and he read it aloud.

"*A Treatise on the Great Families of the Nine Lands, Their Origins and Lineage.* What is it?"

Her eyes sparkled as she regarded him. "The beginning of a great journey through the last many centuries, if I guess right."

TWELVE

Wordlessly he stood and made his way to the staircase she had shown him. It was wrought in iron and turned in a circle, one even tighter than the staircase from the Academy's first floor up to the dormitories. It ended at the second floor, and another nearby staircase led to the third.

On the third floor, the railing was eight paces away. He went to it to look over. His hands gripped the railing tightly, and he found it hard to breathe. He must have been at least fifteen paces in the air, mayhap twenty. The figures walking about the first level were now tiny; he could hide them with his thumb. His chest tightened as he turned away, moving closer to the wall.

The south end, Jia had said. He went there quickly, keeping his gaze from the railing. Soon he had reached it, and he scanned the shelves. Every book there was bound in leather, and they were of all colors and sizes. On the parchment, beside the title, Jia had scrawled the words: *Second shelf, third down. Red.*

He found the second bookcase, which had seven shelves. The third down was filled with many tomes, several of them red—but none of the titles scrawled upon the spines matched the one he had been sent to find. Puzzled, he looked at the parchment again. He had not misread it. The book was not there. There was one hole in the shelf, a space where a book might be, but nothing more.

Mayhap Jia had misremembered where the book was. Or mayhap it had been moved. He glanced at the other shelves quickly, but none of them held his prize. Then he moved to the next bookcase, and the next. Mayhap he had missed it. He went back and forth across all of them, finding every red book and reading the title carefully to ensure he had not made a mistake. Then he looked at the other colored books, too. Still nothing.

He ground his teeth. Mayhap he should find an-other title. But no, she had been very clear about where he should begin. He wondered for a moment if the missing book was some cruel joke by Lilith. He looked about, but he could not see her anywhere.

But his wandering eye did catch on something. At one of the tables, another student sat deeply engrossed in a tome. A stack of other books sat by the boy's left hand, and at the bottom of the stack was a red book. Ebon took a step closer. There, glistening with gold foil that had been worn off in places, he read the title: *A Treatise on the Great Families of the Nine Lands, Their Origins and Lineage.*

Ebon took another tentative step forwards. He tried to lean over, to place himself in the boy's field of vision. But the boy did not move. Another step. Still the boy read on, his nose only a few fingers from his book. He could not have seen more than fourteen years. His eyes, now squinting as he read, were close together, and his hair shone with a copper tint in the light of the lamps that hung on the library walls.

Though he felt at a loss for a moment, Ebon quickly chastised himself. The boy was just that—a boy, at least two years younger than Ebon was. All his attention was focused on his book, except when his eyes darted to the side to take notes with a quill. He was not even reading the book that Ebon needed.

"Ahem!"

He cleared his throat far louder than he had intended. Every student within ten paces jumped in their seats and turned to him with glares.

"Sorry! I am sorry!" he whispered, trying to reinforce the apology by waving his hands.

Slowly they turned back to their books. All but the boy with copper hair. Now at last he was looking up at Ebon. His blue eyes were wider than Ebon had at first realized, and now they seemed to take up the larger part of his face. His head was cocked to the side slightly, button nose reminding Ebon strangely of his sister Albi's, though otherwise the two of them could not have looked more different.

Ebon stepped still closer. Now he was at the table, standing above the boy. "I was told to read this book by instructor Jia," he said in a whisper. "Will you need it for much longer?"

The boy's gaze dropped to the book. "Yes," he said, and resumed his reading. His quill darted across the parchment.

Ebon stood stock still for a moment, unsure how to respond. At last he pulled out the chair opposite the boy and sat down. That drew the boy's attention again.

"I am sorry—mayhap I did not speak clearly. Jia told me to read the book. Might I use it—at least until you require it again?"

The boy blinked his blue eyes twice in quick succession, and then his brow furrowed. Again he looked at the book, as though he was hearing Ebon's words now for the first time. "Wait. You say that Jia told you to read it? It is a tome of history."

"I know," said Ebon. "I told her that was what I wished to read, and she pointed me this way."

The boy's eyes shot wide. "You asked to study history? Sky above, I cannot remember meeting another student who found it interesting." Then he drew back, looking suspicious. "Is this a jest? Are you playing some joke?"

"It is no jest," said Ebon, taken aback. "Why—why would it be?"

The boy sighed and shook his head. "Because older children always play jokes on me. And this is a beginner's tome. You are older than I am. Certainly you must have studied beyond it by now."

Ebon spread his hands. "I have not. I swear it. May I please borrow it? You may come and fetch me when you need it back."

Once again those blue eyes widened, and the boy leaned forwards, though his whisper only grew louder. "You *are* a beginner. How can that be? How old are you? I would guess at least sixteen."

Quickly Ebon darted a look over his shoulder, but no one had taken any notice. "Do you need to shout it?"

The boy only gave a little smile. "That settles it—certainly you are new here. Well, you are in luck, friend. I have read the treatise through and through, more times than I have kept count of. Jia told you, I imagine, that it is meant to point you to something else you might care to read?"

"She mentioned something of that sort. Why?"

The boy grinned. "Because I can tell you already what you should read instead—you will enjoy it far more, if you have any sense at all, which I suspect you do. It is a history of the Wizard Kings."

The room seemed to grow darker for a moment. Ebon felt the urge to look behind him again, but he fought it away. Even saying such words felt like a crime. "Do you mean this place has books about them?"

"I am not sure if it is even supposed to be here." The boy leaned forwards, his thin forearms pressing down into the book on his lap. "I found it one day, searching for something else entirely. It bears no title, either on its spine or its cover. I think the library's attendants simply missed it."

A secret book, possibly against the rules. Ebon found himself yearning to read it. He stuck out a hand across the table. "Then show me. I am Ebon, by the way."

"Kalem, of the family Konnel," said the boy. He reached out to grasp Ebon's wrist. "Come. I have hidden it away, to keep it from being found."

They stood, the red book forgotten. Kalem took his hand and dragged him away, down the walkway and around to the other side of the library. But he stepped far too close to the railing for Ebon's liking, and Ebon drew back.

Kalem blinked at him. "What is it?"

Ebon eyed the railing distrustfully. "I do not enjoy heights."

He thought the boy might laugh at him, but Kalem only gave a solemn nod. "I did not either. Then I spent three years on this floor of the library. The feeling shall pass in time, but for now we will walk closer to the wall."

So they did, until they reached the other end of the floor. There on the northern wall, Ebon found to his surprise that there were two passages leading into the granite. Kalem took him through and into a room that mirrored the library on the other side—just as wide, just as long, but with only a single floor below it. He realized that this second part of the library must extend back into the citadel quite a ways, until it butted up against the back walls of the dormitories.

"It is even bigger than I thought," breathed Ebon.

Kalem grinned back at him. "You had not seen this yet? Is it your first day?"

"My second," said Ebon. "How could so many books have ever been written? It must have taken a thousand scribes a thousand years."

"I do not doubt it," said Kalem. "Come."

There were far fewer people in this part of the library, and Ebon saw none at all on the same floor as them—all the students he could see were on the floor below. The lamps were less well-tended, and there was no amber skylight to fill the place with a warm glow, so that they passed from light to shadow and back again. In the farthest, darkest corner of the library, Kalem stopped at last.

"No doubt you received some training wherever you came from," said Kalem. "You can come here and do this any time you like. Only remember where it is."

So saying, he went to the narrow space between two bookshelves where the granite wall showed through. Placing his hands to the wall, he concentrated for a moment. From behind him, Ebon saw the glow of his eyes. Under Kalem's fingers, the stone shifted, turning liquid and sliding aside. When he took his hands away, a perfect hole, like a shelf, had appeared in the rock. Upon that shelf sat a book bound in blue leather. With careful, reverent hands, Kalem reached in to withdraw it.

"Here it is," he said. *"An Account of the Dark War and the Fearless Decree."*

Ebon shuddered as though an icy draft had blown down his back. "You say you found this shelf? How did you know it was there?"

Kalem shook his head quickly. "I found the book in the library. I made the shelf myself. It is no great feat, only you must remember to shift the stone back so that it does not crumble."

Ebon turned his gaze away. "I . . . I am untrained. My father never wanted me to learn magic. He only sent me here after my aunt convinced him."

Kalem's blue eyes widened and glistened in the lamp light. It shocked Ebon how expressive the boy's eyes could be, reacting often to even innocuous statements. "That is a great sorrow. Magic is a gift, and not one to be cast lightly aside. But come. You are here now, and have much interesting reading to do."

He led Ebon to a corner where a small table waited with two plush red chairs beside it. Ebon risked a look around before they sat, but still no students were in sight on their floor. Kalem saw his look, and his copper brows drew close together.

"Why do you keep looking about? No one is here to see us read it."

"It is not that. I only . . ." Ebon stopped. How could he tell this boy that already he was mocked for having to study with children, and he had no wish to give Lilith and her friends further cause to torment him?

But Kalem must have read something in his face, for once again he looked solemn and nodded. "I am young. You think I am a child, and do not wish to be seen with me."

"It is not that," Ebon said quickly, wishing he had been quicker to find a lie. "I . . . that is, a tome of the Wizard Kings . . ."

But Kalem waved him to silence. "Do not trouble yourself. I am well used to it by now. They placed me in a class more advanced than my years, for I learned my first transmutation lessons quickly. Now I am two years ahead. None of the other students in my class wish to spend much time with me, either. I am somewhat used to it." But despite the gentle words, Kalem avoided his gaze.

Ebon's attention caught on something else entirely, however. "Did you say you are an alchemist?"

Kalem blinked in surprise. "Are you indeed so unused to magic? Of course I am a transmuter—and you should not use the commoner's word for it, by the way. You saw me shift the stone. What else would I be?"

Ebon cursed inwardly. He should have recognized it at once, but he was unused to seeing such spells. "You and I share a gift. I am an alch—that is, a transmuter."

Kalem's mouth dropped open, his cheeks growing flush with joy. "Sky above. You are in Credell's class, then?"

"I am, sadly." Ebon shook his head and lowered his eyes.

"Sadly? What do you mean?"

Ebon shook his head and hit his hand upon the table, harder than he had meant to. "Credell seems terrified of me. He quivers too much to give me any sort of lessons. I only hope he gets over his terror long enough for me to pass beyond his class."

Kalem nodded sagely. "Ah, I see. I suffered much the same fate when I studied with him, though not so bad as you make it sound."

"Did you? Why?"

Once again the boy's cheeks flushed, and he lowered his gaze. "I imagine you must not know much of the kingdom of Hedgemond. We Konnels are of the royal family there, a smaller clan, yet still holding close to some power. You must be royalty as well if Credell is so frightened, though from your look I would guess you are from Idris. I suppose that makes us kin, though no doubt very distant?"

Ebon let that pass without correcting him. At last it seemed he had met a friendly face here, and he would do nothing to drive the boy away with the name of Drayden. And if he invited scorn by befriending Kalem, what of it? It seemed that to Lilith he was already a laughingstock, and to the other students he was someone to be avoided. Kalem's friendship could hardly hurt. "How, then, did you deal with Credell? For you said you took to your lessons quickly, or at least quickly enough that you eventually graduated his class."

Kalem did not seem to notice that Ebon had avoided his question. "I did the best I could, listened when he instructed the others, and practiced in my every spare moment. Once you pass the novice test, you will move to the second class."

"What is the novice test? No one made mention of it to me."

Kalem gawked at him. "Indeed? You must be of much higher birth than me, if Credell is that scared of you. The novice test is to turn a rod of wood into one of stone."

Now Ebon understood the wooden sticks he had seen in the hands of the other students in his class. "Turning wood to stone? Is that possible?"

"Have you really never seen such magic?" The boy smirked, but quickly hid it. "I am sorry. I cannot imagine what it must have been like for you, being so sternly kept away from what should have been a great joy."

"My father thought magic was . . . unseemly."

Kalem drew back and narrowed his eyes. "Are you—are you, by some chance, your father's eldest child?"

Ebon felt he had drifted upon some dangerous ground, but he did not know what it was. "I am. I had an older brother, but he was killed."

"You are the heir, then? The next head of your family?"

He swallowed hard, wondering how long he could maintain the deception of being royalty. "I am my father's successor, yes."

"Do you think your father meant to keep your talents hidden, and try to put you upon the throne?"

Ebon blanched. "No one would try to put a wizard upon a throne. That would invite the High King's wrath. You know this."

"I do," said Kalem, looking at his fingers where they toyed with each other in his lap. "Yet I have heard rumors that some have tried it. Always they are found and put to death, by the Mystics and the King's law both. Yet still some try."

"That was not my father's aim, I promise you. He would sooner see me in exile than holding any power, I think."

Kalem looked at him. "I am relieved to hear it, though it is a sad thing indeed. My father never had to worry about such—my sister waits to take his place at the head of the family, and I have two older brothers besides. Also, we are far removed from the line of succession to Hedgemond's throne. Sometimes I think my father scarcely notices me. And he is . . ."

He blushed and looked down. Ebon leaned forwards. "What is it? You may tell me."

The boy was silent a moment. "He is more concerned with our coin than with me, I think. We do not have the wealth we once did, and sometimes I have heard him and my mother speaking of what they might have to do if our coffers should run dry. I sometimes wonder if they will be able to keep paying for my teachings here. I do not know what I would do if they could not."

Pity flowed through Ebon, much to his surprise. Of all the many causes for concern his family had often given him, worry of their wealth was not one of them. It seemed that the Drayden accounts were bottomless. And with that thought, he had a flash of inspiration. He turned his chair to face Kalem and leaned forwards intently.

"Then let me make you this bargain, Kalem of the family Konnel. I will learn nothing while I am under Credell's tutelage. So you shall teach me instead. If you do, I shall give you a portion of my allowance. You can save it, and if your family cannot pay for your schooling, you will do it yourself."

Kalem looked at him, eyes shining. "You would do this? Why?"

Ebon shrugged. "Coin is of little concern to us. I am much more worried about how fast I shall learn my spells. It seems that each of us may solve the other's problem. What do you say? Is the bargain struck?"

Kalem grinned and thrust forth a hand. "It is."

Ebon shook his wrist. "Done, then. And I propose that we celebrate our pact. Let me take you out upon the Seat tonight, and we shall toast our bargain until we cannot see to find our way home."

The boy's smile vanished, and his eyes grew wide. "Do . . . do you mean to say we shall *drink?*"

Ebon smiled. "As an alchemist you may be the master, but it seems I have much to teach you as well."

THIRTEEN

THEY LEFT THE LIBRARY THE MOMENT THE BELL rang. Ebon greatly wished for better clothes to wear out, but neither of them had anything grander than their simple black robes. But on the other hand, that meant there was no delay before their departure. He half thought that if Kalem were given any chance at all, the boy would turn tail and run as fast as he could.

"It is only that I have never had wine or ale before," Kalem said, as Ebon practically shoved him through the Academy's front door and into the street. "My mother and father viewed drinking much the same way your father, it seems, viewed magic."

"Then they are all wrong, though for different reasons," said Ebon. "There is much joy, and mayhap even some wisdom, to be found in the bottom of a cup, as you will soon learn. But we should find a place as far from the Academy as we can, so long as we can still find our way back."

They were not the only ones leaving the Academy. All around them, students in black robes flooded the streets, all of them seeming to have the same intent as Ebon: to forget the day's lessons and worries with the bounties of grape and grain. Ebon saw many taverns as they walked, but black-robed students entered all of them, and so he passed them by. Soon the streets thinned out, except for the Seat's usual crowds: trades-men bringing their wares home for the day, and mer-chants and the nobility traveling here and there to at-tend parties and balls. It was a chillier day than the one before, and as the sun lowered, a brisk breeze snapped at their ears. Ebon put his hands in the pockets of his robes to warm them.

He found he was much more comfortable than the last time he had walked upon the Seat, when Tamen had been at his side and he had worried that any mis-deed might be carried straight to the ears of his father. Now he spun as he walked, looking all about him at the buildings. Some were tall and mighty, and others were small and modest, but all felt warm and comfortable.

"The Seat is nothing like back home," he said, only half speaking to Kalem. "Even in the capital, all the buildings are made of white plaster, and they glare in the sun until they hurt the eyes. Everyone wears veils to protect themselves. Only the king's palace is different—lavish, built from stone and steel, and shining with gold spires and great domes. It is a pretty enough sight, I suppose. But I prefer the Seat."

"I still miss home," Kalem said quietly. "Our king rules from Highfell, and that is certainly no place so mighty as the Seat. Yet though the buildings are simpler, they seem more welcoming, and though the palace is nowhere near so grand as the High King's, still my breath was stripped away when I first beheld it."

Ebon looked at him in surprise. The boy spoke with surprising passion. Ebon wondered what it was like to be homesick—truly homesick, not like his earlier vague desire to flee the Academy back to Idris. He imagined yearning for the place from which you hailed, rather than for a few people whose company you enjoyed there.

They had not seen a black robe on the last many streets, and so Ebon cast his eyes about for a tavern. Soon he found one, a place with no door barring its entry and a wide window in the wall. He thought, with a flutter in his stomach, of the window through which he had spied a blue door. Had that really only been a few days ago? It seemed a lifetime. Well he remembered that place, far to the west of here, and in the back of his mind he decided that he might visit it again, if the chance arose. Had not Adara told him that she hoped he would return? They were the words of a lover, and mayhap spurred by coin. Yet now he could find out for himself.

But he drew his mind back to the here and now as he pulled Kalem towards the inn. "Come, we shall drink here. It seems a fine place—and just near enough that we shall not have trouble finding our way home."

"Are you certain?" said Kalem, looking up at the sky. "Already the day nears darkness."

"Then we shall walk home in torchlight. Come."

They stepped in through the door. Ebon was gratified to see that no one gave them a second glance. He still feared that Kalem might try to escape, so he kept his hand on the boy's arm on their way to the bar at the back of the tavern. There a stout man with great growths of brown hair on his cheeks surveyed them with a keen eye. His thick nose was red, and he wore an air that said he could be friendly enough, but would brook no disturbance of his domain. Ebon had seen it in many barkeeps over the years.

"Academy whelps," he said. "And not ones I have seen before."

Ebon felt a moment's trepidation. "Is our coin less welcome here than another's would be?"

The man shook his head. "Coin is coin. Only that boy with you looks a bit young."

"I will care for him," said Ebon, reaching into the purse at his belt. "And coin is coin, as you say."

He flipped a weight into the air, and the man caught it easily. His eyebrows raised slightly, and he bit down on the gold. "So it is, young master. They call me Leven, and I am at your service."

"Then let us have some wine, Leven; and make it something fine, from Calentin, but no cinnamon, if you please. I am Ebon, and my friend here is Kalem. I do not think we will drink enough for that weight tonight—but I ask that you do your best to help us try. If you do, I shall bring more of them."

Leven nodded and turned to fetch a flagon from a shelf. This he gave to Ebon, as well as two goblets of pewter—finer things than the wooden cups held by most of the tavern's other patrons. Ebon nodded his thanks and shoved his way back into the crowd, seeking an empty table.

Kalem was gawking at him. "A whole gold weight? That must be fine drink indeed."

"Not so fine as the price I paid," said Ebon. "But here is your first lesson of taverns, Kalem: pay the proprietor well when you can, and better than you should. If they are of a good sort, they will remember it when your purse weighs less. Now help me find a table—it is dim in here."

The boy gulped and nodded. At last Ebon spotted one in the corner—a low table, with benches set to either side of it, and both of them shrouded in darkness.

It was perfect. Even if another student from the Academy were to come, he doubted they would see Ebon or Kalem sitting in the shadows.

"Here, Kalem. This will do nicely—ulp!" Ebon shot up in the middle of sitting down, for his rear end had struck someone.

"What do you want?" snapped a voice. Ebon peered closer, and saw bright eyes peering at him out of the darkness. He had guessed right about the shadows—the girl had been invisible, so complete was her concealment. Then he leaned closer, and saw that there was still another reason for it: as well as her walnut-dark skin, she wore the same black robes as Ebon and Kalem and had her hood up. Another student from the Academy.

"I—er, that is, I did not mean . . ."

The girl only stared at him, and to his relief Ebon did not think he saw much rancor in her eyes. "Did not mean to place your fat rear upon me? I should hope not."

Ebon swallowed. "I—we can find another table."

She studied him for a moment. Beneath the hood, her hair was the color of sun-dried wheat, but he could see that it was dyed that color, and cut in a short bob. Her light eyes were sharp, peering at him over a thin nose. Slowly those eyes turned downwards, spying the flagon in his hand.

"You could sit elsewhere. But then how could two whelps like you hope to drink all that wine?"

Ebon looked to his right. Kalem's eyes were fixed on the girl. Hoping her words were an invitation, Ebon nudged Kalem to take a seat on the other bench, and then slid in to sit beside him. The girl had a wooden cup before her, and Ebon carefully filled it before doing the same to the pewter goblets. Once the drinks were poured, he raised his and poked Kalem to do the same.

"To the hospitality of strangers in taverns," he said.

The girl neither answered nor raised her cup. Instead she threw the wine back in one long pull and clapped the empty cup down onto the table. Ebon hastened to follow her, but he could only drink half his goblet at once. Kalem seemed to have forgotten he was supposed to drink his at all.

The girl closed her eyes, running a tongue across her lips. "Sky above, that is fine stuff." Her eyes snapped back open, narrowing at them. "Fine indeed. The two of you are goldbags, then?"

Ebon balked. Mako, his aunt's guard, had used the same word, but he had never heard it before that, and had not wanted to ask the man for its meaning. But beside him Kalem blushed and ducked his head.

"We do not use that word where I come from," said Ebon, feeling the need to bolster the boy. "It does not sound very polite."

"That it is not," said the girl. She reached for the flagon and poured herself another cup, draining it in another long swallow. Ebon expected her to explain further, but she spoke no word. Kalem still had not touched his goblet. Ebon nudged him, and the boy took a tentative sip. His eyes widened, and he looked to Ebon.

"That . . . that tastes wonderful," he said.

The girl arched an eyebrow. "And this one is a gold-bag whelp."

Ebon found his hackles rising, but he tried to stay calm. "If you intend to keep calling us that, at least tell me what it means."

But Kalem spoke before the girl could answer. "It is just what it sounds like. Goldbags—wealthy."

Ebon blinked. The girl leaned forwards, smiling at him, but not very kindly. "Wealthy, eh? I suppose some would put it that way. Some others would say greedy. Sitting in your palaces and manors, hoarding your gold. What do you lot do with all that coin, anyway?"

He held her gaze. "Just now, we pay for you to drink a fine Calentin wine."

She stared, and Ebon feared she might strike him—either with her first, or with magic, he was not sure, and did not know which would be worse. But then she burst out laughing and leaned back against the wall behind her.

"Fairly spoken, and more well-mannered than I have been. Never let it be said that only your kind are polite. I am Theren."

Ebon noted carefully that she did not give a family

name, but he did not think it wise to ask why—he thought he could guess. "I am Ebon," he said, leaning forwards and extending a hand. "My friend is Kalem."

"Of the family Konnel," Kalem piped up. Ebon winced. Already the girl seemed irritated at their status. It seemed unwise to dangle their parentage before her eyes.

Sure enough, she sneered. "Oh, sky above, a *royal* goldbag." But when Kalem flushed and looked back towards his lap, she snickered. "Come now, child, I mean nothing by it. Goldbags are all alike to me—I think only you lot hold royalty in higher regard than the rest of us."

"You are a student, I can see," said Ebon, hoping to move the conversation onwards.

"As are you."

"Of what branch? And what year?"

"Inquisitive, are we? A mentalist, seventh year."

Ebon glanced at Kalem, and saw the boy looking at Theren with the same awe Ebon was certain must show in his own face. "You are nearly finished with your training, then?"

Theren shrugged. "Mayhap. They have not found a spell to teach me that I could not master. As long as they keep trying, I will keep learning, I suppose."

Ebon thought of the words he had had with Jia earlier. "And then? What will you do after? Surely your patron must be eager to have you back."

Her lip curled, and he knew he had made a mistake. "Of course you would assume I have a patron," she said. "But then again, a goldbag *would* think that a common girl could not be at the Academy without the help of some wealthy lord."

"I meant no offense." He did not break her gaze, hoping she could see his earnestness. "I am unused to the Seat, and unused to the Academy especially. It seems I have much to learn before I can even speak without making a fool of myself."

Her glower softened, and she turned away. "It seems so. And besides, you speak true. I have a patron, though I do not relish it. Not all of us have it so easy as you two, no doubt sent here with a mountain of your parents' coin to waste. Though I cannot complain at how you choose to waste it." She lifted her cup for emphasis, and then reached for the flagon again.

Ebon shrugged. "My family was not my choice, I assure you of that. Each life comes with its own struggles, and ours are no exception." She snorted. He ignored it, though it rankled him. "But if I am not fond of where my coin comes from, and if you and I both appreciate good wine, then help me waste it, I say."

She wagged a finger at him. "Now at last you speak wisdom. I suppose you are not so bad as all that—for a goldbag, at any rate. But if you mean what you say about being wasteful, we shall need another two flagons at least."

Wordlessly, Ebon reached for his purse and produced another gold weight. She rose and took it, studying it in the lantern light for a moment. Then she looked up at him once more.

"Very well, Ebon," she said. Ebon did not miss the fact it was the first time she had used his name. "Can you find it in you to forgive words harshly spoken? And you as well, Kalem?"

"Can you find it in you to get the damned wine?" said Ebon, smiling at her. "The flagon is nearly empty, and we do not have all night to drink."

Theren left them with a laugh. Ebon turned his smile on Kalem.

"I think I like her," said Ebon. Kalem did not speak a word, his eyes fixed on Theren from across the room. Ebon shoved his shoulder. "Leave off, little *goldbag*. If you stare any harder, your eyes may melt. Or mayhap she will melt them for you—can a mindmage do that?"

That shook Kalem from his reverie, and he glared at Ebon. "A *mentalist*, Ebon, honestly. And no, she could not—though I could, if I learned the spell to shift living flesh."

"You can turn stone and not flesh?" said Ebon in surprise. "But stone is so much stronger."

"Yes, and simpler. That is the key. Stone is much the same through and through. But our bodies are made up of so much—water, they say, and fire, and . . . well, flesh. That is why you are set to work upon a wooden rod. Wood, and all plants, are somewhere in between flesh and stone. It is easier to turn something complex into something simple than the other way around."

Ebon felt as though his head was spinning. "I fear I do not understand."

Kalem leaned forwards, eyes sparking with interest. Ebon had a feeling that the boy did not often get the chance to speak of such things with someone who cared to listen. "There are hierarchies, you see. Stone is one of the simplest, then wood, then flesh, to speak broadly. To turn wood to stone is easy. Flesh to stone is harder, but still easy for any second-year transmuter. Flesh to wood is harder still. Then stone to wood, stone to flesh, and wood to flesh. And then there is *shifting*. That is when you do not simply *turn* matter—you melt it, or turn it to mist, or make it vanish entirely. That is . . . not *easier*, perhaps, but different, in a way many find easier to grasp. Do you see?"

Ebon did not see. In fact, Kalem had said *stone* and *wood* and *flesh* so many times that, together with the wine, Ebon was having difficulty remembering which word meant what. But just then, three black-robed figures strode through the tavern door, and Ebon's heart quailed as he recognized Lilith and her cronies.

Quickly he turned his head to the side, trying to hide his face.

"Shift yourself over," he said quietly. "Sink into the shadows."

Kalem blinked at him. "What? Why? What is it?"

"Those three who just entered, they are—"

"Is that my jester?"

Ebon groaned and looked up. Lilith wore a smile

as she approached his table, standing there at the end of the bench so he could not rise without pushing her out of the way. Her companions stood behind her, still silent, arms folded as they looked down at him.

"Leave us be, Lilith," said Ebon. "What are you doing here, anyway?"

"I came seeking another, but now I think it would amuse me to drink with you instead. And may I remark how adorable it is to see you beyond the Academy walls with one of your classmates. He must be a first-year."

"I am not," said Kalem at once. "You have seen me before. I am in the—"

"Quiet, child," snapped Lilith, before turning her gaze back on Ebon. "I learned something of you today, jester. Do you want to know what it was?"

Ebon felt the blood drain from his face. He knew, or thought he could guess, what she was about to say. He had to distract her. "You know that if you fight me, neither of us will be welcome within the Academy again."

Lilith laughed at him, and turned to her friends. "Oren, Nella, did you hear that? My jester is worried for me. How kind of him to think of my education. But why would I fight you, little jester? You did not let me tell you what I had learned about you—Ebon, of the family Drayden."

Ebon glared at her. From the corner of his eye, he could see Kalem looking at him with wide eyes.

She smiled at Ebon's expression. "Yes, it was quite a shock. But I suppose it makes sense. A worthless student from a worthless family. Why did they send you away, jester? Had they run out of water for you to lick up from the ground?"

Before he knew what he was doing, Ebon shot to his feet, but Nella, the girl by Lilith's side, shoved him back down onto his bench. He tried to rise again, but found himself unable to move. His muscles strained against some unseen barrier. With wide eyes he looked down, but there was nothing there. Then he saw Oren's eyes glowing white, and he realized: this was magic.

Lilith leaned down, one hand resting on the table so that her face was only a few fingers from his. "What is wrong, water licker? Did no one ever teach you to deal with a *real* wizard?"

Ebon held her gaze, letting his hatred show. But then he saw movement over her shoulder: Theren, returning with two new flagons of wine. She stopped just behind Oren and Nella and glared. Then her eyes glowed white.

Lilith cried out as her foot shot up into the air behind her. Her head bounced off the table on the way down as she was lifted up.

The glow died in Oren's eyes as he turned in shock. An invisible force struck him in the chest, and he fell back against the wall. Nella spun in midair and fell next to him, and Ebon saw her grunting and straining against some hidden force.

Lilith's bonds slackened, and she crashed to the tavern's wooden floor. At once she shot to her feet, hands twisting before her as her eyes began to glow—but then she saw Theren and stopped. For a moment, all was still.

Then Leven the tavern-master was there, pushing himself into the space between Theren and Lilith, barrel chest blocking each of them from the other's view as he thrust his arms in either direction.

"All right, you lot have had your fun. No spell-casting is allowed in my barroom, as *you* know full well." He thrust a finger just under Theren's nose.

She smirked at him. "What spell-casting? The moment they saw me, they grew frightened and fell to the floor."

Lilith pushed forwards, but with a hand on her chest Leven stopped her. "That is enough. Leave here now, and mayhap I shall not send a letter to your masters."

The Yerrin girl glared at him, and then at Theren, but Theren's smirk only widened. With a huff, Lilith whirled and strode from the tavern—but not before she gave Ebon one last look of hate. Nella helped Oren to his feet, and they scuttled out the door after her.

The tavern had grown quiet as the fight broke out, but now slowly the other patrons turned back to their drinks and resumed talking. Leven watched as Lilith and the others left, and then turned his considerable girth on Theren, hands bunched to fists on his hips.

"You swore to me you would not begin another wizard's duel here."

Theren still held a flagon in either hand, but she swept one foot behind the other to dip in a low bow. "And it gives me great pleasure to have kept my vow. I did not begin a duel at all. In fact, to my mind, I ended one."

Leven shook his head. "I mean it, girl. I will not have you breaking more tables—not to mention my finest bottles."

Theren straightened and wiggled the flagons before his eyes. "Even if I have a new friend, who is willing to pay handsomely for such fine bottles?"

The alemaster shook his head, and his scowl weakened somewhat. But his voice remained stern. "Just remember: become more trouble than you are worth, and you will no longer be welcome here."

She stepped past him, planting a brief kiss on his cheek. "You have the heart of a king, Leven." But Ebon noted that that was no answer.

Leven walked away, and Theren resumed her seat across the table. She pushed one flagon towards Ebon and took a long pull directly from the other. "Well. It seems I misjudged you. If Lilith dislikes you so, you must be very nearly honorable—at least for goldbags."

Ebon shrugged. But Kalem had ducked his gaze, and at Theren's words he made to stand. "I should be returning to the Academy," the boy mumbled. "It is very late."

"Kalem, sit down," Ebon urged him. "Please. I am sorry, for I dealt with you dishonestly, though I did not lie."

Theren arched a thin eyebrow. "Oh? Dissent among the ranks?"

Ebon sighed and fixed her with a look. "I shall tell you as well, I suppose, since I would rather not anger you later, with your command of magic. I failed to mention my family's name earlier. But I am Ebon, of the family Drayden, and I hail from the capital of Idris."

Theren became very still, except for her fingers, which drummed on the neck of her wine flagon: *tap-tap. Tap-tap.*

"I am sorry," said Ebon, lowering his gaze now. "Only . . . only that name has plagued me all my life, and it seems that everyone I meet hates me because I carry it. I thought that here, where we all wear the same black robes, mayhap I could leave it behind. Yet I cannot. Lilith will not let me—and now, it seems, neither will the two of you. I should not have come here tonight." He made to stand.

"Oh, sit down," said Theren, eyes rolling. "Honestly, you wealthy ones are so prone to dramatics."

Ebon hesitated. Looking back, he saw Kalem still gazing at his own lap. After a long moment of silence, the boy finally looked up at him. "I thought you were royalty, like me."

"I am not," said Ebon. "Would you have befriended me, if you knew? I have not had a friend in many a long year. Forgive me, for I saw a chance at finding one, but I should not have lied to make it come true."

For a moment Kalem looked out the window, to the street where constables were just now coming around to light the street lamps. His hands twisted in his lap. "I suppose I can understand that," he said quietly.

Theren took Ebon's goblet and handed it to him. "Drayden or not, and whether you summon it by gold or by alchemy—only keep the wine coming, and you will have my friendship."

Ebon smirked, and he saw Kalem give a little smile. He took his seat, and together they raised their cups to drink deep.

FOURTEEN

WHEN HE WENT TO BREAK HIS FAST THE NEXT MORN-
ing, Ebon sat at an empty table as he had done before.
But soon, to his slight surprise, Theren came and sat
wordlessly on the bench beside him. After a moment,
Kalem sat on his other side. Theren looked none the
worse for wear, but Kalem held a hand pressed hard
over his blue eyes, and his coppery hair was greasy, as
though he had yet to bathe.

"Why?" he muttered as he sat with them. "Why
does it hurt so?"

Ebon smiled. "You have found the sweet pain of

wine, my young friend. I fear that I did not watch you as closely as I should have. You drank too much for your own good."

Kalem peered at him from between his fingers. "Is it always like this? Do dragons scream within your head as well?"

"They do not, but then I do not think I drank so much as you," said Ebon diplomatically.

"You had more, and so did I," said Theren, missing his attempt at kindness—or mayhap not caring. "But we can hold our wine."

"Do not say that word," said Kalem, quickly pressing a hand to his mouth. "The very sound of it makes me want to vomit."

Ebon clapped him on the back, and the boy winced. "You should be proud you have not done that already."

"I have. Twice."

Theren had finished her food shockingly fast, and now she shoved the heel of her bread into Ebon's bowl to soak up some of his broth. "It occurs to me that after last night's fisticuffs, which I rather enjoyed, our conversation did not range so far as it might have. We seemed more interested in wine than words."

"*Please,* do not say that word."

Theren ignored him. "What did you do to invite Lilith's wrath, Ebon?"

Ebon shrugged, though secretly he was pleased that she no longer called him 'goldbag.' "I only met her the day before last. She seemed to hate me from the start, though as you heard, she did not learn my family's name until yesterday. Mayhap she only meant to mock me at first, because I . . . that is, I am . . ."

Theren frowned. "What is it? Come, spit it out."

Kalem looked at her, lips twisting. "He is untrained. His father never let him study magic."

Theren stared. "You cannot be serious."

"I wish I were not."

Theren's eyes glowed as she twisted a finger, and the empty bowl before her lifted up until it was standing on one edge. Spinning her finger in little circles, she sent it twirling on the spot, until it was only a blur before her. Ebon did not know if she did it to torment him, or only because her mind was working, but he wished she would stop it. "You mean to say that you cannot do even the simplest of magic? How did you learn you were an alchemist, then?"

"Transmuter," said Kalem.

"Wine," said Theren. Kalem groaned.

"I did the testing spell when I was a child," said Ebon. "But the moment my father learned the truth, he forbade me from ever trying it again. My valet was required to report it if I was ever seen trying a spell. I managed the testing spell again only two days ago, but when I tried it yesterday, it did not work."

"What did Credell say when you told him?" said Kalem.

Ebon stabbed his spoon into his soup, making some of it splash out on the table. "It was hard to tell around all of his gibbering. He is more frightened of me than he would be of a viper in his bed. At this rate I shall never be an alchemist."

Theren snorted. "Poor little goldbag. You know, do you not, that some of us do not have a family name to help us in our training here?"

He glared at her. "My name has not helped me at all. If anything, it has made things worse."

She dismissed him with a wave. "Spare me. The dean is a Drayden, and no doubt some distant cousin of yours." Then the glow faded from her eyes, and she leaned forwards with interest. Her bowl stopped spinning, and her voice dropped to a conspiratorial whisper. "Say. You could appeal to him for special permissions. We could leave the Academy after hours if we wanted. Mayhap you could have him speak to my instructor to teach me higher spells."

"You misunderstand his view of me," said Ebon. "He only sees me at all out of pompous vanity and some small sense of duty to my aunt. And his visit made Credell's treatment of me all the more difficult to bear."

Theren glared at him. "Poor little goldbag," she said again. She leaned back, her eyes glowed, and her spoon flew into her bowl with a little *clunk*.

Kalem watched her spells with a little pout. "I wish I were a mentalist," he said wistfully. "Or an elementalist, even. How wonderful it must be to have such power. Transmutation often seems the weakest of the branches."

Theren shrugged. "I will not deny that my gift can be amusing."

Ebon, too, was impressed by her effortless command of her magic. And watching her lift her bowl into her hands using only her mind, he was struck by an idea. "Theren—could you teach me?"

She blinked at him, the glow in her eyes dying. "Teach you what?"

"Magic. Kalem agreed to help me learn my spells, but you are more advanced than he. Mayhap you could even help both of us."

Kalem and Theren gawked at each other before looking back to Ebon. "Sky above," Theren said quietly. "Do you honestly know *nothing* of magic?"

He felt his cheeks burning, and he ducked his head. "I have told you as much already."

"You said so, yes, but . . ." Theren chuckled. "Oh, this is rich indeed. I was determined not to pity you, Ebon, but you test my limits."

Ebon leaned away from the table, folding his arms. He knew he must look like a pouting child, but he did not care. "Stop your mockery. Tell me what I said wrong."

Kalem put a gentle hand on Ebon's arm and spoke with a slow patience that grated on his nerves. "The different branches are utterly unlike each other. Theren could no more teach you magic than a bird could teach you to fly."

"I do not understand," said Ebon, brow furrowing.

"Magic is magic. Does it not all come from the same source?"

Theren shook her head sadly as Kalem went on. "Mayhap, but it becomes different by the time we are able to use it. Elementalism is chiefly cast through speech, mentalism through the eyes. Therianthropy takes place in the mind, and transmutation is cast through the hands."

"But we all envision our spells as we cast them," said Ebon.

Kalem's lips pressed together, and he looked helplessly at Theren. Again she shook her head. "Yes and no. It is . . . well, it is difficult to explain, even for me. Even, I sometimes think, for our instructors. I can tell you only that once you have attained command of your gift, it comes ever more naturally. Likely you do not remember learning to walk, but you have seen babies trying to master it. They try and try, but they cannot keep their balance. Then, one day, they are able to take their first steps. From then on, they simply . . . walk. You do it without thinking now—but could you explain it to an infant?"

"And transmutation is to mentalism as walking is to a fish's swimming," put in Kalem, "or like a bird's learning to fly."

Ebon shook his head miserably. "I still do not understand."

Kalem put a hand on his shoulder and smiled brightly. "You shall. I will do my best to teach you.

Soon you shall turn wood to stone as though it were pouring wine into a goblet." His face soured. "Ugh. I may need to retch again."

Ebon sighed. "I tried that this morning. I snuck into my classroom to fetch a wooden rod." He pulled it from his robes. "Yet it is still wooden, and I cannot seem to grasp the first thing about turning it otherwise."

"You will learn it soon," said Kalem.

"I hope so," groused Ebon. "It would be nice to have a victory, even one so small. My instructor is afraid of me, the dean only makes it worse, and for some reason I cannot comprehend, a Yerrin girl has decided to make me her own personal whipping-boy. Finding I cannot use magic after all would only seem to fit the pattern."

Theren's eyes glowed, and the rod floated from his grip into the air. She spun it before her eyes as she pursed her lips. "Well, I do not envy you. Learning my first magic after the testing spell seemed to take ages. But it came easier after that." The glow died away, and she caught the rod as it fell. She leaned forwards with interest, pointing the rod at Ebon like a baton. "Say. Mayhap we can solve one of your problems, at least. You have started some quarrel with Lilith, or the quarrel has come to you regardless. How should you like to repay her for shaming you?"

"Theren," said Kalem. His voice held a tone of warning. But Ebon leaned towards her, his interest piqued.

"I do not wish to invite the instructors' wrath for fighting," he said.

"*Fighting,*" said Theren with a quick shake of her head. "Sky above, nothing so crass. Only . . . she has the best of you in magic, yes? Yet you have strengths. Your family name is stronger than hers, and your pockets are deeper. And you have me." Her teeth flashed in a grin.

"Ebon, this is a terrible idea," said Kalem.

"You have not even heard it," said Theren.

"Say on, then," said Ebon.

"Not here." Theren looked about as though someone might be listening. "But let us gather after the day's studies, and we shall see what might be done."

"Why?" said Kalem, narrowing his eyes. "Why would you help him fight Lilith?"

Theren only shrugged. "She and I have had our own tussles in the past. Surely you can imagine how a girl like her might have more than one foe."

A bell clanged, reverberating about the dining hall. "Well, let us go to our classes," said Kalem. "This afternoon I shall do my best to help you learn your spells, and mayhap you will forget all about this foolish plan of Theren's."

"Fare well," said Theren. "I shall see you this evening. And know this, Ebon: I have not forgotten my plans for you. Some day soon you will speak to the dean on our behalf." She fixed him with a stern look and turned to go.

"She left her dishes," grumbled Kalem, scooping them up from the table.

Ebon realized later that he had not the faintest idea where to find Theren after their studies. But he need not have worried. When he and Kalem left the library at the end of the day, they found Theren waiting for them in the hall just outside. She stood on one foot and leaned against the wall, arms folded, but she straightened as soon as she saw them.

"There you two are. It took you long enough. Do not tell me you are bookworms as well as goldbags. I can only forgive so many flaws."

"Theren, I have been thinking," said Kalem. "Mayhap all that is required here is a calm, measured conversation with Lilith. I am certain that she and Ebon can work out their differences if only—"

She ignored him, falling into step beside Ebon and speaking so abruptly that Kalem fell to silence. "Allow me to instruct you in the manner of your revenge. I am quite proud of this idea. It relies for its success on the general prudishness of most goldbags, and particularly those of the family Yerrin."

"Prudishness?" said Kalem.

"You royal types are so concerned with concealing yourselves. The family Yerrin have adopted the affectation as well, mayhap because they aspire to your station," explained Theren. "Any commoner in the city or the forest thinks nothing of shedding some clothing on a hot day. But you would rather sit sweating in your carriages than reveal so much as your chest. In the highest circles, I am given to believe that being caught half-naked is the height of embarrassment."

"Well, certainly!" said Kalem indignantly. "You cannot tell me you would enjoy walking about naked. Our bodies are for spouses and lovers."

"Spoken like a true goldbag," sneered Theren. "And so does Lilith believe."

Ebon himself was not overly fond of being seen disrobed, except when it came to servants. But he said only, "I am listening."

"You should be watching instead. Lilith will be in the common room by now."

So saying, she led them on through the halls and up the narrow staircase towards the dormitories. When they reached the door leading to his common room, Ebon balked. But Theren gripped his shoulder with an easy smile.

"Now, then. All you must do is enter the room and speak with Lilith, and I will take care of the rest."

"You want me to attract her attention?" said Ebon. "I think she dislikes me enough as it is. She will set my robe on fire, if she thinks she can get away with it."

Theren shrugged. "Mayhap. But you will not have to suffer her torments long. I promise you that."

"Why will you not come with us?" said Kalem.

Theren's eyes hardened. "Because if she sees me enter with you, she might be less inclined towards torment."

"Oh, well, that *is* reassuring," said Ebon. "You mean to use us as bait."

"Come now. You may be a goldbag, but you do not strike me as a coward. Go, brave warriors! To battle!"

She opened the door and shoved them inside before slamming it behind them. The room was filled with students, some sitting in the chairs and couches, others standing beside them. The sharp noise of the door drew every eye, and for a moment the room was filled with perfect silence.

"Er . . ." said Ebon, his cheeks flushing. "Good evening."

"The jester has arrived!" Lilith's already too-familiar voice sang out from the other end of the room. "Fellow students, our evening's entertainment is here, and not a moment too soon."

She sat in a broad leather armchair, resting upon it as though it were a throne. Oren and Nella completed the picture, standing to either side of her like attendants. At her words, every student averted their gaze. Lilith was clearly on the hunt, and none of the others wished to become prey.

"Well met, Lilith," said Ebon. He wondered if he should go to her, or if he should act as if he were going towards his dormitory. Theren wanted him to speak to Lilith, but would it not be suspicious if he did so directly?

"And you have brought another plaything," said Lilith, nodding towards Kalem. "You must promise to keep him around. Two jesters are twice the fun, after all."

With a sigh, Ebon made his way across the room to her. Until Theren made her move, they would have to keep Lilith's attention. As they drew up before her, Kalem stepped forth and offered his hand. "Er, ah . . . well met. We have not been introduced. I am Kalem, of the . . ."

"Away, whelp. I saw enough of you last night—or at least, what little there is to see." Lilith waved a hand dismissively, and Kalem stepped aside as if she had moved him with mind magic. Her eyes fixed on Ebon. "So. Here he is. The jester of the family *Drayden.*"

She said the name loud enough to be heard throughout the room. From the corner of his eye, Ebon saw that the few students brave enough to look at him quickly turned away.

"I am no jester."

"Yet I find you laughable. And what other purpose does a jester have?" She smiled at him, and then at Kalem. "The two of you are a remarkable pairing. A royal son whose family has great power, and no coin. And a merchant son whose family has great coin, but whose power wanes across the nine lands. What a sight."

"You know nothing of my family," said Ebon, surprised at the fervor in his words. Anger made his stomach clench and the back of his neck prickle. He almost did not hear the sound of a door opening behind him, and then closing again quietly as Theren snuck in.

"Who does not know of the family Drayden?" said Lilith. "So dark and terrible a clan. Yet what have you lot done lately? You sit in your desert halls, planning trade routes and scrimping your coins. How the mighty have fallen. It is said that your grandfather ruled Idris with an iron fist, the royal family serving as his puppets. Your dear aunt must not have the spine for power."

"Do not speak of her," snapped Ebon.

At Lilith's side, Oren and Nella tensed. But Lilith only smiled. "I shall speak of what I wish. After all, we are friends here, are we not? Or at least, we are young people joined in mutual endeavor. To learn our magic. How fare your studies, by the by?"

Ebon's hands balled to fists. Were it not for Theren's command, he would have strode away to find comfort in solitude. Though Lilith sat and he stood, the scorn on her face made him feel as though she were looking down on him.

And then suddenly, she was. Without warning, Lilith's chair rose into the air. At first Ebon thought it was her doing, some trick of firemagic he had never heard of before. But the look of shock on her face soon told him it was otherwise. With a glance over his shoulder, he noticed Theren lurking in a corner, half-hidden behind a couch. Her eyes were glowing.

"What are you doing?" said Lilith. "Put me down at once!"

Ebon spread his hands, stifling a smile. "What do you mean? I know no magic. And I am a transmuter besides. Is this transmutation? If so, I have never seen its like before. Mayhap I have turned you into a bird."

The ceiling in the room was quite high, and now Lilith was very close to it. Then, the chair began to tip. Very, very slowly, it tilted forwards. Now every head in the room was turned towards her, watching as she scrambled to keep her seat. For a moment, Ebon was afraid she would fall to the stone floor. It would not be fatal, but surely it would injure her. But he reassured himself; Theren must know what she was doing.

"It is mindmagic!" cried Lilith. "I can feel it! Oren, stop them!"

"I cannot!" said Oren, whose eyes were glowing now. He ground his teeth in frustration.

"Which one of you is it?" said Nella. She went from chair to chair, seizing students by the front of their robes and looking into their eyes, searching for a glow. "When I find you, I will melt the skin from you!"

Then the chair flipped all the way over. Lilith barely held on to one of the legs, dangling there in midair. But then her feet lifted up, and suddenly she hung upside down in midair. Gravity did its work, and dragged her robe down around her shoulders, exposing her underclothes and a great deal of skin. Kalem yelped and averted his eyes. Throughout the room, reluctantly, students began to giggle. The laughter swelled, and soon was reverberating throughout the room and off the walls.

"What an audience I have tonight," said Ebon, turning to them all with a smile. "It pleases your jester very much to have brought you such mirth." He placed a hand to his waist and bowed, as fine as any courtier. The students only laughed harder.

"Put me down this instant!" cried Lilith. "Theren! Theren, I know it is you!"

She stopped moving through the air at once. Then, swiftly, she came back down. The chair turned over in its descent to land right side up. Lilith was not so lucky, landing hard—but not too hard—on her head. She shot to her feet and replaced her robes, her face a mask of fury. Quickly she made for Ebon.

Theren appeared as if from nowhere, standing beside Ebon with hands balled into fists. Kalem stood to his other side, though Ebon saw the boy gulp in fear. But fright, it seemed, was baseless; Lilith stopped a pace away, staring at Theren with . . . not hatred, nor even anger. Ebon recognized the look with a start, for it was the last thing he would have expected to see: sadness, along with a deep pain.

"You have a forked tongue, Lilith," said Theren softly. "And I care not what you do with it. But you will not use your magic against my friends again."

Oren and Nella came for Theren, but Lilith stopped

them with outstretched arms. Her jaw spasmed again and again, but she spoke no word to Theren. Instead she turned her gaze on Ebon, and familiar hatred reappeared in her eyes.

"Until the morrow, *jester*," she hissed. "You find yourself in fortunate company."

She spun on her heel and swept from the room. Oren and Nella followed after only a moment's hesitation.

The other students in the room turned quickly away. If Ebon had thought to earn more friends, those hopes seemed dashed. But Theren was smiling, and even Kalem wore a nervous little grin. That seemed enough, at least for now.

"I have not had such fun in months," said Theren, grinning. "Come, goldbags. Let us see if we cannot get ourselves a drink before nightfall."

FIFTEEN

They spent their time in the library the next day reading Kalem's hidden tome on the Wizard Kings. Or rather, Ebon read it while Kalem sat by and worked on his own lessons. Often Ebon would have some question about the text, and he would ask Kalem. The boy's knowledge was incredible, and he would always answer Ebon with some tale from another of the library's volumes. Often Ebon would take down the names of other books that Kalem thought he should read, and soon his parchment was full of them. He looked upon the list with some dismay; it seemed half a lifetime's worth of reading.

When he tired of study he would take out his wooden rod, and Kalem would try to teach him how to turn it to stone. But try as he might, Ebon could not summon the magic to do it.

"Take your time," Kalem told him. "It is only your third day."

"You do not understand," said Ebon. "As long as I am in Credell's class, my time here is wasted."

"I passed his class early, and yet still it took me half a year," said Kalem. "You cannot expect to do it in a week, especially when you have never been allowed to practice before."

That day passed, and the next, and the next. Soon Ebon found himself settling into a comfortable routine—comfortable, at any rate, outside of Credell's class, although even that became more tolerable. The instructor still looked at Ebon with wide-eyed terror whenever he spoke or moved. But the other children seemed to forget their fear of him, since he did not do anything particularly frightening, and Ebon began to learn their names. The wild-haired girl he had seen on his first day was called Astrea, and she seemed to take a particular liking to him, though she still feared to speak with him. Often he would catch her staring from across the room, but she turned and blushed whenever he looked her way. Though Astrea looked nothing like Albi, his sister, still something in her manner reminded him of home. Whenever he could manage it, he would catch her gaze and stick his tongue out at her.

She would giggle behind her hand and turn quickly back to her lessons.

Every afternoon, he would huddle in the library with Kalem. He would find tidbits from the history of the Wizard Kings that prompted him to start a catalog of other books to read. But in those tomes he would often come upon something that gave him some question, and then he would refer back to the great blue tome. He and Kalem spent as much time trying to learn spells as they did reading, though Kalem warned him often that they were supposed to use the time for studying, and Jia would be cross if she found out.

After two weeks, Ebon began to feel at home. When he thought back to his first two days, they seemed to have happened to someone else. Even Lilith's torments had lessened, though she still gave him an evil look whenever they passed each other in the hallways, and sometimes she jostled him in the dining hall when she walked by. But she gave him a wide berth whenever he was with Theren, which was often, and if Theren ever caught her nearby, she stared until Lilith scuttled away. Ebon suspected there was some history between the two of them, but when he asked Theren, she only shrugged and said, "Some, yes. She knows better than to create any more."

On some days, Ebon would sneak out of Credell's class and into the training grounds. The instructor could not possibly have failed to notice his absence, but mayhap he was relieved not to have the young

Drayden in his classroom. Ebon knew he would get in trouble if he were ever discovered, but there were many hedges that ran along the Academy's wall, and he could go there to hide himself and watch the other students practice their spells.

Sometimes he watched the classes of the other three branches, the mindmages and firemages and weremages. But most often he went to the smaller grounds to see the alchemists practice. Their spells were less spectacular, not the sort of magic he often heard of in tales and the like. Yet Ebon knew, or hoped, that this magic lay in his future, and so it kept his interest better than any of the others. He did not see the student who had turned her instructor's arrow to dust, but he saw the others performing similar spells with the cloth balls they threw between each other.

When he watched the weremages, one instructor often caught his attention. He was a somewhat older man, black hair dusted with grey, and he wore his beard thick but trimmed close to his face. Ebon thought he had the look of one from Selvan. There was something familiar about him—but mayhap it was only because he looked so kindly. Always he spoke to his students in a calm and measured tone, and Ebon noted how he would show them a spell over and over again until they had learned it. Then he would leave them, but keep watch carefully from the corner of his eye. Ebon often thought wistfully how he wished Credell were such an instructor—but this man was a weremage, and could not have taught Ebon even if he wanted to.

One day he was in the library with Kalem. His wooden rod rested in his hands, and he tried to see into the wood, to change it. But he could not make it swell in his vision, the way a cup of water did when he cast the testing spell.

"Instead of seeing it, try to feel it," said Kalem. "Sometimes that works better."

"Of course I feel it," said Ebon. "I am holding it in my hands, am I not?"

"I do not mean feel it, I mean . . ." Kalem waved his hands about vaguely. *"Feel* it," he finished lamely.

Ebon's nostrils flared. "That makes it all much clearer. Quick, run to fetch Credell! I am ready for my test." He shoved the rod back into his robes. "Enough of this. I have found a book written by a member of my own family, many hundreds of years ago, and to-day I meant to start it. I will return in a moment."

He stood and strode away from their table, among the bookshelves that stood tall about him. The right section was easy enough to find, for he was now well practiced in seeking out the library's many works. Slowly he scanned the spines, looking for his book.

"How go your studies, goldbag?"

Ebon nearly jumped out of his skin, and he gripped the bookshelf to steady himself. When he turned, he could not believe his eyes for a long moment. Before him stood Mako. The man leaned casually against the bookshelf behind Ebon, the wicked knife at his hip shining as bright as the sparkle in his eyes. His thick, tattooed arms were folded over each other, but in one hand he held a book, which he had opened to the middle and appeared to be reading. With a start, Ebon realized that it was the very book he had come here to find.

"Mako? What are you doing here?" Something made Ebon's skin crawl, something more than his normal reaction to the man. How did Mako get to the third floor of the library without causing some sort of commotion in the Academy? Guests were not allowed to roam these halls unescorted. Yet no one else was in sight.

"Your lack of hospitality wounds me," said Mako, frowning. "It seems an eternity since last I was privileged to lay eyes upon you."

Ebon swallowed hard. "It has not even been a month."

"The days seem like years, and all that drivel." Mako slapped the book shut and made to return it to the shelf. But then he caught Ebon looking at it, and he held it up in mock surprise. "Oh, were you looking for this one? Here it is, young lord. Take it with my compliments."

"How did you know?"

Mako's too-friendly grin widened. "How did I know what, Ebon? There are far too many answers to that question for me to give them all here and now."

"Never mind. What do you want?"

"That question, too, comes with a host of replies.

And why should I answer your question, when you have not answered mine?"

"Yours?" said Ebon, blinking.

"The first thing I asked you: how go your studies?"

Ebon looked about, unsure. "They go well enough, I suppose," he said. "Though I find it—"

Mako clapped his hands sharply, and Ebon's words died in his mouth. "Quite enough of that. I have come for another purpose. The family requires something of you."

The library was utterly silent about them. Ebon could hear his heartbeat thundering in his ears. "The family—by which I suppose you mean my father. What does he need?"

Mako looked down at the fingers of his right hand. His left drifted to the hilt of his knife, and Ebon's hands tightened on the spine of his book. But when Mako drew the knife, it was only to pick under his fingernails with the tip. It glistened in the dim orange glow of the library's lamps.

"What sort of question is that?" said Mako lightly. "He is your father, and the reason you attend the Academy at all. Are you not happy to fulfill his heart's desire, whatever that may be?"

"Of course," Ebon said quickly. The last thing he wanted was for Mako to run back to Father with tales of his ingratitude. "I only meant to ask, how may I be of service to him?"

"There will be a package left for you. Tonight, after

the Academy's lanterns have been dimmed and that white-haired old bat no longer guards the front door. Too, there will be a special permission slip from your loving cousin the dean. It will allow you to leave the Academy."

Ebon's throat caught, and his voice grew weak, as though he were being strangled. "Leave?"

Mako took his meaning and grinned. "Not forever, boy—only for tonight. You must bring the package to the west end of the Seat, where you will find an inn called the Shining Door. A man there will recognize you, and you must give him the package."

"What is in it?"

"You need not trouble yourself over that."

"Could you not bring it yourself? This seems an awful amount of trouble." Mako's eyes went cold, and Ebon shivered. "I mean only that, certainly my father would like it to be done fast. It will be many hours until I can leave this place."

Still the bodyguard stared with ice in his eyes, though the grin never wavered. "He has patience enough for this. And besides, I am somewhat well known in that part of the city, and not in any way one would consider complimentary. But no one there will think you are up to anything nefarious."

"And will I be?"

Mako gave him a wink. "Why should you be? You are only delivering a parcel. If you get up to any mischief, it shall be on your own account."

Ebon felt as though the jaws of some unseen steel trap were closing about him. "But if I am doing nothing wrong, why must it be done so late at night?"

"Who would not enjoy a nighttime adventure? And you have the dean's special permission."

Ebon wanted to refuse. He wanted to tell Mako he would not do it, and that the bodyguard could deliver the parcel himself. How did he know that this was actually at his father's request? It might be Mako's own scheme, into which he meant to ensnare Ebon against his father's wishes. But Mako must have seen something of these thoughts on his face, for he sucked a slow breath between his teeth and shook his head.

"Ebon," he said genially. "Could you truly be so eager to disappoint your father? Halab may have spoken for you, but he could withdraw you on the slightest whim. Do this for him, out of respect and gratitude. He cares for you so very much."

The words carried no obvious threat, but still Ebon heard one. He could imagine being cast from the Academy, his tuition no longer paid, his allowance cut off, and he himself bundled into a ship bound for home. Again he saw in his imagination the triumphant sneer on Father's face as Ebon marched in through the doors of the Drayden mansion.

"Very well," said Ebon. "I will bring the package, if that is what my father wishes."

"He does," said Mako. He pushed himself off the bookshelf and gave Ebon a little bow—but Ebon thought he saw mockery in the gesture. He turned away from the bodyguard, opening his book as if he meant to read it right there.

"One more thing, little goldbag—do not look inside the parcel."

Ebon turned to look at him, but Mako had vanished. He leaned out to look around the bookshelf, but the aisles on either side were empty.

SIXTEEN

THE DAY ENDED QUICKLY—FAR TOO QUICKLY FOR EBON'S liking, for he dreaded his errand. But soon the daylight had faded through the Academy's many windows, and he felt an uncertain anxiety settle about him. He sat with Kalem in the boy's common room—not the one outside Ebon's dormitory, for Kalem feared to go where the older children lived. Ebon had taken to visiting Kalem instead, three floors higher. The children here were of Kalem's age, and they looked at Ebon somewhat fearfully and left him alone. He found that he much preferred it that way.

As day turned to night at last and attendants came to light fires upon the hearths, Kalem began to yawn heavily in his chair. His eyes were bleary, and he rubbed at them. "I slept poorly last night. Or rather, I slept not enough. I became caught up trying a new spell my instructor showed me yesterday."

"Hm?" said Ebon, looking up. He had only been half listening.

Kalem looked at him oddly. "What has gotten into you? You are half bouncing in your seat, and I do not think you have heard a word I have said all night."

"It is nothing," said Ebon. "If you are tired, I will leave so that you may go to bed."

"I can stay up a bit longer, if you wish to talk. We have not tried your spell yet."

"I myself am weary." Ebon stood, and felt at once that he had done it somewhat too quickly. "I will make my way to my own room. Good night."

"Good night," said Kalem, yawning once more. He stood and retreated to his dormitory.

Ebon made his way quickly downstairs. Curfew approached but had not yet come, and so he was somewhat unsure what to do with himself. He did not wish to return to the common room outside his dormitory, for fear of meeting Lilith there. Instead he stole down to the first floor and made his way to the dining hall. Some spare loaves had been left out on the serving table, as they were each day, and Ebon snatched one up to tear into it. Something about his anxiety had raised his appetite.

He took the loaf with him as he went out through a white door into the training grounds. There was a stone bench he often liked to sit upon. He went there now, clutching his robes a bit tighter against the chilly night. The moons were just rising in the eastern sky, their glow drifting down to paint the grass in silver. The stars were bright that night, and Ebon watched them make their slow way through the sky. Soon it would be time, and he would have to go. But for a moment he could rest here on his stone bench, and pretend it was where he meant to spend the rest of his evening until he went to bed.

Voices sounded on the air, coming from around the corner. Without thinking, Ebon dove over the back of the bench and into the hedges by the Academy wall.

Around the corner came two instructors, obvious by their age even when the night turned their dark grey robes as black as a student's. Ebon recognized one of them: it was the kindly-faced weremage he would sometimes watch when he snuck out into the training grounds. The man walked with another instructor, one Ebon did not know by name, though he thought she might be a mindmage. They walked slowly, and their talk seemed without purpose.

But as they passed by, a curious thing happened. The weremage paused for a moment, and he turned so that he was looking straight at the spot where Ebon hid. Ebon's pulse raced so fast that he thought his heart might burst from his chest. But after a moment the instructor resumed his walk, taking two quick steps to catch up with his companion. Soon they had passed beyond the next corner of the Academy, and Ebon let loose a sigh of relief.

It was time, or past time now. He snuck out from the hedge, wolfing down the last scrap of his bread loaf, and made his way back to the Academy's entry hall. He half hoped to find Mellie standing guard there as she always was, but Mako had spoken true: it was a new woman, tall, thick, and matronly. Ebon had never seen her before. Her fat cheeks puffed as she stood to greet him. Under her arm was a parcel wrapped in brown cloth.

"You are the Drayden boy," she said. Ebon was unsure if it was a question, and so he did not answer. She shoved the parcel into his arms and led him to the front door.

"When you return, knock twice, then thrice, and I shall know it is you," she said. Then she very nearly pushed him out the door before closing it behind him.

Ebon sighed, looking up and down the street. A few figures moved about in the light of torches, but none seemed the least bit interested in him. He knew it was not unheard of for Academy students to go out after hours for one reason or another, but still he felt nervous, as though at any moment a constable would snatch him up and inquire about his business.

Quickly he set off into the streets. Then he changed his mind, thinking it might be better to stay out of sight as much as possible. Nearby was an alley that looked like it ran west for a ways. He made for it, blinking hard to help his eyes adjust as he slipped into shadow. But they did not adjust fast enough—he ran into another figure with a crash and a yelp.

"I am sorry," he stammered, stepping back into the moonslight. But then his eyes became accustomed to the darkness at last, and he recognized who he had run into: it was Theren. She looked just as surprised to see him as he was to see her.

"What under the sky are you doing here?" she said, sharp eyes narrowing.

"I might ask the same of you," he said defiantly, trying in vain to hide the parcel behind his back.

"And I will answer you readily. I am off to visit a house of lovers. Now it is your turn."

"I . . ." Words failed him for a moment. At last he found them, too late. "As am I."

"Truly?" she said, and he could hear in her voice that she did not believe him. "Then what is that package behind your back? It is too fat to hide, or you are too thin, I cannot tell which."

"It is nothing," said Ebon, trying to turn it sideways to conceal it better.

Her thin nose twitched. "Very well. Keep your secrets. It is no business of mine what a man does with his lover. But if we are of a purpose, then let us walk together. These streets are dark, and they can be dangerous."

Ebon scoffed. "Do not mock me by saying you wish for my protection."

"I would never dream of it. I mock you by saying that you require mine."

"I can fend for myself," he said, hoping she could not see his cheeks burning in the moonslight.

She thrust a finger under his nose, eyes alight. "Wait. I know what you are about. You have spoken to the dean, just as I said, and he gave you permission to leave the Academy."

"I did not! I . . ." He trailed off lamely, averting his eyes as he searched for an answer.

"I knew it." She folded her arms across her chest. "Yet you would not even extend me the same courtesy. I might have known better than to think a goldbag would help one so lowly born."

"Theren, I give you my word, I did nothing of the sort. I wish I were not here at all, and I—" He decided he must take the plunge. "I am not out to visit a house of lovers."

"Of course you are not. What, then?"

He looked over his shoulder and then back at her. "I was given a task. By my father. He wishes me to bring this package to an inn, a place called the Shining Door. The dean gave me permission to be out, indeed, but I did not request it. Nor do I wish to be here. I do not like anything about this."

"What is in the package?" She reached out a hand curiously.

Ebon snatched it away from her. "I am not allowed to look inside."

"How intriguing." To his shock, her eyes sparkled in the moonslight. "What is this? Some black business of your family's? Do you walk beyond the King's law?"

"I do not know," he insisted. "I only know that my father asked this of me, and he is the only reason I am at the Academy in the first place. So I mean to do as he asked and then promptly forget the matter entirely."

"An excellent plan," said Theren, drawing herself up. "And I shall come with you."

He balked. "No. You should not. Go to your lover, and pretend you never saw me."

She waved a hand in dismissal. "What pleasures could I find that would be grander than the intrigue of a midnight plot? Besides, what if you should find yourself in trouble? What will you do, turn water into oil and throw it in their faces? You need me."

"I shall not get into trouble. I am only delivering a parcel."

"So you think." She gripped his arm and dragged him into the alley. "Yet one never knows the perils that may lie in one's future."

He tried to think of how to dissuade her, but she pressed on so determinedly that he soon resigned himself to his fate. But he shook her grip off his arm and walked beside her in sullen silence. Theren, for her part, seemed to take this all as some glorious nighttime adventure, though to his relief she stopped asking him any questions.

As they neared the western end of the island, Ebon began looking about for someone to ask directions of. But Theren tapped him on the shoulder and pointed. "I know the Shining Door. It lies this way. Come."

She set off, and he hurried to follow her. Soon they found the place: a squalid little building tucked in between two larger ones. The thick beams that held up its roof were bent outwards, like a child taking a deep breath, or a body about to burst with pox. From the smell that drifted from its open front door, Ebon thought it was more likely the latter.

Inside, the common room was dim, and every conversation was muted. Many wary eyes glinted at them in the darkness. Ebon was acutely grateful for his plain students' robes; if he had appeared here in the finery to which he was accustomed, he would have feared to find a knife slid between his ribs, the assailant hoping to find a fat purse.

He wanted to leave immediately, but he forced himself to take another step beyond the threshold. His eyes roved about, seeking someone who recognized him. No one paid him any special attention at first, but then he caught sight of a sudden motion. In the back of the room, a figure beckoned him forth. Ebon did not want to approach, but neither did he want to be in this place a moment longer than he had to. With Theren by his side, he wove his way quickly between the tables until he reached the one where the figure sat.

It was a man, his skin pale to the point of being ghostly. This was certainly no man of Idris, and Ebon wondered why he would be in league with the Draydens. A thin mustache clung to his lip, dipping down into a sparse beard. His eyes were rat-like and flitted all about. His cloak and hood were blue, but his tunic and leggings were grey.

"You know who I am?" said Ebon, fighting and failing to keep his voice steady.

The man sneered and held forth a hand. Ebon gave him the brown parcel. The man quickly undid the string holding it shut and lifted a corner, peeking inside. Ebon craned his neck, trying to see, but the man drew it back.

"I was told you would come alone," he said in a rasping voice. He did not wait for a response, but stood quickly and left, making for the rooms at the back of the inn.

Ebon released a long sigh he had not known he was holding. "Let us leave this place, for I feel as though I grow dirtier the longer I remain." He nearly ran for the door, Theren beside him, and once in the open air he drank it in with long, deep breaths.

"Well, that provided no answers whatsoever," said Theren.

"I am glad," said Ebon. "The less I know of what just transpired, the better, I suspect. If I could drink enough to forget it ever happened, I would."

"There might be time enough for that yet," said Theren. "It is not very late."

"The moons are halfway through the sky," said Ebon. "Let us return and sleep, or else tomorrow's classes shall be a torture."

"If you insist, alchemist. I will show you the way."

"You do not mean to go to your lover?"

She shrugged. "I think I have had thrills enough. She will still be there if I visit her on another night."

Ebon blinked at her. "She? Oh, dear. Should I have words with Kalem?"

Theren grinned at him, teeth flashing in the moonslight. "You do not mean he is enamored of me? Oh, the dear boy. Yes, do let him know that he would have no hope of turning my head, even if he were not so young."

Ebon shook his head with a little smile and followed Theren as she set off through the streets. They walked in silence, and soon Ebon found himself wondering what it was, exactly, that he had just done. He feared to know, and yet he found himself even more fearful of ignorance. Always he had taken great pains to avoid any inkling of his family's dealings. It was common knowledge that the Draydens were spice traders, but Ebon knew of his father's late-night meetings, of Mako's strange work that seemed to take him all across the nine lands. He saw the terror that shone in others' eyes when they heard he was of the family Drayden. Always he had shied away from such things. And now he suspected that, unknowing, he had been thrust straight into the middle of it all.

Theren must have entertained thoughts not unlike

his own, for after they had walked together a while, she glanced at him. "Tell me true: what was that all about?"

Ebon sighed. "I said I do not know."

She shook her head. "You cannot mean to persist in that lie. I know only rumors of your family's doings, but if even half of them are true . . ."

"If you know only a rumor, you know more than I," said Ebon. "Never have I involved myself in . . . in whatever it is my family does that makes others fear us so."

Theren scoffed. "More Drayden favoritism," she muttered.

"It is not," said Ebon, growing angry. "If you would for but a moment forget your abject, ignorant hatred of those who are wealthier than you, you might see that. I never wished to be my father's son."

"I cannot *imagine* such difficulty," said Theren. She feigned irony, but Ebon could hear true resentment lurking beneath it. "What anguish to ride in a golden carriage, hiding your face to avoid seeing the dark deeds that paid for it."

Ebon wanted to answer—or rather, he wanted to shout at her. But he was keenly aware that he might lose one of his only two friends at the Academy if he did. Besides, he did not quite know where he was, and did not wish to spend any time wandering lost on the Seat. So he walked beside her in silence, biting his tongue until it nearly bled.

Soon he saw the familiar shape of the Academy looming above the buildings before them. Though he knew he could enter the front door, he found himself curious about how Theren had snuck out. So when she turned left, he followed. She took him around the corner, where he found a small collection of wooden sheds pressed up against the Academy's outer walls.

Seeing his questioning look, Theren explained. "They keep brooms and such within, and use them to sweep the surrounding streets."

He thought she might enter one of them, revealing a hidden door. Instead, she stepped close to one of the sheds, eyes glowing. She crouched and leaped high in the air to land atop the shed. Again she crouched, lower this time, and gave another mighty jump. The Academy's wall stood ten paces high—she just managed to grip the edge of it with her fingers, and Ebon saw her eyes glow once more as she used her magic to climb up. She turned for just a moment and waved, a black shape against the stars, and then vanished.

"Well and good for her," Ebon muttered to himself. "But not for me, I suppose."

He trudged back to the front door and knocked upon it, twice and then thrice. After a moment it swung open, and the stern woman from before gave him a little nod. He ignored her, climbing the wide stairway quickly and making his way to his dormitory, where he dived beneath the covers and tried to forget the whole affair.

SEVENTEEN

By morning Ebon felt little better, and he was exhausted besides. Somehow he made it through his morning class, though often times he caught his head nodding. Once he barely snapped awake before crashing nose-first into the table. Credell could not have missed it, but the instructor, of course, said nothing.

Well, if I cannot concentrate, and Credell is too frightened to say anything about it, mayhap I should take advantage of the situation, thought Ebon. So he slid down the bench until he reached the wall, slouching against the stone. Soon the murmuring buzz of the other students lulled him into peaceful slumber, and he dozed comfortably.

It was a while later before he felt a tugging on his sleeve. He opened his eyes, expecting to see Credell—but it was Astrea, the young girl with the wild hair, her eyes wide as she stared at him. The moment he awoke she jerked her hand back from his sleeve.

"Class is over," she said softly. They were the first words she had said to him since the first day, when she thought he had come to the wrong classroom.

Ebon blinked hard and looked around. It was true. The room was empty. He had not even heard the bell ring.

"Thank you, Astrea," he said, and then yawned wide.

"I do not know why Credell is afraid of you. I like you."

Almost before the words had left her lips, she turned and ran for the door as though her life depended on it. In a moment she was gone. Ebon stared after her, blinking hard. But when he finally stood to leave, he found that he was smiling.

The dining hall buzzed with voices. Ebon stumbled between the other students, heading towards his usual table. Theren and Kalem were there already, and looked to be half done with their meals. Theren regarded him with a small smile as he sat, but Kalem's eyes were wide with questions.

"You are very late."

"I am," said Ebon. He spooned up a bite of soup with a grimace. They had had the same thing twice already this week.

"What were you doing?"

"Sleeping, as it happens," said Ebon.

Kalem blinked. He looked to Theren and then back to Ebon. "Sleeping? In your bed?"

"In my class."

The boy's jaw dropped, turning his face to a perfect mask of shock. He could not have looked more surprised if Ebon had changed to an Elf right before his eyes. "You . . . that . . . but your instructor!"

"Credell fears even to speak to me. If he tried to reprimand me, he might die of terror."

"The tragic life of a goldbag," muttered Theren, picking at her nails.

"Leave off, Theren," said Ebon. Her cheeks turned crimson, and she looked away.

Kalem had not recovered from his shock, and still gaped like a fish. "How could he let you sleep through his class?"

"What harm is there?" said Ebon. "It is not as though he teaches me anything when I am awake."

"Still . . . I can scarcely imagine it." Kalem shook his head and then, after a moment, his eyes narrowed. "But why should you be so tired? You went to bed just as I did last night."

Ebon felt sick. He ducked his head, picking at his sleeve as though something upon it had suddenly captured his interest. "Yes, well . . . in fact, that is not quite what happened. I went out upon the Seat."

"We both did," Theren said brightly. Ebon wished she would keep her mouth shut. "Why not tell him what you did, Ebon?"

"I scarcely know myself. My father sent me a message, asking me to deliver a package to some inn on the west end of the Seat. He arranged special permission for me to be out after hours."

Kalem leaned forwards and spoke in a voice hardly above a whisper. "What was in the package?"

Ebon shrugged. "I was not supposed to open it."

"Though I greatly wanted to," said Theren.

"You went with him?"

"Not by intent. I pursued other interests, but we encountered each other upon the streets. He was so cagey about his purpose for leaving the Academy, I decided I should follow him and see what he was up to. But I learned nothing, for Ebon would not give me any answers."

Ebon felt his temper was dangerously close to breaking, and his weariness did not help. "I have told you—"

"Yes, you have told me," said Theren rolling her eyes. "No need to do so again."

"Well, I think you were both terribly idiotic," said Kalem, folding his arms across his chest with a scowl. "You should not have delivered the parcel if you did not know what was in it, Ebon. And neither of you should have gone wandering the Seat at night."

Theren shrugged. "I do it often. No one seems to mind."

"I doubt anyone knows that you do it," said Kalem.

"But that is saying the same thing."

"I would not have done it," said Ebon, speaking quickly before Kalem could think up another retort. "But my father is the reason I am here at the Academy. How could I be so ungrateful as to refuse to aid him?"

"But you do not even know what you did," said Kalem. "And forgive my saying so, but . . . but a favor for your family . . ."

Ebon looked angrily into his lap. "Say what you mean to say. A favor for my family is likely a dark deed. And yet what would you have done? What else could I have done?"

"You could have refused."

To Ebon's surprise, Theren spoke in his defense. "Mayhap we are trying overmuch to craft guilt out of innocence, Kalem. Ebon may be a Drayden, but he does not seem a bad *sort* of Drayden. What harm could come from a little parcel? And the adventure was somewhat amusing, at least."

"What harm? How can we know, without knowing what the parcel held? What if it was poison, or a dagger? Or . . . or even *magestones.*"

He said the word in such a hushed whisper that Ebon felt compelled to lean forwards. He looked to see if anyone else was listening. Theren's eyes grew dark, and she gripped Kalem's arm until he squirmed.

"Do not even whisper such things here, you fool!" she hissed.

"I do not understand," said Ebon. "What are ma—that is, what are those things you just named?"

"Of course you would not know," said Theren, rolling her eyes. "Tell him, Kalem—but *not* here, nor any place where curious ears might hear you. You two have your lover's nest in the library; speak of it there."

She released Kalem and left them. The boy stared sullenly after her, rubbing his arm where she had squeezed it. When he looked at Ebon, dark disgruntlement showed in his eyes.

"It is *not* a lover's nest."

Ebon could think of no words to cheer him up. It seemed to him that Kalem was right and Ebon was a fool. Yet even with that knowledge, Ebon suspected that one day his father would ask another favor of him—and he doubted he had the will to refuse.

"Come," he said quietly. "The meal is nearly over, and our next class beckons."

They cleaned their table and made their way into the Academy halls. Ebon's feet dragged with every step.

Once they had safely sequestered themselves on the library's third floor, Ebon leaned in close. "What are these magestones you spoke of before? Why did they bring such fear to Theren's eyes, when she fears almost nothing?"

Though there was no one in sight, Kalem still shushed him and looked around. "You should be very, very wary of speaking that word within these walls, even in the most shadowed whisper. Theren was right—it was foolish of me to say it in the dining hall."

"But what *is* it?" said Ebon, growing exasperated. "Or rather, what are they?"

"*They*," said Kalem, taking great pains to avoid the word, "are black stones, or crystals, I think. I do not know where they come from—no one does, except those who sell them, and they have no wish to share the secret. Though they look like a shiny rock, they break easily in the hand or between the teeth. When a normal person eats one, there is no effect. But if a wizard should eat one . . ."

He fell silent, shivering, and once again he looked over his shoulder. Ebon shook him gently. "There is no one there, Kalem. You have looked at least a dozen times."

"Still I feel as though we are watched," said the boy. "Mayhap I am overly fearful. If we were found to be speaking of this, it would go ill for both of us."

"Well, finish the tale, so that we need never speak of it again."

"As you say. If a wizard consumes a magestone, their powers are increased manyfold. Even a modest elementalist could summon flames hot enough to melt stone, and an alchemist could turn a house to straw with a touch. If a wizard is mighty already, the stones can turn them nearly Elf-like in power. And some other, darker side of our magic is unlocked—for alchemists it is a corruption, like a plague we can imbue in matter that spreads to anything close enough. Whatever it touches withers away to nothingness, until the magic is spent. They call it blackstone."

Ebon had leaned forwards without realizing it, and now he was gripping the arms of his chair, as though his limbs had readied themselves to flee of their own accord. He forced his shaking limbs to relax.

"That sounds powerful indeed," he said. "But if it increases the strength of our magic, where is the great harm?"

"The stones do not only strengthen our gifts. They consume the mind as well. From the moment a magestone passes your lips, it fills you with an aching hunger for more. At first the craving is slight, just a tickling at the back of the mind. But if you deny it, it soon grows to a raging desire that will drive away all rational thought. Wizards who take magestone will kill to acquire more. They will cast aside all bonds of friends and family if only it allows them another piece. As long as they can keep up their supply, they may appear rational. But if for even a moment their store of magestone is threatened, they will destroy all the nine lands to secure it."

The library around them was utterly silent. Ebon let loose a long *whoosh* of breath. "Was that, then, the power behind the Wizard Kings?"

Kalem nodded slowly. "It was. There is an entire section of the blue book that speaks of it. You will read it before long. That is one of the reasons I am sure it is forbidden."

"But if you learned of it in the book, what of Theren? Surely she has not read the same words."

"She has not. But every student in the Academy knows of the magestones, or learns of them in time. It is strictly forbidden to speak of them, and so of course everyone does so. But if an instructor ever learns of such discussion, the punishment can be severe. Some students have been expelled."

"Just for speaking of it? That seems unfair."

"It may be, but then again, who wishes for students to graduate the Academy with a desire to find the stones? In fact the Academy's punishment may be considered light. If a wizard, having graduated, is found to have consumed magestones, the penalty is an immediate and messy death."

Ebon swallowed. "I will remember that. Where would you find magestones, if you wished to?"

Kalem's face went bone-white. "Ebon! After hearing my words, how can you ask that question?"

"I do not mean to go and secure some right this moment—or ever," said Ebon, frowning. "I only won der, if they are forbidden by the Academy, and outside the King's law, then how do they even exist? They must come from somewhere—why does the High King not track down the source and wipe it out?"

"Why do you think I should know? The last I checked, neither of us were the High King's lawmen, nor seated at her councils."

Ebon smirked. "A fair point, I suppose, though wryly made. Very well. I still have a great deal of reading to do this day, and you have kept me at this discussion overlong."

"Do not let me stop you," said Kalem. He selected a book from their table and leaned back, waving a hand airily. "Go on about your business."

Ebon shook his head with a smile and rose to walk among the bookshelves. He was looking for a new tome, the biography of an ancient king of Calentin who many said was responsible for raising it to its present heights of culture and power. Soon he was lost among the shelves, peering at the books' spines in the dim light, here where the lanterns were often ill-tended.

"What a good little goldbag you have turned out to be."

The words nearly made him leap out of his skin. He recognized Mako's voice and ground his teeth together. When he turned, he found the man leaning against a shelf again, just as he had been last time. In his hand was a book, and Ebon knew without looking that it was the very book he had sought on the shelves.

"What are you doing back here?" Ebon whispered. "You must leave, before the instructors see you prowling about."

"Why should they eject me? Former students of the Academy are welcome to return at any time, if they seek some ancient wisdom in the library's vast wealth."

Ebon glared at him. "You never studied here. You are no wizard."

"Are you so certain of that?"

A shudder rippled through Ebon. What *did* he know of Mako? No, he had never seen the man use magic. But what of that? Only an overly boastful wizard would go about casting spells needlessly. Mako was many things—unnerving, overly friendly, and mayhap cruel—but he rarely boasted.

Mako was looking into Ebon's eyes now, and he smiled at what he saw. "Good, little goldbag. You are learning caution. Remember that our second thoughts are often wiser than our first, and the third are wisest of all—but the fourth bring only inaction."

Ebon shook his head, feeling as though he was ridding it of cobwebs. "Enough riddles. What do you want?"

"I wished only to congratulate you on the excellent service you rendered to your father."

"It was my pleasure to aid him." Ebon grimaced. Even saying the words felt like swallowing moldy bread.

"Yet you made a grave error. You brought your little mindmage lover for company."

Ebon gawked, his mouth working as he struggled for words. He was suddenly terrified for Theren. Mako did not truly care if they were bedmates. But if he knew that Theren had gone with Ebon, he knew she had seen the parcel.

Mako must have seen the terror in Ebon's eyes, for his grin widened. "Fear not, little goldbag. I mean your mindmage no harm. And I have not brought word of this to your father."

Ebon sagged against the bookshelf with relief. "Then why make any mention of it at all?"

"So that you know never to do anything so foolish in the future. I will keep only so many secrets on your behalf. If one of your little friends should accompany you again, they may find themselves drinking deep of the Great Bay's waters and making a little house of their own in its depths."

Ebon spoke through a throat of desert sand. "You mean to say, then, that my father will require more favors of me?"

"Dear, dear boy. Did you ever doubt it?"

"What was in the parcel?"

"You know better than to ask. You are happier without that knowledge; therefore remain ignorant. And the next time your father barks, and you jump to obey, leave your friends at home."

"I will remember."

"Good. Now return to your reading." Mako threw the book at him. Startled, Ebon barely caught it before it hit the ground. When he looked up, the bodyguard had vanished.

Fear had seized Ebon's limbs, and he found it hard to return to the table where Kalem waited. Now he knew what he had already thought—that Mako and his father were not done with him yet. Worse, he could no longer confide in Theren or Kalem, and would have to keep the truth from them. They might try to interfere; at least Kalem would, and Theren might involve herself out of curiosity. That could spell their deaths.

Miserable and alone, Ebon left the bookshelves and made for the table.

EIGHTEEN

KALEM SEEMED TO SENSE THAT SOMETHING WAS wrong, for he asked Ebon many times that day what was troubling him. Ebon only shook his head and denied it, and after a while Kalem stopped asking. But he looked often at Ebon, his brow furrowed in deep thought, and he spent too long reading each page of his book.

After their studies, Theren met them in the hallways. "I have had a fine day," she declared. "Fine enough for celebration. What say the two of you to a night of drinks? I promise not to make you regret this one, little goldbag." She reached out and ruffled Kalem's hair.

He grinned, but Ebon's mood was still dark. "I have no cause to celebrate, myself. I think I shall remain here."

"No cause? Then come and drink until you find one. Come, dear Ebon. You are far too dour, and have been ever since last night. Together we can banish the dark thoughts that plague you. Tell him, Kalem."

Ebon barely kept himself from the retort that he was dour, in part, because of Theren's obvious distrust of him. She seemed polite enough now that she wanted him to pay for her wine. But before he could voice any such thought, Kalem looked at him doubtfully and shrugged.

"She may be right—it could help improve your mood. Answers can be quick to find if sought for by an easy mind, my instructor always says."

"That has the sound of fool's wisdom," grumbled Ebon. "But if the two of you insist, then I shall come with you."

"Excellent," said Theren, clapping her hands. "For in truth, I have no coin for wine, and need yours instead."

"Of course you do. How are you so impoverished already? Last night you had coin, at least, for a lover."

Kalem's face fell as he looked at her. "Ah . . . you are seeing a lover, are you?"

Theren gave him a little smile and ruffled his hair

again. "I am afraid that was my aim, little goldbag. And for many months now have I enjoyed *her* company." She arched her eyebrow even as she stressed the word.

Ebon thought Kalem might grow even more distraught. But in fact the boy brightened, as though Theren had said more words that Ebon could not hear. "Oh! Oh, I see. Well. I am happy to hear it, then."

"I thought you might be. Come, wealthy patrons! Tonight we drink until our problems leave us at last!"

As she led them out of the Academy, Ebon drew Kalem back to whisper to him. "I had meant to tell you about her, but had hesitated, for I feared to upset you. Yet you seem cheered by the news."

Kalem shrugged. "And why not? I had thoughts of her, yes, but I thought it likely she would see me only as a child. But now I know that, even if I were older, things would be no different. It is not ill luck at the year of my birth, then, but another sort entirely."

Ebon frowned. "Still, ill luck is ill luck."

"My mind is eased regardless."

That made Ebon shake his head, even as Theren dragged them both into the streets. They made for Leven's tavern, passing through the usual flood of other students in black robes. But Ebon's thoughts kept up their endless wandering, mulling over Mako and his father and the parcel—and, more urgently, what they might ask him to do next. Once, he almost spoke of it to his friends. But then he cast a wary look over his shoulder, wondering if Mako lurked in some shadow, watching him. And, too, anyone on the streets about them could be one of Mako's agents, listening in to ensure that Ebon said nothing. Nowhere seemed safe anymore. Not even the Academy.

And then he thought of Theren, alone on the streets last night, and had an idea.

"I have changed my mind," he said, stopping in the street. "Forgive me, but I do not think I will drink with you tonight."

"Come *on,* Ebon," said Theren. "How will you deny me my right to a warm fire and flushed cheeks? And you seem as though a good drunkenness would do you well."

Ebon reached into his pocket and drew forth a gold weight. "Never let it be said I stood between you and a good flagon. Enjoy yourselves."

"Do not return to the Academy alone, Ebon," pleaded Kalem. "You should be with friends."

Ebon ducked his head, blushing. "I do not mean to return to the Academy."

Theren seemed to take his meaning at once, but Kalem's brow furrowed. He opened his mouth as though to ask a question, but Theren threw an arm over his shoulder and spun him around, marching him off down the street.

"Come, little master. Our goldbag needs to be alone, and I can answer your questions without him." Soon they were out of sight.

Ebon was somewhat unsure of himself on the streets, but he knew his destination lay to the west, and so he headed that way. Soon he began to recognize a few of the buildings, and his steps came quicker and more certain. A few times he made a wrong turn and had to double back. But before very long he found himself on a familiar street, with a tavern behind him and a blue door just a few paces ahead.

As before, his throat grew tight and constricted, and he felt a tingling in his limbs. He looked down the street in both directions before chiding himself for being ridiculous. Who there would mind that he visited a house of lovers? He no longer had to worry about a retainer who might bring word of his deeds to his father, and no one else cared a whit.

He twisted the knob and opened the door.

Perfume, silk, and the strumming of a harp. Immediately his eyes went to the corner—but it was a man playing the strings. Ebon's heart skipped a beat. The house's matron arrived, sweeping up to him just as she had before, and wearing the same warm smile.

"Well met once again. How may we serve you this evening?"

"You remember me?"

She shrugged. "I have a gift for faces. Is there any sort of lover you are looking for tonight?"

Ebon licked his lips, for they had gone dry all of a sudden. "Is Adara here?"

Her smile widened slightly. "Of course." Turning, she beckoned. Adara rose at once from the shadows of the room's far corner. She had been sitting there all along, Ebon realized, and from the way she smiled as their eyes met, he suspected she had been watching him from the moment he stepped in the door. She wore Idrisian clothes, just as before, though this time the cloth seemed finer, and when the lamplight caught it, it shimmered. Too, she had a sheer blue veil over the lower half of her face. Though it did not entirely stop him from seeing her full lips, it drew his eyes to her own, where he found himself lost in wonder.

She took his hand. "Hello again, Ebon."

A short time later, she lay with her head on his chest, the two of them naked and nestled in the satin sheets of the bed. Ebon lay there silent for a long while, sometimes closing his eyes, sometimes opening them again. The quiet held only contentment. His troubles seemed far away, tiny things with simple solutions, only waiting for him to sweep them aside like so much dust. Adara must have sensed his desire for peace, for she said nothing, only traced her fingers across his chest in little patterns.

At last, Ebon lifted his head to kiss her. "I wish I could have returned earlier."

"As do I." She gave him a soft smile, and he returned it. They were lover's words, he knew, but that did not change the thrill they sent through him.

"How have I retained your lessons?"

"Not as well as could be hoped, but mayhap better than I expected." She smiled wider. "You must promise to let me teach you more often."

"I wish I could promise that," he said with a sigh.

She frowned. "What troubles you?"

He pursed his lips and looked away. She studied his face for a moment. He thought she might press him further.

Instead she pulled away, rising from the bed and going to a side table. His eyes were drawn to her movements and, if he was honest, her naked form. He watched as she brought him a pitcher and cup.

"I remembered what you asked for last time," she said. "I have kept these in my room ever since your first visit."

He sat up and looked inside the pitcher, and then he laughed. It was half full of clean, clear water. She smiled, eyes shining, and pressed it into his hands.

"Come. Show me a spell."

He shook his head, still smiling, and filled the cup with water. She took the pitcher back and put it on a table. He stirred the water, focusing on it through his finger. Kalem had practiced this with him often in the past few weeks, and now it came easily enough. The world grew brighter, and Adara gave a little gasp at the glow of his eyes. Soon the water was thick and soupy, and he withdrew his finger. The glow faded, and he handed her the cup.

"There. It is nothing very impressive, but it is magic nonetheless."

She took the cup gingerly and looked inside with awe, as though it held liquid gold. "That was wonderful to see," she said, her voice very small.

"Come now. Surely you know other wizards. I cannot be the only student of the Academy who comes here."

Carefully she put the cup down beside the pitcher. "You are not. But if the others wish to talk—which is rare—they only want to talk of themselves. They never offer to show me spells. And I rarely ask. I do not enjoy their company as I enjoy yours."

Lover's words. Yet still he smiled. "I only wish I had more to show you. I cannot learn my next spell, and I fear I will rot away in my class before I ever master it."

"What is it? Why does it trouble you so?"

He rose from the bed and went to his robe where it lay on the floor. From its pocket he drew his wooden practice rod. "I am supposed to turn this to stone. But for the life of me, I cannot seem to master the magic. I try and I try, but still it is made of wood, as you can see."

Sitting beside him, she ran her fingers over the rod. Her hand brushed his, making him tingle with delight. "Truly? You are learning to turn wood to stone?"

"I am supposed to. My friend Kalem says it is no great feat. He can do it in the span of a blink, though he is three years younger than I. It is the passing test of the first-year alchemist. Wood is the dead substance of something that was once alive. We learn to turn it to something that never lived in the first place. That which is alive is made of many things. That which is dead is usually much simpler. Kalem says that is the purpose of the test—not to see the wood for its complexity, but to envision the simplicity of the stone. But still I cannot do it."

She put her hand on his arm, running her nails along the skin. "I have faith that you will. It is only a matter of time. But I also sense that this is only one reason you look so concerned, and mayhap not the greatest reason of all."

He sighed, letting his hand fall to the bed. "You guess right. There is something . . . or some*one*, rather, who is much on my mind. I . . . my family has begun to give me errands. Only one, so far. Yet I fear more will come."

"What sort of tasks?"

"They had me deliver a parcel."

She giggled and stifled it behind a quickly raised hand. "That sounds like no dire deed."

"I do not know what was in it," he said. "But Mak—but the man who instructed me to do it is no man given to idle errands."

"Was it your father?"

He turned away. "I do not wish to speak of who."

"You may trust me."

"I do." He took her hands in his, and raised them to his lips. "Some might say it is foolish, yet I do. Only it troubles me. And it troubles my friend. She thinks I know more than I let on, and am withholding it from her."

"She?" Adara smiled broadly. "Ebon, if I were a jealous woman . . ."

"You need fear nothing of that. She prefers the company of women."

Her eyes flashed with recognition and—delight? Amusement? "Truly? Do you mean you have befriended Theren?"

Ebon rounded on her in surprise. "You know her? Wait . . . do you mean that you and she . . .?"

Adara frowned at him, and it seemed to Ebon that the affection in her eyes dampened. "I am not her lover. But Ebon, you should not be dismayed if I were. You do not hold any claim to me."

"Of course not," said Ebon quickly. "Only . . . I suppose I do not like to think of it."

She folded her arms. "You may as well. It is childish to do otherwise, and avoiding the thought may lead to darkness down the road. I have seen it before."

Ebon shook his head. "I am sorry. You are right, of course. Forget I made any mention of it at all."

Still she wore a little frown, but she relented and took his outstretched hand. "Very well."

He lifted her fingers and kissed them. "It is only that I am troubled. I do not know when Mako will return for me with some other task from my father, and I do not know what I will tell him when he does."

"You will do what he asks, of course."

He looked at her quickly. "You say it so easily. Does it not worry you?"

She shrugged. "Why should it? You only brought a parcel to someone in a tavern. If there is darkness in such an act, it comes before, or after, and is not your responsibility."

"Yet I bore the parcel."

She sighed and pushed his shoulders until he lay back upon the bed. Slowly, intently, she climbed atop him.

"Never do kings behead messengers for bearing words, even when those words displease the king. And if bearing such parcels keeps you upon the High King's Seat, and here in my arms, then I command you: bear them, Ebon. Bear as many as you must. Only do not leave me."

He found it impossible to muster any reply.

NINETEEN

THOUGH EBON'S FEARS HUNG DARK ABOUT HIM, IT seemed that for a time, at least, Mako and his father were finished with him. He saw nothing of the bodyguard as the days became weeks and true winter came to the High King's Seat. At home in Idris, the turning of the season had meant relief from unbearable heat; but on the Scat, Ebon had found autumn quite pleasant, whereas he now found himself chilled as he passed through the granite halls.

One day he entered the library for his studies and found Jia sitting at a desk on the first floor, reading a short letter. He gave her a wave, as he always did, but then he stopped. Jia was rarely jovial, but today she was more solemn than usual. Her face was grave, brows drawn together, and she hunched over the letter with worry.

Slowly he approached. She did not look up, or indeed seem to notice him at all. Soon he stood at the table, but she had not so much as batted an eye.

"Instructor Jia?" he said tentatively. "Is everything all right?"

She jerked in her seat and looked up at him. With a quick sigh, she folded the letter and tucked it away in a pocket before she stood.

"No, it is not," she said. "Yet it is nothing you need trouble yourself with. Do you require assistance?"

He shook his head. "No, Instructor. But what troubles you so? If I could help . . ."

"It is this battle in Wellmont. No doubt you have heard of it?"

Ebon frowned. "I have not. Wellmont—is that the city upon the border of Dorsea and Selvan? They squabble constantly. Surely it is no great worry."

"They do," she admitted. "But this seems to be something more grave. It has lasted longer than usual, at any rate. And even a border skirmish there would trouble me. I grew up in that city, as did a former student of the Academy, one who I cared for very deeply. The last I heard, she was stationed there, but I have not received word from her in months. And there is something else . . . something that happened in the battle . . ."

Ebon wanted to put a comforting hand on her shoulder, but it seemed inappropriate. Instead he merely stammered, "I am sorry to hear that. You taught this student weremagic?"

"I teach weremagic to no one."

He could not help a small smile. "Therianthropy, I mean."

Jia shook her head. "No, I was not her instructor. She was a mentalist. But never mind; this is nothing for you to worry over. We can do little about it in any case, here so far away from the fighting—and a good thing, too. Carry on with your studies, Ebon, and remember: wisdom in the right head may stop such wars before they begin. You should hold that endeavor as paramount, as should all people of learning."

"Yes, Instructor," he mumbled.

As he left her, he thought of the war, so far away, and wondered what it would feel like to have a loved one stuck in the thick of it. That thought drew him to his brother Momen.

He scarcely remembered when Momen rode away from home. Much clearer were his memories of the day they learned he had been killed. It had been a dark day, a day that seemed to go on forever, full of hurt and tears and hatred in Father's eyes. He doubted he would ever forget it; in fact a small part of him hoped he would not.

A thought struck him, and it seemed odd he had

never thought it before. Ebon did not know how Momen had died. As far as he could remember, Idris had never been involved in any border wars with the three kingdoms next to it. Idris was a desert; it lacked the fair green lands that made Selvan so attractive a target. And the Camar, the royal family of Idris, were almost as fearsome as the Draydens. He had never mustered the courage to ask his father how Momen died, and now he likely never would. Mayhap Halab knew. He would have to ask, the next time he saw her.

Kalem was waiting at the table when Ebon arrived, and immediately he put down his book. "Let us see it," he said.

Ebon sighed and drew the wooden rod, handing it over. Kalem took a deep breath. His eyes glowed, and under his fingers, the rod turned to stone. He blinked, and it returned to wood.

"There. Did you feel it this time?"

Kalem had told him that wizards could sense other wizards using their spells if the magic was of an aligned branch. Weremagic and alchemy worked in tandem, he said, as did mindmagic with firemagic. Ebon could sense when a weremage or another alchemist was using their powers. Now, as he often had before, Ebon could feel a tingling on his neck and a turned stomach when Kalem transformed the rod. But it was no more help than it had been before.

"I sensed it, yes. But I still do not see how that helps."

"The feeling it gives you—try to emulate it. Try to recapture it when you cast your spell."

Ebon rolled his eyes and took the road. He tried to do as Kalem asked, picturing the tingling on the back of his neck and the vague roiling of his stomach. But that only distracted him from seeing the wood for what it truly was. Nothing happened to his eyes, and he soon cast the rod aside in frustration.

"It is no use. When I focus on the sensation, I lose sight of the rod, and when I think of the rod, I cannot think of the sensation."

"Just focus upon them both. It is quite easy."

Ebon thrust a finger under his nose. "If you tell me, even once more, that it is easy, I will—"

Kalem smiled and touched Ebon's robe. The whole sleeve turned to iron, and at the sudden change in weight, Ebon tipped over out of his chair. He yelped as he landed hard on his arm—but, as it was encased in metal armor, it did not hurt as badly as it might have.

"Change it back," he growled.

Kalem sighed and did as he asked. "Ebon, you grow frustrated too easily. A calm mind is the best facilitator of magic."

"I have few places to find calm in my life."

"Then I hope you are resigned to a life without spells," said Kalem with a shrug. "Because that is all you will ever have. When you struggle to clear your mind, let this encourage you: if you master yourself, wizardry will follow swiftly. Then all the physical world will be at your command; you will control earth, buildings, even the oceans and the winds. Is that not worth learning to cast aside fear and doubt?"

"What do you mean, the oceans and the winds? Those spells are of mind magic."

"Elementalism, Ebon. You could at least pretend that proper terms matter to you, for I can assure you they matter to everyone else."

"Elementalism, then," said Ebon through gritted teeth. "But you have not answered my question."

Kalem seemed to take this as an apology, for he nodded magnanimously. "I do not speak of elementalist spells like summoning water and wind. Those depend on motion. Our magic is the magic of change. You can turn water to oil easily enough. One day you will learn to change the air as well."

Ebon's curiosity was piqued. He had never thought of this before, nor seen an alchemist at the school do it. "How? What can you do with the air?"

"Some simple things," Kalem said with a shrug. "They teach more advanced spells in the next class. But I have learned the spell to make mist."

"Can you show me?"

Kalem looked surprised and more than a little pleased. He crossed his legs beneath him, and after a moment his eyes began to glow. Before Ebon's eyes, a mist seemed to spring out of nowhere, but as he looked closer he could see it emanating away from Kalem's body. Soon it filled the space all around them, spreading further and further until it reached the library's railing. The mist grew thicker and thicker, until Ebon could not see more than a few paces in any direction.

"That is all I can do for now," said Kalem. "My instructor says he could fill the entire Academy with fog, if he so chose. I do not know if I believe that, but then again, it is a very simple spell." He blinked, and the glow faded from his eyes. The mists rushed back and vanished, and the air was clear again.

"That is wondrous," said Ebon. "I would give much to be able to cast such a spell." He felt his own lack like an ache in his heart.

"You will learn it. In fact, it seems simpler to me than turning wood to stone. Air is a very simple thing. Not like wood."

"Mayhap I could try it," said Ebon.

Kalem looked uncomfortable. "I am not sure that is wise. They teach us our spells in a certain order, and they do so for a reason."

"What reason? If I can make mist, why should I not try it? Mayhap it will turn my mind towards other spells—even the spell for stone."

"Mayhap," said Kalem. "I suppose I cannot see the harm in it . . ."

Ebon closed his eyes and tried to envision the air around him. He spread his fingers until he could feel its coolness on his skin. At first he felt no different. Then he remembered how it felt when he turned water to oil. He did not picture the water in his mind so much as he *saw* it through his fingers. He tried it now, and soon it was as though he could see the air's tiny currents as they wove about him. He opened his eyes and focused. To his delight, the world brightened, and he knew his eyes were glowing. Thin wisps of mist sprang into being, twisting in little spirals about his fingers.

Joy shot through him, joy strong enough to break his concentration. The glow died, and the mists vanished. But rather than disappointment, he only felt his joy increase until he laughed out loud. "I did it!"

Kalem's grin matched his own. "You did at that. That seemed to come to you easily."

Ebon studied his fingers closely. He still felt that he could see the air's currents. "It was so much easier than the wood. I could see it as plain as the floor beneath my feet."

"As I said, air is simple. But still, even I did not learn mist so quickly. You should be proud."

"Have you ever used it? It seems to me that mists would be a powerful spell for sneaking about."

Kalem's face fell, and he looked to the ceiling as though for help. "Sky save me. Of course you would immediately think of how to use it for mischief."

Ebon gave his shoulder a little push. "Oh, calm yourself. I have no schemes to sneak about the Academy and wreak havoc. At least, not yet."

"You would find it a hard prospect even if you did. Any alchemist or weremage would sense what you were doing and put a stop to it."

"*Transmuter* or *therianthrope,* Kalem," said Ebon, wagging a finger in admonishment. "Honestly, you could at least pretend that proper terms matter."

Kalem scowled.

TWENTY

THE DISCOVERY OF A NEW SPELL, AND ONE THAT ACTUALLY
seemed useful, filled Ebon's days with joy. Whenever he
could, he practiced spinning his mists. When he grew
bored in Credell's class, in between reading books in the
library, in the common room outside his dormitory—all
were perfect opportunities to steal away by himself and
practice. And now he found himself wondering what
else he might be able to learn. Suddenly his wooden rod
seemed utterly unimportant. Oh, certainly he would
need to turn it to stone one day—but why worry over it
now, when he could learn other spells instead?

But not all his time was so joyous. Every so often, thoughts crept in of the parcel he had delivered for Mako and his father. Despite sharing his worries with Adara, and the conversations he had had with Kalem and Theren, he could not help but wonder what he was now involved in. If indeed he was part of some nefarious scheme, he doubted the King's law would care that he had not wished to be involved.

One morning he woke with an idea. He toyed with it all through Credell's class, turning it over and over in his mind. By the time of the midday meal, he knew he had to bring it to Kalem and Theren.

"I have been thinking hard," he said, as soon as they were all seated in the dining hall. "And I want to know what was in the parcel."

"I am sure we would all like to know," said Kalem. "But that carriage, as they say, has driven on already."

"Mayhap not for good."

Theren leaned in, eyes alight. "My dear goldbag. You cannot be proposing what I think—no, what I *hope*, you are proposing."

"Mayhap," said Ebon with a grin.

Kalem looked back and forth between them, utterly lost. "I do not understand. What do you mean to do?"

"I shall return to the inn where I brought the package. If the man is still there, I mean to find the package and learn what was inside it."

Kalem could only gawk. "You cannot be serious."

"He is, and it is glorious," said Theren. She laughed out loud and slapped her hand down on the table. Many students looked over in shock, but she ignored them. "My dear little goldbag. I take back all the nasty things I ever said about you. Well, not all of them, but the greater part of them at least."

"You will help me, then?"

"She will *not,* because you will *not* do this mad thing," said Kalem. Though he whispered, it was so loud and harsh that Ebon doubted it did much to hide the words. "You do not know what you are involved in. You could be killed."

"I doubt that. The man we saw is some agent of my family's. He would not dare raise a hand to me, for then he would face their wrath—or at least my aunt's, for I doubt my father cares whether I live or die."

"You do not know that," said Kalem. "What if he hired your family to do this thing for him? If they are in his employ, and not the other way around, that is a very different situation."

Ebon scoffed. "My family, playing the part of lackey to some man in a rotten hovel of an inn? That is hardly likely."

"You are quick to say so, yet what if you are wrong? It could go ill for all of us."

"All of us?" said Ebon with a smile. "Do you mean to come with us, then?"

"Say you will, little goldbag," said Theren, shaking Kalem's shoulder. The poor boy flopped all about as though he were a rag doll. "It would not be a proper adventure without you."

"I do not *want* it to be a proper adventure!" whined Kalem, shoving her hand away.

Ebon leaned in closer. "Think, Kalem. You have heard rumors of my family's doings, have you not? It seems I am being drawn into them, though I did not will it. Will you not help me fight off their influence? I do not mean to grow up and become another agent of whatever mischief my father wishes to get up to."

"Then leave it behind," said Kalem miserably. "Refuse to follow his orders, and keep your nose out of whatever is happening."

"Too late for that," said Theren. "His nose is already well stuck in."

"And I cannot refuse him," said Ebon. "He will withdraw me from the Academy. Mako said as much."

Kalem seemed to know he was defeated. It made him sullen, and he folded his arms in a pout. "This is a terrible idea."

"Mayhap, but it is the only thing I can think of to free myself. I see you as a friend, Kalem. A true friend. Will you help me?"

The boy rolled his eyes and looked around. "Of course I will. You idiot."

Ebon and Theren cheered as they embraced him.

That night, Ebon met his friends in the hall outside of Kalem's common room.

"All right," said Kalem, looking thoroughly disgruntled. "If we mean to go through with this mad scheme, then let us get on with it. How do you mean to sneak out?"

"Theren has a way."

"And I shall not leave you behind this time," she said with a grin. "But I do not think all three of us can approach the wall without being seen."

"You need not worry about that," said Ebon. "I have learned a new spell."

He focused on the air around him, and the world grew brighter. Mist sprang from his skin, swirling about to surround him. Soon he could not see the others, though he could still sense them standing close. His chest swelled with pride—but then he heard Kalem and Theren burst into raucous laughter through the mist, which they swiftly hushed.

"What?" said Ebon. "What is it?"

"Ebon, you look ridiculous," Theren managed to choke out. "Stop that foolish spell at once."

He did not understand, but he let the image of the mist slip from his mind. The world darkened, and the fog receded. Kalem still clutched a hand to his mouth, his eyes bugging out from laughter, and Theren's dark face had darkened further as she fought to remain silent.

"Do you not think the Academy's attendants

would notice a perfectly student-sized cloud of mist scuttling about the halls?" said Theren. "It practically held to your limbs. You were as inconspicuous as a two-mast ship falling through the ceiling of the High King's palace."

"It looked like this." Kalem's eyes glowed, and mist sprang into being around him—but it held only a few fingers away from his skin, so that he was like a little boy made all of fog. He crouched and slunk down the hallway in a low run, head swinging back and forth as though looking for pursuers. Theren clapped both hands to her mouth again and nearly fell over laughing.

Ebon's cheeks were burning, and he looked down at his shoes. "Stop that. It is easy enough for the two of you to mock me; you have been here for years."

Kalem let the mists die away, and Theren put a comforting hand on his shoulder. But they could not hide the glints in both their eyes. "Indeed, it is unfair," said Kalem. "I am sorry. And you should be very proud of how quickly you have learned the spell for mist. But on this outing, at least, I think I should be responsible for concealing our escape."

"Very well," grumbled Ebon. "Then let us get on with it."

He led them through the halls and then down the wide staircase to the front hall. Mellie was there by the door. She straightened in her chair and fixed them with wide, suspicious eyes. But Ebon only gave her a little wave and turned around, heading back down the hallway to the white doors leading outside.

"Turn left," said Theren. "We should leave by the eastern doors, for I need to use the sheds."

Ebon did as she said, and soon they had reached the training grounds outside the citadel. A few other students stood here and there in pockets, scarcely visible in the dim light. There, too, Ebon saw Jia and the other instructor he had often seen on the training grounds, speaking with each other as they strode down a path.

"We shall have to wait for Jia and Dasko to pass," muttered Kalem. "They are both therianthropes; if I cast my mists now, they will detect it."

Dasko. So the instructor had a name.

Jia saw Ebon and gave him a nod, which he returned, but the two instructors took no other notice of them. Soon they had vanished around the corner of the citadel. Ebon waited a few moments just to be safe, and then he gave Kalem a nod.

The boy's eyes glowed, and mist filled the air all about them. Ebon heard a few muted sounds of surprise from the other students in the training grounds, but he and his friends were already running for the wall. He would have run straight into it if Theren had not stopped him with a quick hand. She guided them all until they stood by the wall together, huddling against it in the fog. A few paces away, Ebon saw shacks built against the inside wall, perfect mirrors of the ones on the outside.

"I will go first," said Theren. "The sheds are easy and will give you a sense of how to make the landing. If I am atop them first, I can help steady you. Then we get to try the wall—that will be the fun part."

"I doubt it," said Ebon. He remembered the sickness in his stomach when he had stood upon the library's third floor balcony and shuddered.

"Up we go, then," said Theren. She crouched, eyes glowing, and then with a leap she vanished into the air.

Ebon gulped hard. Then he felt something under his arms where they joined the shoulders. He looked down, but there was nothing there. *Theren's magic,* he realized. Steeling himself, he jumped as high as he could.

An unseen force gripped him, throwing him through the air. Then he was coming down, the shed roof beneath his feet. It came too quickly, and he fell with a crash. Soon Theren had gripped his arm and hauled him up.

"All well?" she said.

Ebon nodded, a bit shaken. A moment later, Kalem came flying through the air to land beside them both. The boy's eyes still glowed from holding the mist in place.

"The next leap will be harder," Theren warned. "Be ready to grip the wall with all your might."

Again she leaped first, the glow of her eyes vanishing into the mist above them. Again Ebon felt unseen hands holding him up. He crouched as low as he could. For a moment he could not will himself to move.

"Ebon?" said Kalem.

"A moment." Ebon took two deep breaths. "Sky above, protect me."

He leaped.

This time he rocketed through the air, the mist stinging his eyes so that he had to close them. Then the cold against his skin vanished. He opened his eyes to see the top of the wall rocketing towards him.

He could see he would not clear it.

Panic froze his limbs. But then his chest struck the wall's lip, and on instinct he reached forth to seize it. His elbows barely cleared the edge, and his shoes scrabbled uselessly against the wall as he tried to help himself rise the last pace.

"Ebon!" Theren fell to her knees and reached for him just as Ebon lost his grip and fell into empty space.

For an instant, time stopped. He could see the world in perfect detail: the horror in Theren's face, plain despite the glow in her eyes; the rough texture of the wall sliding away under his hand; his robes fluttering in the air that rushed past him.

But then Theren's hand closed over his wrist, and he slapped against the wall hard enough to knock the breath from him. Theren swung him one way, then another, and her eyes glowed brighter. He felt another unseen push, and an invisible rope tugged him atop the wall.

He collapsed on his back, panting, clutching the granite beneath him until it scraped his fingers. Theren must have thought he was hurt, for she knelt above him and looked into his eyes.

"What is wrong? Are you injured?"

Ebon could not speak, but he shook his head. She grinned at him.

"I would wager you never thought the Academy would be like this, goldbag. Come. Kalem is waiting, and likely wondering what we are up to."

She stood and went to the edge. Ebon closed his eyes, willing the world to stop spinning.

"Aieee!"

Kalem screamed as he landed beside Ebon. He cleared the lip easily and landed facedown. Like Ebon, he seized the wall's top as though he might never let go.

"My apologies," said Theren. "You are much lighter than either of us. I may have brought you up too quickly."

"Yes, you may have," said Kalem, voice shaking.

"I cannot go back down," said Ebon, voice breaking on every other word.

"What?" said Theren.

"I cannot do that again. I cannot move. Please. Please, I cannot."

Kalem pushed himself up to a sitting position and looked ruefully at Theren. "He deals poorly with heights. I had forgotten."

Theren shook her head and rolled her eyes. "Come now, Ebon. It is only a little jump. Going down is much easier, for I do not have to lift you—only stop you from falling to your death."

Ebon's limbs shook harder. Kalem, still sitting, slapped Theren's leg. "Leave off, Theren! Can you not see you are frightening him?"

"It is not her, Kalem," said Ebon. "Look how high we are. I was mad to think I could do this."

Kalem came crawling to Ebon's side. "Come, Ebon. You must go down, one way or another. It may as well be on the outside, rather than into the training grounds again."

"I cannot move. Tell one of the instructors I am here. They can lift me. I care not if they punish me, or even expel me. I *cannot* move, Kalem."

Kalem frowned and put a hand on his shoulder. "But you can. Because you must, and because you were right before. Your family has some evil work afoot. We can put a stop to it, but not without you. Come, my friend. Sit up, first. Then we will take the next step."

Sit up. That seemed easy enough.

Ebon took another deep breath and forced his hands to slide across the stone until he could lift himself. Soon he was half-sitting, though still he tried to keep himself low to the stone.

"Good, good," said Kalem, speaking softly. "Now. Theren will go down first, as she did before. And I will be here with you until you are ready."

Theren shook her head, but she did as Kalem said, stepping off the edge of the wall and vanishing into the darkness. The only thing they could see of her was her eyes, faintly glowing in the darkness ten paces below.

"It is so far," Ebon said, trying not to wail.

Kalem squeezed his shoulders. "You can do it. Come now. You are older than I am."

"That only means I am larger. What if she should drop me?"

"You heard her—going down is much easier than going up. If it helps, I will push you."

"If you do, I will pull you with me."

They both chuckled, though Ebon had to force it. "All right," said Kalem. "Whenever you feel yourself ready."

Ebon slid closer to the edge of the wall. It was just there now, right beside his hand. He did not even have to jump. He could simply fall. His heart still hammered in his chest, and spots of light danced before his eyes. He thought he might faint. *That would get me off the wall in short order,* he mused. The thought summoned a bitter laugh.

He slid his feet over the edge and pushed off.

Panic seized him again—but this time it did not matter, for Theren caught him. He could see her as he drew closer, the glow in her eyes brightening, hands held up. The closer he fell to the roof of the shed, the slower he moved. By the time he was two paces above her, he was no longer even afraid, for he moved slower than a brisk walk. He came down upon the roof easily, but still his nerves made him fall to his hands and knees.

"Did I not tell you?" said Theren. "Easier than going up."

"You were right," said Ebon. He forced himself up and embraced her. She started in surprise, but hugged him back after a moment. "Thank you."

"Yes, well," said Theren, clearly uncomfortable. "Leave off, or our little alchemist will dive into the abyss without me to catch him."

A moment later, Kalem was down. He and Theren jumped easily off the shed roof. Ebon elected to climb down, hanging from the edge before dropping to the street. Then they ran off, and soon the Academy was out of sight.

They had come over the east wall, and so they ran in a wide loop until they were heading west again. As they went, Kalem looked about in excitement. His young face glowed with a silver tint in the moonlight.

"This is terribly, terribly stupid of us. We could get in a great deal of trouble, or even be expelled from the Academy. It is all rather exciting."

"I fear we have proven a poor influence on our young friend, Ebon," said Theren, teeth flashing in the dark.

"Mayhap, but mayhap he shall be better for it. You are a bit prudish when it comes to rules." Ebon ruffled Kalem's hair. Kalem batted his hand away.

"Leave off. You speak as though you have done this often, instead of once, and then with special permission from the dean."

"Lucky for you both, then, that I am an old hand at this," said Theren.

"How many times have you snuck out?" asked Kalem.

"You mean this month?"

Ebon shook his head and smiled. In truth he was far more worried about this excursion than he had been the last time he was in the city after dark. But now the journey was his own choice, and besides, he had his friends with him. That was more comforting than ignorantly doing his father's bidding.

Before long Theren had led them to the Shining Door, which looked every bit as dirty and irreputable as the last time. "Don your hoods," said Ebon. "I would not have anyone here recognize Theren and I from when we came before."

"They will see our students' robes," said Theren. "That may be more than clue enough."

"That we cannot help."

With their hoods raised, they entered the inn. Almost immediately, Ebon felt Kalem draw closer to him. The patrons in the common room gave them evil looks. With their hoods up, gazes lingered a while longer as some tried to see their faces. Ebon ignored them as he made his way to the back, where the innkeeper stood with his hands spread on the counter.

"Well met," said Ebon, trying to deepen his voice. "We seek a man who roomed here, or mayhap rooms here still. He had a thin beard and Elf-white skin. When last I saw him, he wore blue and grey."

"I may know many men," said the innkeeper. "And

it does me no good to discuss any of their business. Shove off."

Theren tensed beside him, but Ebon put a hand on her arm. From his purse he drew a gold weight, sliding it to the barkeep. The man eyed the coin for a moment, but he did not move. Ebon sighed and extracted another, placing it beside the first. "That is all you will get, and is more than a fair price for loosening your lips."

The innkeeper scowled, but he took the coins and tucked them into his pocket. "The one you seek is not here at the moment, though he still holds a room."

"What use are those words?" snapped Theren.

"They are the only ones I have."

"What room has he taken?" said Ebon.

The innkeeper pointed to the hallway leading to the back. "First on the right."

Ebon withdrew another coin. *No matter my allowance, at this rate I shall soon be a pauper.* "For your willing assistance," he said. If the man caught the irony in Ebon's tone, he did not show it—but he took the coin.

They moved towards the hallway, Ebon in the lead. But before they reached it, Kalem tugged at his sleeve. "What do you mean to do?" he whispered.

"Search the man's room."

"Are you mad? What if the innkeeper is wrong? What if he is here, and even now slumbers within?"

"Well, if he is slumbering, then we shall have no trouble," said Theren brightly.

"Unless he wakes. Or unless he does *not* slumber, and is sitting there waiting in lamplight for some foolish Academy students to come bumbling to their deaths!" Kalem's voice rose with each word until he was nearly screeching, though still in a whisper.

"Our only other choice is to turn back and make for home," said Ebon.

"That seems an excellent idea."

"For cowards," said Theren.

"I am going," said Ebon. "Kalem, if you wish, you may withdraw. We shall find you on the street in a moment."

Kalem looked as though he might, but then he looked around. Many eyes were now upon the three of them, for they stood near the center of the room.

"Oh, very well," he muttered. "Only I think this is the height of idiocy, and speaking of the two of you, that says quite a lot."

They reached the door. Ebon pressed an ear to it for a moment, but he could hear nothing inside. He turned the latch and stepped through. The door gave a long *creeeak* as it swung slowly open. There were no lanterns within. The only light came from the common room itself, and that was too dim to reveal anything.

He squared his shoulders and took another step in. The room was dead silent. Theren and Kalem's footsteps sounded like thunder as they came in after him and swung the door shut.

It took a moment for his eyes to adjust, and even then they could not see into the shadowed corners. But faint moonslight through the cracks in the drawn shutters revealed a dirty, unkempt bed and a single chest of drawers. There was a lamp on the floor by the bed, and for a moment Ebon thought to light it. But that might be folly; what if the man returned and saw the light glowing beneath his door?

"Look quickly," he said. "The package was soft, wrapped in brown cloth, and tied with simple string. I think it was mayhap two hands wide. Find it, if you can, or anything unusual that might have been inside it."

They set about their search. Theren moved to the bed, lifting the straw mattress and the pillow. Her nose coiled in disgust. Ebon understood why as he dropped to the floor and searched under the bed's frame—the floor smelled of something untoward, a smell he could not place and did not like. But there was nothing underneath, except some rubbish of paper that held no words.

But from the chest of drawers, Kalem whispered, "Ebon."

Theren went to him at once, and Ebon joined her a moment later. In the bottom drawer of the chest was the brown cloth parcel. Ebon recognized it at once.

"That is it," he said. "Open it."

"Why should I?" said Kalem, voice shaking. "You open it."

Ebon reached for it with shaking fingers and undid

the string. The brown cloth fell away. But in the darkness, he could not see what lay within. He reached for it and drew it out, holding it under the moonslight.

It was a tabard, that was plain: white with gold edges, and large enough to be worn over a suit of plate armor—or mayhap chain, if the wearer were particularly large. It covered chest and back and upper arms as well, and a lifetime of wealth told him the cloth was very fine. But more importantly, upon the breast was displayed a sign: a four-pointed star with a red gem in the middle. Ebon knew he had seen it before, but it took him a moment to place it. When he did, his heart skipped a beat.

"The High King's sigil," breathed Theren.

"This is worn by the palace guards," said Kalem. "I went there once. Every one of the High King's personal guard wore a tabard of just this make."

"Why would I have been asked to deliver this? And to a man like the one we saw, in such a flea-ridden place?" said Ebon.

"Mayhap there is more to be found," said Theren, and she returned to the drawer.

But just as Ebon was about to join in her search, a sound made him freeze The door's latch turned, and before he could tell them to hide, it flew open. There in the doorway, wreathed in the lamplight from the room beyond, stood the pale man with the thin beard.

TWENTY-ONE

KALEM GAVE A SHARP CRY AND STRETCHED OUT HIS hands. His eyes glowed, and a thick mist filled the room. At the same time, Ebon leaped forwards to drag Theren back from the chest of drawers.

Together the three of them pressed back into the room. Ebon did not know what to do, but he knew that trying to escape through the door would mean capture.

Theren tore from his grasp, and he lost his grip on Kalem. Then a form came forwards through the mist, wiry hands grasping at empty air. The pale man.

He seized the front of Ebon's robe and dragged

him in. Even so close, the mists were too thick to see his face.

"Help!" cried Ebon. He tried to strike the man, but found his wrist caught in an icy grip. His assailant's skin was cold and clammy, his arms all wiry muscle.

The other hand released Ebon's robe. Then Ebon heard a *snikt*—a drawn dagger. The steel flashed in the mist as it came up, ready to plunge into Ebon's heart.

Something invisible struck the man. His head flew back, and he dropped the blade. His ankle flew high, flipping him upside down. Ebon had seen it before when Lilith had attacked him in the tavern. It was Theren's magic.

"Run!" she cried.

Ebon ran for where he thought the door was. But he misjudged and struck the wall instead. A small form crashed into his back—Kalem. Ebon grabbed the boy, and together they pressed through the door into the hallway beyond.

Theren was there, but she did not waste time with words. Together they fled through the common room. The innkeeper cried out, but they ran on, heedless. Soon they were in the cool, clean air of the streets beyond, but they kept running until they had left the Shining Door far behind.

At last they stopped in an alleyway, far from any main street. Kalem collapsed against a brick wall, sliding to sit on the filthy ground. Eyes closed and head thrown back, he cast down his hood.

"Did he see us?" said Theren. "Does he have our description?"

"Our hoods were raised," said Ebon. "And though he held me by the wrist, I could not see his face in the mist. I think we are safe."

Kalem's panting slowed at last. His gaze fixed angrily on Ebon. "Safe? You nearly got the three of us killed!"

"How was I to know he would return while we were in his very room?"

"How could you simply assume he would not?" said Kalem. "He meant to murder us. What if he had? Can you imagine your parents receiving a letter that you had been killed upon the Seat?"

Ebon felt his cheeks burning, and he looked down at his shoes. The street was silent for a moment. "My father would read the letter and then most likely throw it in a fire. I doubt he would even tell my mother."

"I came from an orphanage in Cabrus," said Theren. Her voice was nearly as quiet as Ebon's. "No one there would care. My patron would see it as an inconvenience. Then she would find another wizard to do her bidding."

Kalem's mouth hung open, but no sound came out. He looked back and forth between them and then dropped his own gaze. "I . . . I am sorry," he said. "I had not thought . . . that is, I thought only of my own parents."

Ebon shrugged. "Who could blame you? I, too,

considered only myself. It was thoughtless of me to bring you here."

Theren pulled the boy to his feet and gave his shoulders a little shake. "Do you jest? We might be dead if not for our brave Kalem here. Your mists were exquisite."

Kalem still looked abashed, but he gave a little smile. "I panicked. I hardly knew what I was doing."

She smiled. "Better a fool who does the right thing than a wise man who does the wrong, I always say."

Their somber mood lifted somewhat, and Ebon gave his friends a smile. But then he frowned again. "I only wish we had learned more. I wonder what he had that uniform for."

"There I may be of some help," said Theren with a wide smile. "For I found something else, just as our unwelcome guest arrived."

Her hand vanished into her robes. A moment later she drew forth a parchment and unfurled it. It was a map of the Great Bay and the High King's Seat, with marks and symbols scrawled all across it.

They made their way back to the Academy as quickly as they could, and Theren helped them over the wall once more. Again Ebon found it a harrowing experience, but already it was easier than the last time.

After sneaking into the citadel, they went to the common room outside Kalem's dormitory. The younger children had all gone to bed, and they huddled together over a table to study the map by firelight.

The Seat itself took up most of the map, though Selvan's coast was depicted to the west. The docks on the east and west ends of the island were drawn in more detail than the city itself. Near the western docks, many ships had been drawn in dark blue ink, while near the eastern dock were more ships drawn in red. From the High King's palace were drawn lines in blue and red, tracing through the city and out to the docks to meet the ships of the same colors.

"What does it mean?" said Kalem softly.

"I do not know," said Ebon. "It looks like a route from the palace to the docks, to ships waiting."

"It could be," said Theren. "But look here."

She pointed, and Ebon saw a smaller drawing that had escaped his notice. To the south of the eastern docks, on the very southeastern tip of the island, was a smaller ship—more of a boat. A rough cave had been sketched around it, and they were both enclosed by a red circle.

"None of this means anything to me," said Ebon. "I know little of ships and sailing."

"Yet the drawings seem more concerned with the island than with the boats," said Theren.

Kalem's expression became grave. "Mayhap this is some plot. Have you heard the tale of the Lord Prince in his youth? Some bandits captured him and hid him in their forest stronghold, where they hoped to extract a mighty ransom from the High King. This may be some plan to do the same again, or something similar, at least."

"I have heard that tale," said Ebon. "But it would be foolhardy now. His guard has been vigilant ever since. And he was captured upon the King's road, not within the palace itself."

"A brash plan may succeed where a more timid one fails, if only because one's foes do not expect it," said Theren.

"And mayhap it is not the Lord Prince," said Kalem. "Mayhap it is some other member of the royal family. Mayhap some king or young prince from one of the outland kingdoms. This is an ill finding. We should tell one of the instructors so that they may warn the palace."

Theren cuffed the back of his head. "Think. How could we tell them we came by this information? What is your plan? I can imagine your words to Jia. 'Pardon me, Instructor, but I snuck out of the Academy after nightfall and found a plot to capture one of the royal family. Or I think I did—you see, I am not sure *what* I found, in truth.' You would be put on the first ship home before you could finish the words."

"Yet great disaster might be averted," said Kalem. "We do not have to tell them it was we who found this map. We could leave it where they could find it and let them deduce the rest for themselves."

Ebon sat scowling down at the map, only half hearing his friends. Finally he spoke in a low murmur. "We do not know what this means. We do not even know the full extent of our own ignorance, for this may lead to some other truth we cannot imagine. What if this is nothing evil after all? What if the man is an agent of the High King herself, carrying out some order?"

Kalem frowned, and a moment passed before he answered. "Ebon, I can see why you would wish to believe that. It would mean your family plotted nothing untoward and that you were blameless in following your father's order. Yet I think it is dangerous to so easily believe that is the case."

"How else can you explain his uniform?" said Ebon. "Surely those cannot be obtained from just any clothier. Mayhap he is in hiding, until he leaves upon his mission and must reveal himself to be the High King's agent?"

Theren and Kalem looked at each other uncertainly. After a moment they shrugged.

"I think we should rest," said Ebon. "Whatever the truth behind this map, it would be foolish to act too quickly upon guesses. The hour is late, and our minds may be befuddled. Can we agree upon that, at least?"

"I suppose so," said Kalem doubtfully.

Theren let loose a mighty yawn. "I call those words wise. Very well. I am only glad we have had another night of excitement. We should do it more often."

"We should *not,*" muttered Kalem.

Ebon rolled up the map and tucked it into his

sleeve. Then he paused a moment before speaking, and he had to duck his head before he could. "I wanted to thank you both, by the by. For coming with me. I would have died were it not for you."

Theren flushed and looked away. "Well, you would not have been able to go were it not for me. I think that may balance things out."

Kalem smiled at her, and then at Ebon. "I believe that what she meant to say is, 'You are welcome.' But now I truly must go to bed, or I will fall asleep in my chair. Good night."

"Good night," said Ebon.

Kalem rose and went to his dormitory. Theren followed Ebon out, and silently they descended the stairs toward the older students' dormitories. But when they reached the bend in the hallways where they were meant to part, Ebon stopped her for a moment.

"I thanked you already. But I feel I owe you an apology as well."

That took her aback. She smiled slowly. "Why? You have done me no harm."

"No true harm, mayhap, but I have sometimes been impatient, or thoughtless, or simply stupid. Yet you have never abandoned me."

Theren shrugged as though bored. "You have not given me sufficient cause yet, I suppose. And besides, I have already said I find you a decent enough sort. For a goldbag."

Ebon stepped close and took her shoulders. He

kissed one cheek, and then the other, before stepping away again.

"What was that?" she said, eyes narrowed in suspicion. Her hand twitched, as though she restrained herself from rubbing at her cheek—or mayhap striking him.

"A greeting, and a parting, for dear family and friends," he said. "The custom of my kingdom—though one in which I am ill practiced, for there are few who I hold dear enough to earn it."

Theren's jaw clenched, and she did not answer. To his surprise, Ebon thought he saw her eyes glistening. But she only said, gruffly, "Well. A bit more kissing than I am comfortable with, but then your kingdom is very strange. Good night. Goldbag."

She turned and quickly made off down the hall.

TWENTY-TWO

OVER THE NEXT FEW DAYS, EBON MET WITH HIS FRIENDS at every opportunity. During meals they would sit together and discuss the map. Every afternoon, Ebon would pore over it in the library with Kalem. Yet no matter how they tried to read the markings, they could find no further meaning in them.

Once, Ebon went to Jia and asked her if there were any special significance to the colors of red and blue when used in mapmaking. She looked surprised at the question, and launched into some explanation of how farmers used them to mark the rotation of crops through the seasons. Though Ebon knew at once it had nothing to do with his own map, he found himself forced to sit and listen to the lecture.

After he finally escaped and returned to Kalem, he slouched in his chair. "I feel nearly dead from boredom. I can think of nothing but cotton and wheat and the best dates for planting them. Only I have them mixed up, and would likely try to grow cotton in the dead of winter."

Some days later, the three of them sat huddled together at the midday meal. All were silent, staring into their bowls with no new ideas springing to mind. Ebon had thought for so long upon the map that he imagined he could see it splayed out on the table before them.

"There is something we might do," said Theren slowly. "Though I doubt Kalem will like it."

"With such an introduction, how could I refuse to hear your plan?" said Kalem, rolling his eyes.

"We could go to the docks and see what we might find to explain the marks," said Ebon.

Both Kalem and Theren gaped at him, but Theren spoke first. "That is just what I meant to say. How did you know?"

"I have thought the same thing myself," said Ebon. "I did not mention it before now, because I thought that if even you had not spoken of it, it must be a terrible idea indeed."

"It is!" hissed Kalem, leaning forwards. "It *is* a terrible idea, and you must put it from your mind immediately! Already you have nearly gotten us all killed. Do you wish to risk our lives again?"

"I know no other way to learn the truth of the map," said Ebon with a shrug.

"And this is entirely different besides," said Theren. "Before, we went in search of a man who we knew—or at least suspected—was up to mischief. Now we are only going to see the docks."

"Mayhap we could go there during the daylight hours, to further reduce any danger," said Ebon halfheartedly. But he knew it for a poor idea, and he saw the same thought in Theren's expression.

"That would likely teach us nothing at all," she said. "Whatever this plot may be, we are unlikely to find it laying plain for us to find. If dark deeds are to be done, wisdom says they would be done in the dark."

"Another nighttime adventure, then," said Kalem. "Well, you may count me out."

"Dear cousin Ebon! Might I have a word?"

The voice shocked them out of their hushed conversation. Ebon looked up to find the dean standing over their table. He and Kalem froze. But Theren only leaned back carelessly, eyeing the dean with casual disinterest.

"Dean Cyrus," stammered Ebon. "Forgive us. We did not see you there."

"Please. 'Dean Cyrus' sounds so formal. 'Dean' is sufficient. Now, about that word . . .?"

The dean looked pointedly at Kalem and Theren. Kalem took the hint at once and leaped from the bench as though he had been stabbed. In a moment he had vanished among the other children in the dining hall. But Theren only looked to Ebon, brow arched in question. He nodded. She removed herself from the table, though much more slowly than Kalem had.

Dean Cyrus took a seat opposite Ebon. He had no food with him, and he leaned forwards on his elbows with a friendly smile. Ebon was keenly aware of the effect it had on the other students nearby. They seemed caught between wanting to watch and wanting to be as far from the dean as possible. He saw many students leaning away in their seats, as though they found even a few extra fingers of distance more comfortable.

"So. How go your studies, Cousin?"

"They progress well, Dean." It was a lie, of course, but Ebon well remembered how Cyrus had treated Credell when he thought the instructor was not teaching Ebon quickly enough.

"I notice you are still in Credell's class."

"Yes, and he is working hard at my instruction," said Ebon earnestly. He tried to smile but was afraid it came out as a grimace.

"Clearly not hard enough," said the dean, sounding annoyed. "A bright boy like you, and especially one so old, should have graduated his class already. I imagine he has you fooling about with that wooden rod trick?"

"Yes, Dean," said Ebon, ducking his head.

"Such a simple spell. The basest alchemists can perform it. Some students come to the Academy already having learned it from a wizard in their homeland. You should be well past it already. I shall have to speak with Credell."

"I assure you that is not necessary, Dean," said Ebon in desperation.

Cyrus waved a hand airily. "Think nothing of it, my boy. Your loyalty is admirable, but you owe nothing to an instructor who does not give you enough attention."

Ebon wanted to sink through his seat and into the stone floor. But he said only, "Yes, Dean."

"Now, then. What of our dear family? How fare they? Have you had any words with Halab recently?" The dean leaned forwards, his fingers spreading across the tabletop, and Ebon caught a curious light in his eyes.

Now we come to it—the true reason for this visit. Ebon knew full well that the dean cared little for his studies. But he could not imagine why he was interested in Ebon's correspondence with the family. Unless . . .

Ebon's heart quailed with terror. Mayhap the dean was in league with his father, in whatever plot centered around the Shining Door. Mayhap they suspected Ebon had been the one to attack the man at the inn, and now the dean was here to investigate the truth.

He chose his words carefully. "I have not spoken with Halab, nor with any other of the family, since I arrived here, Dean." *Other than Mako,* he thought. But if he was right, and this visit was about the happenings at the Shining Door, then Cyrus would already know of Mako's visits. And if he was wrong, Ebon doubted the bodyguard would appreciate a loose tongue.

Cyrus' eyes glittered. "Oh? Are you certain? Have none of them written to you? You may tell me, of course."

"They have not, Dean. Honestly. Mayhap . . . mayhap they have been too busy to write."

Come to think of it, it was odd that he had not received a letter. Father would never have sent one, of course, but enough time had passed that Albi could have. Then he realized that he himself had not yet written home, and his ears burned. It had been nearly two months since he left home. Albi would likely be furious with him.

The dean smiled and shook his head. "Oh, Ebon. You cannot think me so simple as all that. If anyone in the family has told you something you do not wish to relay, let me rid you of your fear: I am fully informed of all goings-on back in Idris. I only thought we might combine our knowledge and see what we could surmise from it. I would be especially interested in correspondence with Halab, for she has not answered my letters in some days now."

Days? That meant Halab was still on the Seat. If

she had returned to Idris, Cyrus would not have expected a response for weeks.

"I have not written Halab," said Ebon. "Though you have reminded me that mayhap I should, to thank her for sending me here. It was only by her grace that I was able to attend."

The dean's mouth twisted, becoming something sour and foul. "Yes. Grace, indeed." Then he leaned back, taking on a crafty look. "Well, we might speak of something else. Have you learned any . . . *other* . . . spells? That is, spells other than what Credell has tried and failed to teach you?"

Ebon swallowed hard. He thought of the mists Kalem had taught him to spin. Did the dean know of that? How could he? Had Ebon broken some rule without knowing it?

He realized he had taken too long to answer, and spoke in haste. "No, Dean. I have learned nothing else. I am trying to focus on Credell's teachings."

Cyrus leaned still closer. "Come, Cousin. I was a student here myself once. I know students will often pass knowledge to each other of new spells they have learned. Has one of your alchemist friends taught you anything new? Mayhap that young copper-haired boy who was just here?"

Ebon swallowed hard. "Kalem said it is unwise to learn our spells out of order. I have tried to persuade him, but he has only instructed me in the spell that turns wood to stone."

Cyrus' expression darkened. His voice dropped to a whisper, one that Ebon could barely make out. "You would not do well to lie to me, boy. You could scarcely have a worse enemy in the Academy than the dean."

Ebon's pulse sang in his ears. His throat had almost gone too dry to speak. "I am not lying, Dean."

For a moment they sat there, staring at each other. Then, abruptly, Cyrus leaned back.

"Hm. Very well." He folded his hands into the sleeves of his robe. His brows drew close, lips pressing into a thin line. "I understand the urge to guard your friends' secrets. As for our family, I ask you this: should you hear from Halab again, please come and tell me at once."

"I will, Dean," said Ebon earnestly.

Cyrus stood quickly and swept off, leaving Ebon wondering as to his meaning. He knew only one thing: the jaws of the trap were closing still, and he could not think how to free himself.

TWENTY-THREE

THE NEXT DAY, EBON WAS SLUMPED AGAINST THE WALL in Credell's class. He watched the instructor go back and forth through the classroom, giving the children advice and answering their questions. Just now Credell was beside Astrea, the wild-haired girl and the closest thing Ebon had to a friend here. The girl seemed to be on the cusp of transforming her wooden rod. Often Ebon had seen her eyes glowing with her magic, the wooden rod swirling beneath her fingers. But when she stopped, she still held only a wooden stick. Credell was turning the rod from wood to stone and back again before her eyes, explaining it to her with murmured words that Ebon could not hear.

It made Ebon's heart ache. Credell was not a bad instructor in truth, for Ebon could see how gently he dealt with the young children. Yet he still could not speak to Ebon without shaking, nor provide any answers to whatever unseen barrier stood between Ebon and his magic.

A knock came at the door. Credell's head jerked up at the noise, and for a moment he only stared. Then his gaze flitted to Ebon, eyes filled with fear. Ebon shrugged.

Credell rose and went to the door. He ducked his head outside to speak with someone Ebon could not see, and when he closed the door he held a message in his hand.

"Er . . . ah . . . Ebon, of the family Drayden," Credell stammered. "You have a visitor. She awaits you outside the Academy. The dean has given you permission to go."

Ebon started in his seat. A visitor? Who would visit him here on the Seat? It could not be his father, for Credell had said *she*. And if Ebon's parents had returned, his mother would never visit him alone. For a moment the thought of Adara flitted through his mind, but he dismissed it as foolish.

Then it came to him in a flash. He shot from his seat and ran from the room, ignoring Credell, who flinched as he passed by.

He burst from the Academy's front door into the street. There she stood: Halab, wearing fabulous golden clothes interwoven with threads of real silver. She turned at the sound of the door opening, and as her gaze fell upon Ebon, she spread her arms.

"Dearest nephew," she said.

"Halab!" Ebon cried, throwing himself into her arms. They embraced for a long moment, and then he remembered his manners. He pulled back, kissing her first on one cheek, and then another. She placed a gentle hand to his cheek.

"Even now you have not forgotten courtesy. I am glad, for you are a long way from home."

"My heart gladdens to see you, dearest aunt," said Ebon. To his great surprise, he found tears springing into his eyes, and against his will they leaked down his cheeks. "I have missed you most terribly. As well as all of the family," he added hastily.

She arched an eyebrow, as though she knew he thought of his father. "Indeed? Then I am only sorry I have not visited sooner. I have arranged for us to spend the day together."

"Truly?" said Ebon. He glanced back at the Academy's front door. "I . . . well, then I am most grateful."

"Oh? Do you not enjoy your studies?"

"Of course I do," he said. "I cannot tell you how much joy I have found here."

"I hope you will tell me all about it," she said, putting his arm in hers as she led him off down the street.

Tell her he did, for nearly two hours as they made their way through the roads of the Seat, apparently without any aim or destination. He told her of the library's many wonders, and of Kalem and Theren, and even Credell, though he left out some details of the instructor's craven nature. Of course he said nothing of his adventures beyond the citadel's walls, and especially nothing concerning Adara. He doubted Halab would disapprove, but he knew his father would, and some whispered word of it might reach home. *Best to keep that to myself*, he thought.

By the time he had finished his tales, his throat was raw from talking. Halab had nodded and made little noises of appreciation at just the right moments. When at last he dwindled to silence, she chuckled and shook her head. "Had I known you would take so well to the Academy, I might have spoken to your father years ago. And yet, in another sense, I think you arrived here at precisely the right time."

Ebon was about to ask her what she meant, but she jerked his arm to the left and down a side street. "Quickly. This way. We do not want to miss the beginning."

"The beginning of what?"

But before she could answer, the thunder of trumpets and bells tore the air asunder. The sound made Ebon nearly jump out of his skin, but Halab stood steady, as though she had expected it. Looking around, Ebon realized they stood scarcely a street away from the High King's palace. They were at the mouth of a main thoroughfare where it met the Seat's greatest road, the one that ran straight west and east from the palace to the wide gates at either end of the island. A crowd had formed around them. As Ebon looked up at the palace, resplendent in white and silver, its great gates began to swing open.

An army marched forth. First Ebon saw many soldiers on horseback, their mounts' hooves dancing gaily as they bounced in parade march. Behind these came more on foot, striding easily even in full plate. All of them wore tabards like Ebon had found in the Shining Door: white with gold edges, and the four-pointed star in the center. The sigil of the High King.

After a time, the High King's army had passed. But after them came still more troops. These were tall and stern, their finely-crafted armor polished until it shone, throwing the sunlight in Ebon's eyes. And all of them wore red cloaks, though their hoods were cast back.

"They are Mystics," said Ebon, voice hushed in wonder.

"Indeed," said Halab. "This is the greater part of all the Mystics here upon the Seat. They march at the command of the Lord Chancellor himself, and he at the command of the High King."

"But where are they going?"

"They go to join the war in Wellmont, in the southwest of Selvan. Or, it is more correctly put, they go to put a stop to it. The High King has at last decided that this border squabble is unseemly, and aims to halt it by strength of arms."

"Can she not simply command them to cease their fighting?"

"Oh, dear nephew. The minds of kings are stern and stubborn and difficult to sway. She might issue such a command, of course, but Dorsea might not listen. And even if they did, resentment would burn like a bonfire in their hearts, only to erupt again into war, and mayhap a worse one. At times, soft words may serve for diplomacy. But a wise ruler knows when to use an ironclad fist instead. Come."

Though the march was not yet over, she turned and led him away. Ebon cast one last look over his shoulder at the red-cloaked soldiers marching by, but they were soon lost to sight through the crowd.

She led him unerringly through the streets, and soon he recognized where they were: the neighborhood that surrounded the Drayden family manor. Before long he saw it, standing two stories above the surrounding buildings, its stones painted gold like their homes back in Idris. His steps faltered, and he felt as though a cloud had passed over his heart.

"Come along now," said Halab, tugging at him playfully. "Your father does not wait within. Today it is only you and I."

He smiled and tried to deny that that had been his thought, but she waved him to silence. They found the gates open and waiting, and when they climbed to the smaller dining hall on the fourth floor, a feast had been laid out for them. From the way it steamed, Ebon guessed it had been hastily uncovered the moment they had arrived.

His weeks at the Academy had nearly caused Ebon to forget how well his family ate. He feasted on lamb and figs and fine spiced soup, and salad dressed with oils that teased his tongue delightfully. Though he never went hungry at the Academy, now he ate like a man famished. When at last he could not down another bite, he sighed contentedly and sank back into the plush cushions of his chair. Halab had finished some time ago, and now she watched him over steepled fingers, a small smile playing across her lips.

"Should I investigate the Academy for starving you?"

"Not at all. It is only that they have so many to feed, and cannot prepare the food so fine as our servants can," said Ebon. "I am ever grateful, and will remember this meal for many months to come."

She reached for her wine goblet and took a delicate sip. That reminded Ebon of his own cup, and he took a deeper pull. "Remember it indeed, and in good health. And now, my nephew, tell me. You have spoken much of your time at the Academy. Have you enjoyed your time here, and your new friends? Truly?"

Ebon frowned. "Of course. Does it seem otherwise? I am happier here than ever I was at home."

Her gaze was fixed on his, and her eyes had grown sharp. "Yet it seems to me I hear something behind your words, some source of discontent that troubles you. Do my senses deceive me?"

He balked at that. She was right, of course. But how to tell her of the errand he had been sent on? Though he felt that he owed his father little in the way of loyalty, still he did not wish to trouble Halab with such matters. Shay was her brother, and it was not well to speak ill of kin to kin.

Halab sighed and put down her goblet. "I see you do not deny it, but are reluctant to speak of it, which I understand. Let me, then, hazard a guess, for recently I have spoken with Mako."

Ebon knew the blood must have drained from his face, and fear put a tingling in his fingers. If Halab knew what Ebon had been up to, mayhap she meant to withdraw him from the Academy. Was that her true purpose here?

But Halab pressed on before he could answer her. "He has told me that your father sent instructions, through Mako himself, to deliver a parcel for him. I know nothing more than that, for neither did Mako. Is this true?"

"Yes, Aunt," said Ebon. His voice betrayed him and broke.

She leaned forwards and patted his hand. "There, nephew. Do not worry yourself about such things. Though we may never know the truth behind your errand, do you truly believe your father would use you for some evil end? Surely you cannot think *that* badly of him."

"Of course not, Halab," said Ebon. The words sounded hollow even in his own ears, and from the look in her eyes, she heard it.

"Shay has always enjoyed his little schemes, even when we were children," she said. "They may be cloaked in secrecy, but they are always harmless. And if he should send Mako to you again, you should not hesitate to obey him. After all, it is by your father's grace that you are able to attend the Academy at all. I spoke on your behalf, of course, for he did not welcome the idea. But if Shay insists, he could withdraw you from the Academy and have you brought home. I do not believe either one of us wishes that."

"No, certainly not," said Ebon, shaking his head quickly.

"Good. Then serve your father as he wishes you to. It is a small price to pay. Now. I have had the gardeners carefully tending the roses, and they have bloomed most admirably for winter. Let me show them to you."

Ebon rose to follow her down and into the garden. But though he smiled and spoke with her through the day, as the sun gave way to dusk and then to moonslight, he thought hard upon her words, and wondered when Mako might come for him next.

The next day, as soon as Ebon could find Kalem and Theren together in the dining hall, he told them what had happened. At first they were both keenly interested in the High King's army marching forth, but as he went on to tell them of Halab's words, their moods dampened. Kalem looked only bemused, but Theren looked troubled.

"I take this for good news," said Kalem. "If you have done nothing wrong, then you have nothing to fear."

"A foolish notion," said Theren. "Many heads have rolled free from bodies that committed no sin. I take this as a sign that something evil has indeed transpired, and your aunt seeks to distract you from it."

Kalem looked confused. "I thought you said your aunt was one of the kind ones in your family."

"She is," said Ebon. "No worse than me, certainly. Therefore I think you are half-right, Theren. I think my father works some dark plot, but keeps it concealed from her. She is, mayhap, *too* loving, and cannot imagine any dark motive on his part. I only wish I knew what he is up to."

"You do not suppose anyone in your family knows what we have done?" said Kalem, voice quivering. "If that truth becomes known, I do not think that any of us will remain students here for very long."

"If they knew what we did and meant to expel us for it, it would have happened already," said Theren.

"Unless they cannot prove it," said Kalem.

Theren scoffed. "Since when have the rich need-ed proof or just cause to punish those who displeased them? Certainly they would not hesitate to cast me from this place, though I do not doubt Ebon would remain."

Ebon frowned. "What? Why me?"

She rolled her eyes. "Come now, goldbag. You are a Drayden. The dean is a Drayden. He has even begun to take meals with you. Surely you cannot still think to deny you have his favor?"

"He has not 'begun' to take meals with me," said Ebon angrily. "He ate with me once, and only to ob-tain information. I tell you, my family cares nothing for me—except Halab. Why do you still take me for a favored son?"

Theren shrugged. "All sons are favored whose cribs are lined with gold."

Ebon slammed his bowl down. The tables around them grew silent. "I think I have had quite enough of your small-minded scorn, Theren." He stood and swept away, leaving his dishes behind.

Let her clean up after me, for once, he thought.

TWENTY-FOUR

THE NEXT TWO DAYS WERE TERRIBLE, AS HE WAS FORCED to avoid Theren in the dining hall and in the passage-ways of the Academy. Whenever he saw her heading towards him, he would turn away and hurry past her without speaking. Theren seemed content to ignore him as well, though he thought he saw her smirking whenever he happened to glance her way.

He still spent his time in the library with Kalem, for he had no gripe with the boy. Kalem seemed nearly as miserable as Ebon. Again and again he urged Ebon to reconcile with Theren. Only to himself would Ebon admit that he was sorely tempted; Theren and Kalem were his only friends here. But no matter what they went through together, it seemed she would never see him as anything more than some rich and pampered child, worthy only of her scorn. It seemed that nothing he said would convince her of the truth: he only wished for his family to leave him alone.

Where once he had visited Theren and Kalem in the common room outside of Kalem's dormitory, now he spent most of his evenings wandering the training grounds. They were expansive enough that he could go for hours without seeing another soul, if he was careful. There were hedges and bushes, planted for the purpose of separating different training grounds, into which Ebon could lose himself easily.

As moonslight lit the grounds on the second day since his fight with Theren, Ebon was sitting on a bench near the Academy's outer wall. It was nowhere near the sheds Theren used to sneak out at night—he had made certain of that. He rested upon a bench, leaning back against the granite wall and picking at his fingernails. But his eyes saw nothing, for his thoughts were far away; he thought of Albi back home, of the subtle scorn in Theren's eye when he saw her now, and especially of Halab and Mako and his father.

A sound drew his mind back to the present: the snap of a twig in a nearby bush. His gaze drifted to the sound, and he sat forwards. "Who is there?"

No answer came, but he thought he heard the rustling of leaves. His pulse quickened, and he pushed himself up from the bench. His hands clenched to fists, but he hesitated. Mayhap he had not heard anything after all, and was now being ridiculous. This was the Academy. Who would attack him here?

An unseen force picked him up from the ground and launched him through the air. He slammed into the outer wall. All his breath left him in an instant as he fell to the grass.

Before he could find his feet, the unseen force struck him again. This time it was a hammer blow to his face. His teeth stabbed into his upper lip, and blood spattered the granite wall.

"What—" he managed to stammer, before another invisible blow struck him in the gut. He cried out, tears spilling unbidden from his eyes. At last he recognized it for mind magic.

Theren?

It seemed impossible. She was angry with him, but not this angry.

The force lifted him up to press him against the wall, and this time it held him there. Though glazed eyes he looked down. But it was not Theren before him. It was Cyrus.

"You saw her," rasped the dean. Though his eyes glowed, Ebon could see his fury in the twist of his brow. "You saw Halab. You spent the better part of a day with her, and yet you did not tell me."

Until this very moment, he had utterly forgotten the

dean's request to inform him of his dealings with the family. Now his mind spun, confused, clouded by pain.

"I . . . what?" said Ebon.

He flew a pace away from the wall and then came crashing back. His head struck the stone hard, and stars exploded in his vision.

"Worthless whelp. Did I not tell you? Did I not ask you, ever so kindly, to tell me if you spoke to our family? Yet you disobeyed. I will be kind no longer. I knew you were in league with them. Tell me why they have cut me off. *Tell me!*"

Again he slammed Ebon into the wall. Then, abruptly, the invisible strings vanished. Ebon fell forwards, so senseless that he could not even break his fall with his arms. The grass cushioned his landing, but still it felt as though he had been punched in the chest. Barely able to see, he pushed himself up to his elbows.

"She told me nothing," he said, voice coming thick and bubbly through the blood that gushed from his lip. "She said nothing of you. I do not know what has—"

Magic seized all his limbs at once. He rose into the air. Not too high—no doubt the dean feared to lift him into view of any other students who might be in the training grounds but Ebon knew he could go much, much higher if Cyrus wished it.

"You lie," he hissed. "You are in league with them. You were sent here to spy on me!"

"I was not," Ebon said, sobbing now. "I do not

know why I was sent here. Halab said nothing to me of you. I swear it. She only asked after my studies."

"Tell me the truth, or I will throw you over the wall and let you splatter to soup on the pavement beyond!" said Cyrus. "This is your last chance. Tell me what you and Halab spoke of."

"I swear it! I swear it to you!" cried Ebon. His guts churned in shame, but he could not stop himself from crying, crying as he had not even when he was a little boy, when word came back that his brother Momen had been killed in some far-off land, far from home, far from family. Now Ebon knew he faced the same fate.

For a moment Cyrus studied him, face contorted in fury. Then he relaxed. He lowered his hands from where they had been twisted to claws before him, and the glow died from his eyes. Ebon crashed to the grass again and lay there shaking.

"A pathetic boy you prove indeed," snarled Cyrus. "No subterfuge can be that complete. I wager if I stepped closer, I would smell that you have soiled yourself."

Ebon gave no answer, but only pressed his face deeper into the grass, groveling. He waited for Cyrus to speak on, but no words came.

After a time he looked up. The dean had gone, vanishing into the darkness that even now deepened in the garden. Letting his face fall again, Ebon wept until his tears had soaked the ground, mingling with the blood that still flowed freely from his mouth.

He heard quick footsteps growing louder, and in

a moment hands seized his shoulders to roll him over onto his back.

"No! No, please, I swear I know nothing!"

"Shush!" said Theren—for Theren it was.

She dragged him up to sit and pulled him close. There she held him, uncaring of the blood that soaked into her robe as she pressed his face into her shoulder. "Shush," she said again, and rocked him like a mother rocking a babe. Ebon clutched her like a solid wall in an earthquake, and his weeping redoubled.

It was a long while before his tears finally subsided. When they did, he sat back. To his shock, he saw Theren, too, was weeping. She tried to hide it at once, swiping her sleeve across her cheeks, but he could see where her tears had left their marks, and could just see the red of her eyes in the moonslight.

"I saw him," she said, her voice shaking. "I saw it all. Forgive me, Ebon. I wanted to intervene, but I was so afraid. He is the dean, and I . . . forgive me."

She clutched at him again, and he found himself comforting her in turn. "I forgive you," he murmured. "I would have been just as scared."

"But you are not even trained," she said. "Mayhap I could have staved him off. If he had tried to send you over the wall, as he said he would, I would have torn down the Academy to stop him."

"I know you would," he said, pushing her back and looking into her eyes. "I know it. You are my friend, after all, are you not?"

In frustration she pounded his chest with her fist, but gently. "A terrible friend I have proven to be. Too craven to stand in your defense, and too foolish to believe what you said about your family."

"Ah," said Ebon, forcing himself to smile. "So at last you believe me when I say I am no favored son of the Draydens?"

"I should say so." Despite herself she laughed, and then swiped at her nose with her sleeve. But then her tears welled anew, and she looked away from him, as though she could not meet his eyes. "Ebon, I wanted so badly to help you. But I would have been expelled."

"Yes, you would have," he said. "As I said, I might have done the same as you."

"No, that is not all I mean," she said. "Ebon, leaving the Academy would be the worst thing that could happen to me. I fear it more than death itself."

Ebon frowned. "Why?"

She stood rather than answering, and then helped Ebon to his own feet. With his arm over her shoulder she led him to the bench nearby, and together they sat. Still she said nothing, not for a time, at least. Her hands were pressed together before her eyes, and she slid them against each other slowly. Her gaze was somewhere far away, as Ebon's had been before the attack.

"When I discovered my gift," she finally said, "I was living on the streets of a city called Cabrus."

"That is in Selvan, is it not?"

"It is, and no decent place for an orphaned girl. I fled the orphanage when I was young, for the matron there was cruel to us. But on the streets I found someone far worse; a weremage who killed any homeless girls who came into her clutches. I avoided her as long as I could, hoping to one day find passage from the city and escape her grasp at last. That is when I learned of my gift, and before long, word of it reached my patron.

"She is a woman named Imara, of the family Keren, and I think she earnestly believes that all things in Underrealm exist to serve her—either to be amusing, or to be useful. She saw me as some mix of both. She tested me to confirm my gift, and then she offered her patronage. I accepted, though I disliked her greatly, for my only other choice was to remain in Cabrus and someday die. And now, if I ever return to Dorsea, I will be her lackey for the rest of my days."

"Can you not earn your way out of her service one day?" said Ebon. "There are laws."

Theren shook her head. "Spoken like a true child of wealth," she said. "Laws can be bent, if not broken outright, and the wealthy have perfected the art. I could try to flee her service, of course. But if Imara is spoiled and vain, she is also spiteful, and full of wrath for those who wrong her, whether she imagines it or not. And so I remain here. I only . . . it is a terrible excuse, yet I only wanted you to know why I did not try to stop the dean. He would send me home . . . home to *her.*"

Ebon looked down at his hands, which gripped each other so tight that the knuckles were white. It seemed terribly unfair. Suddenly, even his own family seemed less onerous than Theren's circumstance.

"I wish I could help you," he said. "Only I do not know how. My family *could* help, of course—our coin purses are deep enough to pay off your service easily. Yet my father would never agree to it."

His father. Thoughts of Shay, of his whole family, whirled in Ebon's head. He still felt fear of them, yes, but now that was overshadowed by anger.

Ebon's silence had never been enough for them. Obedience had never been enough. Still they all despised him, except Halab, and Albi, and mayhap his mother. He had followed their unfair, uncompromising rules all his life, or tried to—and despite it, Cyrus had very nearly killed him.

He would never be free of them, unless he acted.

His hand moved of its own accord, gripping her arm hard. "Theren. Come with me. We must find Kalem."

"What?" she said, frowning. "Why?"

"Trust me. But you will have to help me walk."

He threw an arm across her shoulder again, and together they hobbled into the Academy, making their way towards the younger children's dormitories. They were careful to avoid any instructors, for Ebon had clearly been beaten and did not wish to explain why. Soon they were in the hallway outside Kalem's common room, and Theren left Ebon leaning against the wall while she ducked in to fetch the boy.

When Kalem came out, his eyes fell upon Ebon and shot wide. "Ebon!" he cried. "What has happened to you?"

"Do not worry yourself," said Ebon. "Only come with us."

They made their way to the stairwell, stopping in between floors and sitting together on the steps. Ebon knew their voices might carry far on the stones, but then again they would be able to hear anyone coming.

"My father is up to something," he said. "I did not wish to believe it at first, but now I know it must be true."

"How?" said Kalem.

"Because of Cyrus' actions. It was he who did this to me, Kalem. He knows something is afoot, but he thinks it has to do with Halab. Yet she, too, is being deceived by my father."

"Very well," said Theren. "I could have told you as much, and I tried, but—" Ebon gave her a hard stare, and she subsided with a gulp. "In any case, what do you mean to do about it?"

"I mean to search the docks, as we both said. We must, for it is the only way I can solve all our prob lems at once. If I can find some proof of my father's plans—"

"You can bring it to the constables," said Kalem.

Ebon shook his head with a grimace. "No. Then

blame might fall upon my whole family. But I could speak with Halab. There will never be a better time. She is here on the Seat, and my father is far away in Idris. Halab knows him only from their youth together, and will not believe me without firm evidence. But if I bring it to her . . ."

"She can address the situation on her own," finished Theren. "That seems wise. Mayhap she could have a stern word or two with Cyrus, as well." Scowling, she cracked her knuckles against each other. "Or she might let me do it."

"I have no doubt she will put him in his place," said Ebon. "But I have not told you all. If Halab deposes my father, I shall be head of my household. Then our gold shall be mine to spend as I wish."

Kalem frowned, but Theren's scowl twisted to a smirk. "A goldbag in truth. I suppose I do not object if you buy finer wines, as long as you continue to share them with me."

Ebon shook his head slowly. "I would not waste wealth on such petty things, Theren. In fact, I would give my seat up to my sister, once she came of age. But first, I would purchase your contract away from your patron. As I said, it would solve *all* our problems—not only my own."

Theren went very still. She blinked hard, tilting her head back and forth—not quite a shake of the head. "You need not—that is not—"

"Come now," said Ebon, spreading his hands.

"What use is gold without a proper reason to spend it?"

"Thank you," she whispered. "You are a truer friend than I have been. If this is your aim, I am by your side."

Kalem still looked doubtful. "This seems a shaky plan at best. It relies overmuch on luck. What if there is nothing at the docks?"

"Then we shall think of something else," said Ebon. "But we must do something. It was easy to be complacent before, but Cyrus has shown us we must act. If he, the dean, is so frightened, then something dark indeed is about to take place. You are a royal son, Kalem. Will you not act for the good of the nine kingdoms?"

The boy stared at his feet. "I think you overestimate the situation," he muttered.

"But mayhap not," said Ebon. "Please. We cannot do it without your mists."

"Very well," said Kalem. "I will help."

"Good. We should all rest well, for we make our move tomorrow night."

TWENTY-FIVE

Ebon took a long bath and went to bed the moment he was done. When he woke he felt refreshed in mind, but rest had made his whole body sore from its injuries. Gingerly lifting his robes, he saw that bruises covered most of his body, and the back of his head was still tender. But whether by design or by fortune, the dean had left his face unmarked except for the deep cut inside his lip. Though he walked tenderly through the day, neither instructors nor students gave him a second look or seemed to see that anything was wrong.

He ate his midday meal with Theren and Kalem. They spoke only a few muted words as they ate, and made no mention of the evening's plan. Ebon thought his friends must be anxious—he himself was more than a little afraid. But he also felt a curious resolution. For once in his life he felt as if he were taking a stand against his father. That more than made up for his bruises and aches.

They made for the city streets as soon as the afternoon's studies had ended, taking a moderate supper at Leven's tavern. The plan was to stay out past curfew, rather than waiting for nightfall before sneaking out. Theren would have to help them scale the wall when they returned, but Ebon was happy to avoid doing so on their way out, for he still did not enjoy being flung through the air.

As daylight began to fade from the sky, Theren led them east at a rapid pace. They had to cross most of the island, and so they wasted little time talking. By the time they reached the eastern wall, it was nearly time for the gate to be shut for the night. Though the guards would have let them pass through to the docks, Theren had warned them against such a course. The guards would surely take note of three Academy students passing just before nightfall, and word might have made its way back to the citadel.

Therefore they drew to a stop between two houses a stone's throw away from the wall, and there they waited for the moons to rise. The gatehouse, a massive structure wrought partly in iron, stood nearly seven paces high. But when the guards lowered the gate at last, Ebon saw that there was a man-sized door in it. That was where they would make their exit.

"I have only snuck out once," said Theren. "It was difficult, but this time the mists should make it easier. I will distract the guards. Kalem, cast your spell once they are away from the gate."

Kalem nodded mutely, his wide eyes shining in the moonslight. Ebon could see the fear in the boy's face, but for once he made no complaint.

Theren raised her hands, and a glow sprang into her eyes. Ebon could see two guards, one to either side of the gate. They clearly did not anticipate any trouble, for they both leaned against the wall in positions of easy rest.

Ebon did not see Theren move, but suddenly both guards pitched forwards as if pushed. They caught their feet and put hands to swords as they peered into the darkness.

"What was that?" said one.

"I do not know," said the other. She squinted down the street. "Who is there?"

Theren shoved them both again, this time away from the gate. Again they stumbled, and this time one of them fell to the street.

"It is some spell!" he said. The air rang as he drew his steel.

"Once more, and then it is your turn, Kalem," murmured Theren.

Her hands twisted, and the guards stepped still farther from the portcullis. Mist sprang to life and flooded the street, thick and soupy.

Theren gripped Ebon's arm and pulled him forwards, and he in turn dragged Kalem. The guards both shouted in the fog, but their voices were several paces away. Together the three friends reached the wall and edged along it until they found the portcullis.

The door had no lock, only a heavy latch that kept anyone outside from opening it. Ebon lifted the latch as quietly as he could and rushed through the door. Theren and Kalem came only a half-step after, and Theren closed the door behind them. They raced from the gate as fast as they could.

The stone road soon turned to old, weather-beaten wooden planks. Theren pulled Ebon and Kalem to the side, where great stacks of crates and barrels stood in rows. Once they had vanished among the cargo, Kalem let his mists fall away. They had reached the docks.

"A fine job," said Ebon.

"It will be harder to get in, but not by much," said Theren. "I can lift the latch from outside."

"Excellent," said Ebon. "Let us be quick, then."

He withdrew the map from his pocket. They spread it out where the moonlight fell down between the crates, studying it in the pale silver glow. The docks were drawn in some detail, and they could see where the ships had been etched. Both were to the south of where they stood now.

"Let us go south," said Ebon, "and see if we can find where these ships lay."

"Very well, but be careful," said Theren. "Look."

She leaned beyond the crate and pointed. Ebon and Kalem followed her outstretched finger. There in the moonslight they could see a figure, and Ebon barely made out the hardened red leather of the man's pauldrons. A constable.

"Likely there are more, but we can avoid them if we are careful," said Ebon. "Kalem, if they should spot us, you will have to hide us."

He made to lead them on, but Theren waved him back. "You are still tender from your injuries," she said. "Let me go first."

So saying, she set off among the cargo and down the dock. They had many stacks to hide behind, but between each one they had to make a harrowing run across open space. Every time they did it, Ebon was sure they would be caught. But Theren always timed their runs well, so that no constable was nearby. Before another hour had passed, they had moved far down the docks until they reached the first spot marked on the map.

"Here we are," said Ebon. "Now let us see what may be seen."

Together they leaned out to peer into the night. But Ebon's heart fell almost immediately. There were two docks before them, each large enough to hold a vast ship. But both lay empty.

"What does that mean?" said Kalem. "The ships are clearly drawn right here."

"I do not know," said Ebon.

"What of the other ship on the map?" said Kalem. "Will that dock be empty, too?"

"I do not know, Kalem!" hissed Ebon. "The only way to find out is to move on."

He caught Theren's eye in the moonslight. She was looking at him doubtfully, brow furrowed in worry.

"There will be something," he reassured her. "There must be."

"But what if it already happened?" she said. "Whatever was plotted, we may have missed it."

"Then we are wasting our time," he said. "But at least we tried. And we can think of something else."

She sighed and led them off down the docks once more.

Before they had even reached the second marking on the map, Ebon had a sinking feeling. No ships loomed out of the darkness above the stacks of cargo. When they arrived, it was the same as before: two spaces ready to hold grand ships, but now empty. There was nothing there. Their venture had failed.

"The same again," said Kalem. He frowned for a moment and then tilted his head at Ebon. "Mayhap that in itself is a sign? Why should these spots be empty? I mean these precise spots. Mayhap the signs on the map mean something other than what we thought."

"We saw many empty spots along the way," said

Theren. "I doubt it means anything sinister. Ebon, what say you?"

But Ebon was frozen. The spots marked on the map were empty, yes. But there was a ship just next to them. It was a small vessel, with only a single mast and space to carry mayhap a dozen passengers. But there were people milling on the dock beside it, and he recognized two of them.

"Ebon?" said Kalem.

Ebon waved him to silence. He leaned forwards, hands gripping the edge of a crate tightly.

Yes. It was them. Liya and Ruba, two of the servants from the Drayden family manor upon the seat. He had almost bowled them over as he ran for the dining hall, the morning after his first night with Adara. Now they carried satchels that looked very much like traveling sacks. They vanished beyond the edge of the ship.

"I need to get closer," he said. "I need to see those people just there."

"Why?" said Theren.

"Just get me closer."

She sighed and looked up and down the dock, but there were no constables close by. Quickly she stole across the planks, and now they were more exposed than they had been at any point along their route. Ebon followed quickly, and Kalem came just behind. Now they were only a few paces away from the figures boarding the ship.

"Be quick," said Theren. "We could be seen far too easily here."

Leaning out once more, Ebon saw that he had been right. Yes, Liya and Ruba were there. And now they stood among a crowd of others he recognized. There were the manor's cooks and cleaners, the gardeners and the stable boy. Ebon was so surprised at the sight that he nearly called out to ask what they were doing, and only stopped himself at the last moment.

"It is them," he whispered. "All the servants from our family manor. They are leaving."

"What?" said Theren. She stopped surveying the docks and looked at the people boarding the ship instead. "What do you mean, all of them?"

"Every one," said Ebon. "I do not recall a face from the manor that is not here before us now."

"But where is your family?" said Theren. "Surely they would not stay to manage the household themselves. Unless . . . have they run short on coin? Mayhap they could no longer pay these servants, and are sending them home."

Ebon snorted. "Not on your life. No, they are being sent away."

"To Dulmun?" said Kalem.

Ebon blinked at him. "What? No. They would be sent to Idris. Why would you say that?"

Kalem pointed to the front of the ship. A green pennant hung there, with the sigil of a white wave breaking across it. "That is a ship of Dulmun," he said. "It is of their king's own fleet."

"Mayhap they hired it," said Ebon.

"They could not," said Kalem. "The king's ships never work for hire. They sail only at his personal—"

"You there!"

The shout made them jump. They whirled to see a woman in red leather armor standing only a few paces away, hand on her sword hilt.

"What are you three doing?"

Ebon glanced over his shoulder. The manor servants had heard the constable, and were looking in his direction. If even one of them recognized Ebon, he and his friends were doomed.

"Run!" he whispered, and shoved the others forwards.

They tried to dodge past the constable and run back the way they had come. But the woman was too quick, and moved to blocked their path. They turned and ran the other direction.

"There are other piers running back to the shore!" cried Theren. "Make for one!"

But looking ahead of them, Ebon saw they were too late. Another constable had heard the commotion and was coming for them now. His sword lay bare in his hand, its steel glinting in the moonslight.

"The cargo!" said Kalem. He ran for the stacks of crates. Ebon and Theren followed a step behind. The constables shouted as they gave chase.

But as Kalem wove through the stacks of crates, Theren's eyes glowed, and she threw her hands wildly from side to side. Barrels swayed where they stood, and then came crashing down to block the pathways behind them.

The constables' angry cries faded as they reached the western edge of the docks. But there were still ten paces of black water between them and the shore.

"Theren, can you carry us across?"

"Are you mad? I can hardly lift you to the top of a wall."

"I may . . . I may have something, said Kalem, though his voice shook. "Theren, could you lower me to the water?"

"No time!" said Ebon. He threw himself to the edge of the dock, grunting at the flare of pain from his bruises. The tide was high, and the water was only a pace away. "Give me your ankles!"

Kalem crawled to the edge and over, with Ebon and Theren clinging to his legs. His robes fell down around his shoulders, so that his underclothes were exposed.

"Not one word, from either of you," he snapped.

"Be silent and hurry," said Theren. "They are getting close." And indeed, Ebon could hear the constables' voices carrying above the crates and barrels, moving around the stacks of cargo towards them.

Kalem reached out his hands until they touched the water. At once, a wave of ice spread from his fingertips. Out and out it spread, until a small platform of ice stretched out for many paces in all directions, securing itself in place by wrapping around the poles of the docks.

"All right!" he squealed. "Let me go!"

They did, and he came down on the ice on hands and knees. He crawled forwards, spreading the ice before him a pace at a time. Ebon and Theren scrambled to climb down from the dock behind him.

But just as Ebon had almost reached the ice, he heard a triumphant cry. Something snatched at the back of his robes. He barely twisted his neck enough to see the constable behind him, one gloved fist holding Ebon's robes. Her sword was held high, ready to strike.

"Let him go!" Theren's eyes glowed, and her hand cut through the air. The woman's head snapped back, and her grip fell away.

Ebon crashed onto the ice. He crawled as quick as he could, just behind Theren.

"Thank you," he told Theren, voice shaking.

"Better than my showing against the dean," she said with a faint smile.

They were halfway to the shore now. Again Ebon heard a cry behind him, but this time much farther away. He glanced back. The constable Theren had struck still lay senseless on the dock, but the other had arrived at last.

The man ran for the dock's edge and gave a mighty leap out onto the ice. But when he landed, it cracked beneath him, and he sank into the water with a yelp.

Ebon froze—but then he saw the man's head break the surface, and his limbs flailed wildly as he fought to remain afloat. At last he got hold of the ice, and there he clung, sputtering and trying to spit the seawater from his lungs.

Ebon and his friends reached the shore and climbed the steep slope leading up to the city's wall. They made their way north until they had reached the eastern gate again. But before they could reach it, Theren reached out and snatched Kalem's cloak to pull him to a stop.

"Wait. We should not go inside yet. There is still the marking to the southeast to investigate—the small boat drawn near the cave."

"You *cannot* mean to go there, too." Kalem's voice rose to a shout. "This is twice now we have nearly gotten ourselves killed, and twice too many. I will not do it again!"

"But we did *not* get ourselves killed," said Theren. "And now they will be searching the docks for us, while we will be on the Seat's southern edge. We will be safer than ever before."

"Nothing about this is safe!" said Kalem, stamping his foot. "If you wish to go running about on more misadventures, then please yourselves. I mean to return to the Academy, now, without any delay. And if you will not come with me to sneak in, then I will march straight back to the gate and knock upon it, and I will not care if they punish me."

Theren's eyes flashed, but Ebon put a hand on her

arm. "Leave it, Theren. I do not think I could last much longer in any case." The crawl across the ice had made his aches and pains worse, and he now found it difficult even to walk. "We can always return another night, when we have rested."

"Yes, and when Kalem has had time to find his courage again," muttered Theren.

Kalem folded his arms. "Call me a coward if you wish, but you know I am right. If there are guards posted where the small boat is drawn, they will be more vigilant now, not less. And Ebon looks as though he might collapse."

"I might, at that," said Ebon.

He smiled, trying to ease the tension, and reached out an arm for Theren. She slung it over her shoulder, and sighed.

"Very well," she said. "Only something in my heart tells me the danger grows greater, not less, the longer we take to discover whatever is going on."

"Be that as it may, we must take a little longer yet."

They walked north again at Ebon's nudge, making for the eastern gate.

TWENTY-SIX

BY THE TIME EBON SAT FOR THE MIDDAY MEAL WITH his friends, he had come to deeply regret their excursion. Now his bruises felt crippling, and his limbs hesitated before obeying his will. He sat hunched over his food, barely able to eat, while Theren and Kalem spoke animatedly about the map.

"Mayhap the blue markings to the west were the right ones, and the red were only a decoy," said Theren.

"But why?" said Kalem. "What purpose for the difference? Mayhap they are both clues, and we simply do not understand what the different colors mean?"

Theren sighed. "I think we will have little luck with guesses. We will only find more answers if we look for ourselves."

"You say that as if it is some simple thing," grumbled Kalem.

Ebon sat silent, staring at his food. His friends had not cared overmuch about the Drayden servants stealing away on the ship, but Ebon's mind had been heavy all morning. Halab had said she was here for family business. This must have been what she meant. The family was withdrawing from its property on the Seat. He could not imagine why.

And another thought grated at him; Halab had spent the whole day with him but had said nothing of this. Had she not imagined that he might come to the manor, visiting it after his study hours? How did she think he would feel, arriving to find it empty, or mayhap even sold to some new owner?

It felt as though his family had abandoned him in truth. That would not be such a terrible prospect coming from Father—or at least it would be no surprise. It was different with Halab.

A black-robed figure stopped beside the table. Ebon looked up to find Lilith looking down at him, smirking. Oren and Nella stood beside her, as always. Ebon barely managed to restrain a groan.

"Well met, jester," said Lilith. She looked to Kalem. "And jester's monkey."

Ebon noted that she utterly ignored Theren.

"What is it, Lilith? I have little patience for jibes today."

"I had heard you went and watched the High King's armies march forth. Did any of your kin march with them? Three wizards of Yerrin are in her ranks."

"I do not know," said Ebon. "If any of my family are soldiers, I have not heard of it."

"Of course you would not have," said Lilith. "Not all families are as proud of their members as Yerrin. Not all families have cause to be."

Ebon scowled, and was surprised at himself for doing it. No matter how little love he had for his family, Lilith somehow made him wish to defend them.

"And are your family taking you on holiday as well?" she went on.

He blinked. The question seemed to come from nowhere. "What? Holiday? No. Why?"

"Winter approaches. My parents are traveling to Feldemar to welcome it, and they are taking me with them. Mayhap the family Drayden is too poor to take such holidays? Or mayhap they *are* taking one, and have simply forgotten you."

Ebon's hand clenched to a fist on the table. Theren shifted on her bench. "Leave off, Lilith," she said.

Lilith's eyes flicked to Theren, but only for a moment. "Well, I must away to prepare for the voyage," she said. "Enjoy your time trapped here in the Academy, jester. When I return, I shall be sure to regale you with tales of my travels."

She sauntered off, out of the dining hall and into the Academy. Oren went with her, while Nella remained, finding a table in a corner by herself.

"That one is simply insufferable," muttered Kalem.

"Her boasting does grow tiresome," said Ebon. "Though in truth, with all we have seen and done in the past weeks, her torment somehow rankles less."

"At least she has given us one piece of the puzzle," said Kalem brightly. "I would wager that that is why your household staff were readying to leave. Your family must be taking a journey for winter, just as hers is."

Ebon was taken aback. "You think she was correct?"

"Why else would they have been loading themselves upon that ship?"

He realized that Theren had not spoken since Lilith left. Her sharp eyes roved across the dining hall, her short bob of hair swinging into her face as she looked back and forth.

"Theren?" said Ebon. "What is it?"

"There are no Yerrins in the dining hall. There were two missing from my class this morning, which I thought was curious." She stopped looking about and leaned forwards. "Are there other Draydens enrolled in the Academy just now? Are they still in their classes?"

Ebon shrugged. "Not so far as I know. It is only me. And the dean, of course."

Her eyes grew dark, and she looked away. Ebon knew she was thinking, as he was, of Cyrus' attack in the training grounds. They ate the rest of their lunch in silence.

Before sunrise the next morning, a hand slapped over Ebon's mouth, jarring him awake.

His eyes shot wide, and he struggled to rise from his dormitory bed. The barest grey glow drifted through the window, casting his assailant as a shadowy figure. Powerful arms dragged him from his bed, still wrapped in a blanket, and pulled him through the door in the back of the dormitory. His screams were muffled under the clutching hand, and no one heard him. He tried to fight, but his injuries kept his movements weak. The hand pinched his nose and mouth until he could hardly breathe.

Once they reached the hallway, he was pressed roughly against the stone wall. There in the torchlight, he at last caught sight of his attacker's face.

Mako.

Ebon froze where he stood.

"Good morrow, little goldbag." Mako's voice was a dagger sheathed in silk. "My apologies for awakening you so. An urgent matter presses, and I could not wait for you to come to the library."

Ebon only stared at him, eyes wide with fear. His heartbeat would not stop thundering in his ears, and it sounded like the march of a giant.

"If I remove my hand, will you promise not to

scream?" said Mako. "If you do, I cannot bring you the message I came to deliver, and that would be very bad for both of us."

Slowly, Ebon nodded. Mako peered into his eyes for a moment. He must have seen what he wanted, for at last he removed his hand.

"What do you want?" said Ebon. Fear and the last groggy remnants of sleep made his voice hoarse and raw.

"I might ask you the same, goldbag. You must want something—or else you would not have returned to the inn with your friends after I warned you not to. And you certainly would not have gone to the docks the night before last. That was foolish indeed."

Ebon's knees went weak. He would have fallen to the floor if Mako's strong arms were not still pressing him to the wall. All his misdeeds were known. Surely Mako would bring this to his father, and then Ebon would be sent home. Or worse, Mako might tell the dean. Then Cyrus might seek to finish what he had begun in the training grounds and leave Ebon's cooling corpse in some dark gutter.

Mako chuckled. It grated from his throat like a panther's growl. "Do not look so frightened. Whether you choose to believe it or not, I am actually somewhat fond of you. I warn you that I know these things not because I mean to tell our family, but so that you know you have been careless at a time when you should be more careful than ever."

"You speak in riddles," said Ebon, trying to sound brave. "Say what you have come to say, and then leave me be."

"Spoken like a true little lord. As, indeed, I hope you shall be one day. But that will never happen unless you heed these words: leave the High King's Seat at once."

Ebon balked. "What? Why?"

"You must trust me. I have learned things, things I should have known long since. Waste no time. Bring your friends with you, if you must. But make for the nearest boat you can find, or crawl upon the ice like you did at the docks. Only leave this island behind you, or face your death."

"Without knowing why? I am not your puppet, Mako."

"I could issue it as a command, if you wish."

Ebon remembered Halab's words. "And would that command come from my father, or from you?"

Mako only grinned. His teeth flashed red in the torchlight, as though they were drenched in blood. Ebon quailed, but forced himself to remain steady as he gave a grim smile.

"You say nothing because there is no strength behind your words. I may be forced to play into my father's schemes, but not yours."

"No strength, you say? I know what you have been up to in the dead of night, Ebon. I could reveal it all to your father, or even to dear Halab. What would you do if she withdrew her support? Do you really think you could remain at the Academy? Yet I have chosen to tell you first. Why would that be, unless I had some liking for you?"

"I can think of many reasons."

"Yet you do not voice them. Trust me in this. Leave the Seat."

Ebon only glared. Mako met his gaze for a moment, and Ebon thought he saw earnestness in the bodyguard's eyes. But then the man's lips twisted in a familiar smirk, predatory once again. He drew back and vanished around the corner. Ebon watched him go, shaking.

TWENTY-SEVEN

The day before, Ebon's injuries had kept him from dressing fast enough to eat in the morning. Now he rushed to don his robes despite the pain and hobbled down the stairs as fast as his legs would carry him. Because Mako had startled him awake so early, he arrived at the dining hall before all but the very first students. There he waited, pacing, until Kalem arrived at last.

"Kalem!" he said, gripping the boy by his robes. "We must find Theren. Something is happening."

"What do you mean?" said Kalem, eyes wide.

"I do not know exactly. But we must find her."

"We should wait outside her dormitory."

Ebon nodded, and they set off through the Academy. His pain spiked with every step, but Ebon forced himself to move on. They climbed the stairs to Theren's room and waited outside her door. Students emerged and gave them curious looks before brushing past. Finally Theren appeared, still rubbing sleep from her eyes.

"Theren, come quickly," said Ebon. "I must tell you and Kalem something."

Her brow furrowed. Ebon took her sleeve and dragged her down the hallway until they found a secluded corner where they would not be disturbed.

"An agent of my family came to me this morning. He warned me to leave the Seat at once."

"What? Why?" said Kalem.

"He would not say. But he said it was a warning."

Theren's face went Elf-white.

"I do not understand," said Kalem. "Does some danger await you within the walls? Mayhap he knows of some plot by the dean to attack again."

"He said I could bring you with me, if I wished," said Ebon. "Why would he say that, unless—"

"I know why," said Theren. "The Seat is going to be attacked."

Ebon and Kalem stared at her. The hallway fell to silence.

"What?" said Ebon at last.

"Think, Ebon. Lilith and the other Yerrins have

fled. I spent the rest of yesterday searching around. Many children of other wealthy families have fled as well. Mayhap they know what is coming, or mayhap they only heard some dark rumor of a coming storm. But they have taken their children and fled. Your manor staff have been removed. You thought it was by your aunt, but it could just as easily have been your father. Something is coming, something powerful enough to endanger every soul upon the Seat."

Ebon shook his head quickly. "No. That would be treason of the highest order. My father may have concocted some dark scheme, but that is a step too far, even for him."

"How else do you explain it?" said Theren. "Why else would they be fleeing this place like rats from a ship?"

"But my parents have not sent for me," said Kalem, frowning.

"Forgive me," said Theren. "But you have told us already that your family's star has fallen. And they are from Hedgemond, an outland kingdom. I doubt they would have heard any rumor of whatever doom is coming."

"Think, Theren," said Ebon. "If what you say is true, then I am part of it. I did my father's bidding, and if his scheme was to attack the Seat, then I played a role."

"You did not know what you were doing."

"I did *not* lend aid to an attack on the Seat," Ebon

snapped. He realized his voice had grown far too loud, and he went on in an urgent whisper. "Others may look upon my family with fear, but not even the rumors of our deeds are that black. Besides, if they were part of this plot, then why would my father leave me here?"

But before the words left his lips, he knew the answer. And Theren and Kalem looked at him with such sadness in their eyes that he felt tears welling up in his own.

"No!" he cried, no longer caring who might hear. He thought he might be sick. "No, you are wrong. My father lost one son already. He would not sacrifice the only other one he had."

Except that he cared, truly cared, when Momen died, he thought. *Do I think he would feel the same way about me?*

"It is the only thing that makes sense," Theren said quietly. "What better way to prove your father's innocence than the fact that his own son died in the attack? It is a perfect deception."

"If it were my family's plot, Mako would have not have found out at the last moment, as he told me. He would have known from the first." Ebon felt desperate now.

"Unless he lied," said Kalem. "Or unless it was kept from him, as well. The fewer who know the secret, the fewer to let it slip."

Ebon turned and leaned his head against the stone

wall. The earliest chills of winter had seeped into it, and it calmed him like a piece of ice held to a fevered forehead. He took a deep breath. Still he would not believe it. His father did not—*could* not hate him this much.

Ebon would not listen to the voice in the back of his mind, the voice that said *Yes, yes, Ebon. He could. Of course he could.*

"I will prove you wrong," he said. "The map is some smaller mischief, already played out."

Kalem looked at Theren uncomfortably and then back to him. "Ebon . . ."

"No. No more words. I will show you. We leave, now."

Ebon marched off down the hallway. He tried to tell himself that he did not care if they followed, but in truth his heart flooded with relief when he heard their footsteps behind him. Together they stormed down into the entry hall. Mellie sat in a chair by the front door, her head nodded to her chest in sleep. Ebon broke into a run and threw open the door, bursting out into the streets beyond. Kalem and Theren followed just behind him. They heard Mellie's squawk as the old woman was startled awake. But before she could react, or even call for help, the three of them had vanished into the streets.

"Well, now we have earned ourselves trouble indeed," groused Kalem.

"I do not care," said Ebon. "This ends now. I am tired of skulking about in search of answers."

His bruises were forgotten now, and he found it easier to walk than he had for days. Indeed, Kalem had to scamper along to keep up with him, and even Theren's long legs swung mightily to match his pace. Ebon eschewed stealth and took the main road east. After a time they were forced to walk around the High King's palace, and then only a short distance remained to the east gate.

Ebon had a moment's trepidation as he approached it. But the gates stood open, and travelers came in and out of it at their will, for it was not heavily guarded during the day. Still he threw up his hood, and Theren and Kalem followed suit as they emerged into the open air beyond. A wave of sea breeze struck them, salty and sweet and carrying the cries of gulls. A morning fog lay upon the Great Bay, a fog thick and tall enough to hide all sight of the horizon, but it ended half a league from the dock's edge. An itch sprang to life on the back of Ebon's neck, but he dismissed it as impatience.

"We will search the southeastern marking on the map first to see if the boat and cave mean anything," said Ebon. "If I am right, I wager we will find an empty cave, its boat long gone. Just as the ships on the dock were gone."

But glancing back over his shoulder, he realized Kalem had stopped short. The boy stood just outside the gate and off to the side, his eyes fixed on the Great Bay. As Ebon looked closer, he noticed Kalem's hands were shaking. Theren, too, had seen him freeze.

"Kalem?" she said. "What is it?"

"The . . . the fog," said Kalem. His voice quaked. "Ebon, can you not feel it?"

Ebon glanced at the fog, confused. "I see nothing."

"Do not look," said Kalem. "Feel."

Ebon closed his eyes and focused. Then he felt it—the tingling on the back of his neck. It was no trick of his mind, but the same sensation as when Kalem spun mists close by.

"Sky above," he whispered.

"What?" snapped Theren. "What is it?"

"That is no morning mist," said Kalem. "It is the work of alchemists—a host of them."

Horns blew on the wall, startling them. And then as they watched, hearts sinking with horror, a host of ships sailed from the mist, drums pounding with war.

TWENTY-EIGHT

EBON WAS FROZEN. THE SIGHT OF THE FLEET SAPPED his courage and his will, so that he felt like one of the training dummies in the gardens—mute, lifeless, unable to move. And above them the horns continued to blare, now joined by bells and the shouts of guards as they saw the ships coming at last.

"What should we do?" said Kalem. "What is this?"

"An invasion," said Theren. "And look at the pennants. Those are Dulmun ships."

"But what do we do?" said Kalem again.

"We must go," said Ebon. "Now!"

His shout finally put life back in their limbs, and they burst into a run. But Ebon and Theren went in opposite directions and crashed into each other.

"Where are you going?" said Ebon.

"Where are *you* going?" said Theren. "That map showed a boat on the southeastern end of the island. It must be for escape. We can use it."

"She is right," said Kalem. "If it is still there, which it may not be. But what other choice do we have?"

But Ebon placed a hand on each of their shoulders to still them. His hands shook, but he forced himself to stand as strong as he could. "I cannot come with you."

"What?" said Theren. "Why not?"

Ebon thought of the Academy, of its thick granite walls and the three floors of its library. He saw Jia and even cowardly Credell. And he thought of Astrea's tiny face, her wild hair that stood out around her head like some hat from one of the outland kingdoms. "The Academy. If indeed my family had some part in this, then I had a hand in it as well. I must go and try to save whoever I can."

"But they are on the west end of the island. They will have plenty of time to escape, for they can run to the western . . ." Kalem's voice trailed off, and his wide eyes grew even wider. "Oh, no."

"Another attack?" said Theren, coming to the same thought. "From the west?"

"Coming from Selvan," said Ebon, nodding. Terror made his voice shake, and tears leaked from his eyes. "The attack will come from both east and west. The Academy will try to get the students out, and they will march straight into the enemy's waiting blades."

Theren stamped her foot and looked away. "You are right. Darkness take us."

"I . . . I will come with you," said Kalem, squaring his shoulders and trying to stand taller.

"The two of you could make for the boats," said Ebon. "I only go to deliver a message. One can do that as easily as three, and this attack is my fault, not yours."

"I went with you to the Shining Door," said Theren.

"And I . . . well, I would not go off on my own, letting you walk into peril," said Kalem.

Ebon swallowed hard against a sudden lump in his throat. "Thank you. But we have tarried too long. Hurry!"

They ran for the gate. Even as they passed through it, it had begun to lower. Just before it closed, Ebon took one last look behind him. Through the portcullis, he saw that the ships were drawing close. Upon their decks were arranged row after row of warriors, all wearing the green and white of Dulmun. Then the iron gates outside swung shut, blocking the portcullis and the ships both.

Not everyone outside had made it into the city before the gates shut. Ebon and his friends fled from the wails that came over the wall.

Ebon ran as fast as he could, and Theren and Kalem lent their hands in support when he needed it. The main road across the island had turned to chaos, with nobles and merchants alike looking about them in terror, unsure of what threat lay beyond the walls. They all seemed half ready to flee, yet they held fast, as though they waited for something to save them.

"Dulmun attacks!" cried Ebon. "Defend the walls or flee to your homes! The Seat is under attack!"

The others took up the cry, and it spread through the streets. Almost immediately he regretted opening his mouth, for the already-thick crowd became a congealed mass of bodies, heaving back and forth as everyone tried to go in all directions at once.

"Come! This way!" Theren led them off the street into the alleys. There they found the way was clearer, and they made good time. Before long they passed the High King's palace on the right, and before much longer the Academy loomed tall and dark before them.

They turned towards the main road again, where lay the front door. Just before they reached it, they heard a great *THOOM* from the west. The sound and force of it stopped them in their tracks. Ebon tried to see the source through the crowd, but the bodies pressed too thick.

"Up!" said Theren. A wagon full of hay sat nearby, and together they climbed atop it. From on high they saw that the western gate lay in ruins, and the portcullis had been raised. Troops wearing blue and grey poured through the gap, slaughtering all in their path. A chill ran down Ebon's spine as he recognized their blue-and-grey clothing—the same colors as the man at the Shining Door to whom he had delivered the parcel.

"Those are no soldiers of Selvan," said Kalem.

"Come," said Ebon. "Into the Academy."

They ran across the street and threw open the door.

The entry hall was full of people, students milling about in confusion while instructors tried to maintain order. More students were filing in from every hallway and down the main stairs. Ebon spied Jia in the press. She stood in the center, directing the other instructors to gather their students and make ready to leave. Ebon ran to her.

"Instructor," he said. "You have received word already?"

"Ebon, rejoin your class," she said briskly. "Obey your instructor's orders. No need to worry, we are leaving by the western docks."

"The docks are taken," he said. "An army has just broken the gates. Even now they are on the streets."

Jia's face became grave, and she looked away. "That is ill news. Curse the dean for his cowardice." Her eyes sharpened as they met Ebon's. "Forget I said that. Those words were spoken in anger."

"What did the dean do?" said Theren.

Jia gave her a wary look. Ebon spoke up instead, trying to feign concern. "Please, Instructor. He is my cousin."

"He is nowhere to be found," said Jia. "I sent for him as soon as I heard, but he does not appear to be anywhere within the Academy. Mayhap he is at the palace on business. It is no matter. There are other ways off the island. Instructors! We make for the south wall! Now, proceed through the front door, as quickly and orderly as you can!"

The students pushed past them in a rush, barely restrained by their instructor's barked commands. Kalem stepped close to Ebon. "Do you think the dean received word of the attack?"

"I doubt it," said Ebon. "From what he said when he attacked me, my family has removed him from their counsel. Most likely he heard the same warning as the rest of the Academy and put the pieces together, just as we did. But never mind him. We must help in the escape."

In a great mass the Academy students flooded the streets, turning east and then south, making their way to the walls. Ebon looked all around and at last spotted instructor Credell. The man shivered with every step he took, and his wide eyes swept about like a sow being led to slaughter. Yet he kept his students about him and ushered them along with the others. Ebon found himself admiring the man for not having fled already.

"Ebon!" Astrea's small, piping voice cut through the din, and she threw herself through the crowd to clutch at Ebon's legs. "Ebon, what is happening? Why are we leaving?"

Ebon scooped her up, though the pain of his bruises nearly made him cry out, and held her on his hip as he kept walking with the crowd. "It is nothing to fear, Astrea. Some soldiers have come to attack the island, but our instructors will keep us safe."

He only wished he believed that himself.

"Where do they mean to take us?" said Theren. "There is no gate in the southern wall. There are towers and places to climb down, but I think that would take too long."

"Jia must have some plan," said Ebon. "We have to trust her."

By the time they reached the south wall, the sounds of fighting pressed close on all sides. Ebon could hear the clash of steel to both sides and behind them as well. But he had not yet seen any of the combatants. The procession stopped at the wall, all the students clumping together in a mass.

Jia barked commands. Some instructors separated from the crowd and went to the wall. Ebon saw Credell join them. Then he realized that all the instructors were alchemists, and some of the older alchemy students had joined them.

"They mean to—" Kalem began.

"I see it," said Ebon. "You should help them."

Kalem looked uncertain for a moment, but Ebon gave him an encouraging nod. The boy scampered away to join the others at the wall.

As one, the alchemists stepped forward and placed

their hands to the stone. Their eyes glowed, and the light of it joined together until it seemed a hundred torches shone upon the wall. Slowly at first, and then faster and faster, the stone beneath their hands began to shift. It spread out and away, above the alchemists and to either side.

In a few moments it was done, and a wide door had appeared in the wall, as neat and as smooth as if it had been carved there in the first place. The alchemists stepped back, the glow fading from their eyes.

"Instructors!" said Jia briskly. "Bring your students through the wall and lead them west. At the docks we will capture ships to bring us across the water."

"Instructor," said Ebon quickly. "What about the rest of the island?"

He saw her eyes waver for a moment, but the thin line of her lips remained firm. "Our duty is to the students. We must see them to safety or lose the next generation of wizards in one fell swoop."

Ebon's throat went dry, but he nodded.

Then someone gave a great shout, and they all turned to look. From the streets to the west poured men in grey and blue uniforms, steel swords bared and glinting in the sunlight. With a battle-cry they fell upon the students trying to flee through the wall.

The instructors leaped forwards to defend their charges. The attackers were driven back in a hail of flame and thunder and invisible blows that sent them crashing to the ground. But they were many, and they pressed forwards with fervor, until soon they had almost reached the mass of black robes.

Then Ebon saw weremages in battle for the first time. Jia's skin rippled as muscles formed beneath it, and hair sprouted all over her body. Her grey robes melted into her skin. In a moment a bear stood where Jia had been—but a bear larger and more fierce than Ebon had ever seen, almost twice as tall as he was, and its claws were long and glinted like steel.

With a heart-stopping roar Jia launched herself into the fray, ripping into the soldiers like an axe through kindling. They cried out in terror as they fell before her. All around, other weremages joined in the attack, until soon blood ran freely on the street.

But they were still few, and some of the blue-clad soldiers edged around them, seeking the students. One came straight for Ebon, and he backed up quickly.

Theren stepped forwards, and an invisible blow hammered the woman into the ground. Her sword went skittering across the pavement, and Ebon picked it up with shaking fingers. He had learned some sword fighting at home, but had never used such a heavy blade.

Another soldier charged, heading straight for Credell's class. The children recoiled and screamed as Credell tried to place himself in front of them.

Ebon struck wildly, giving the soldier pause as he avoided the blow. But the man took only a moment to recover. He swung with practiced ease to bat Ebon's blade out of the way. An overhead strike came quickly, too quickly for Ebon to block it—but then Credell was there, his hand raised to catch the weapon. Ebon cried out a warning—but the moment the blade touched Credell's fingers, it turned to water, and splashed harmlessly across them both.

The soldier stood dumbfounded for a moment, until Credell leaped forwards and seized his throat. Iron rippled out around his fingers, transforming both cloth and flesh until the man's whole neck had been turned to metal. He fell to the ground, unable even to gasp, eyes bulging from their sockets as he fought desperately for life. Credell stepped back, staring at his own hand in horror, shoulders quivering.

"The children," said Ebon. Credell did not hear. Ebon shook him. "The children! Get them through the wall!"

Credell shrank from the words and the sight of Ebon's face, but at last he nodded. He turned and ushered the children onwards with quiet words. Ebon turned back, seeking Theren and Kalem.

Before he found them, he saw Nella. The girl stood near the edge of the crowd of students, her eyes flying wildly about in fear. A soldier in blue leaped forwards through a gap in the teachers, trying to attack the students. Nella screamed and tried to reach for her magic. Her eyes glowed, and flames sprang from her fingers. But they guttered out almost at once as she lost her concentration.

The soldier pressed forwards, sword jabbing for

her gut. Nella tried to step back, but tripped upon her own feet and fell.

Ebon sprang and swung. His sword struck the soldier on his breastplate, and the man stumbled back. Ebon held the sword forwards like a spear, while with his other hand he reached down to drag Nella to her feet. But he had only a moment before the soldier recovered. Ebon barely managed to parry a blow.

Nella found her strength, and this time lightning arced forth. It seized upon the soldier's metal armor and set his limbs to spasms. He collapsed in the street, shrieking, while Ebon and Nella backed away and into the crowd.

Ebon turned to her, and she met his eyes. He saw fear in her gaze—but also confusion, as though she could not understand why he was there.

"Are you all right?" he said.

She nodded. "Th-thank you."

Ebon dropped his gaze and turned away, seeking Theren and Kalem once more.

At last he found them at the rear of the procession, helping to guard the other students from attack. At least Theren was fighting—Kalem stood behind her, eyes glowing, but he could not find a place to strike. Ebon knew the boy's magic was still young, far weaker than Credell's. He could not use it without placing himself in striking distance.

Theren suffered no such restrictions. No soldier could come close. She battered them back with unseen force.

The glow in her eyes was like an inferno, and her hands were twisted to claws as she lashed out again and again. But then the instructor beside her took an arrow to the throat and fell to the street. Theren's eyes returned to normal for just a moment as she looked down in horror.

"I am here," said Ebon, stepping in beside her to fill the gap. "Keep your eyes to the fore. He is beyond your help."

Her eyes glowed as she touched her magic again, but her voice shook when she answered. "What do you hope to do with that little pigsticker, goldbag?"

Ebon had to laugh. "Not much. But mayhap I can take a blade instead of you."

"See that you do." She struck at another soldier, knocking him away.

Their foes were finally forced to retreat under the onslaught, ducking behind the edges of buildings and hiding from sight. Many of their corpses lay littered about the street. But Ebon also saw bodies in black robes, and more in the dark grey of instructors. He was relieved to see that Jia was not among them—she had retaken human form and was once more directing the withdrawal.

Now the last few students were passing through the doorway that had been carved in the wall. A few more instructors held back, hands held up warily and eyes glowing in readiness for another attack. Ebon's eyes roved, searching for danger.

But then, between several buildings and at a great distance, he saw a flash of dark grey.

An instructor?

He took a cautious step forwards, squinting. The figure passed into view again.

Not quite an instructor—the dean. He was fleeing south and east, away from the fighting, and away from the rest of the Academy. But it was not the sight of Cyrus that stopped Ebon's heart. It was the girl at his side: a girl in fine blue robes and soft shoes. A veil covered the bottom half of her face, but he knew her at once.

Adara.

"Ebon, watch out!"

In his distraction he had stepped into the open. Two soldiers in blue sprang from behind a shop. They came for him, while a third fired an arrow from behind them.

Ebon flinched as it struck him—only, it did not strike him at all. It froze in midair mere fingers away, and then Theren was there by his side.

Before he could so much as raise his heavy sword, she battered one of the soldiers aside. But the other struck too quickly, and his sword tore into her arm. Theren cried out and fell to the ground.

With a scream, Kalem leaped forth. He seized the man's breastplate, and it turned to stone. The man swayed back, off balance. Theren fought to her knees and punched the empty air. As though she had struck the man himself, he flew up and off his feet, crashing into the archer. They landed and lay still.

"Theren!" cried Ebon, falling to his knees beside her. "I am sorry. Are you all right?"

"It is only a scratch," she said. But she grit her teeth hard, and her face had gone pale.

"Come, let us get you to safety," said Kalem, helping her the rest of the way to her feet. Ebon lent her a hand—but his eyes had turned to the east again.

He could no longer see the dean, but he had seen which way they were going.

He looked back. The last students were gone, and the instructors after them. Kalem was helping Theren through the wall, and Jia was there, the last to leave.

She looked past them for a moment and saw Ebon. Their eyes met. Her brow furrowed, and she opened her mouth to call to him.

Ebon whirled and vanished into the streets, chasing after the dean.

TWENTY-NINE

THERE WAS NO FIGHTING IN THIS PART OF THE CITY, and so Ebon was able to move quickly. Before long he spotted Cyrus again. The dean walked fast, but was not quite running. Adara walked freely by his side. Every once in a while Cyrus would take her arm, but to steady her, not to drag her along. Ebon guessed that he had already threatened her to get her to come with him.

He still carried his blade, but he did not know what to do with it. He was not willing to kill the dean, even if he doubted Cyrus would show him the same courtesy. But Ebon had to know where he was taking Adara, and for what purpose. Did he mean to flee the Seat? Or did he have some deadlier goal in mind? Ebon only knew that he could not abandon Adara to Cyrus' company, for the dean had shown himself to be half a madman already.

Before long Cyrus reached the wall, and now he moved along it as though searching for something. They passed some towers with doors leading in, but Cyrus passed them by. Ebon doubted the dean would enjoy the idea of climbing down with a rope. *He probably thinks it beneath him,* Ebon thought bitterly.

At last Cyrus reached a tower and went inside. Adara followed close behind. Ebon thought it looked just like the other towers, and so for a moment he waited and watched. But when neither of them reemerged, he stole forwards to the door.

It opened easily, and he poked his head inside. There was only a nondescript guardroom—yet in the floor a wooden hatch lay open. Stairs led down into the darkness, and no torches lit the way.

Ebon gulped. But Cyrus and Adara must have gone into the hatch; there was nowhere else to go. He crept to the edge of the hole. He could see to the bottom of the stairs, where a stone corridor ran away beneath the ground.

There was nothing for it. He took one step down, and then another. His sword shook in his hand. When he reached the bottom, he had to put a hand on the

the wall to guide himself. But fortunately the passage ran straight and true, and he was able to edge his way along without much trouble.

Suddenly there was a terrible, shuddering groan, and Ebon ducked back. But then he saw a light far, far ahead—the bright blue light of day. He had to squint against it for a moment. Two figures appeared in silhouette and then vanished, leaving the door open behind them.

Ebon moved faster now that the way was lit. Soon he saw that the passageway ended in a door leading outside. There was a small platform, and steps heading up to the left. But beyond the platform was only empty space, and he could hear the roar of waves.

When he reached the end, he could see why: he had emerged into the cliffs on the south of the Seat. Along the island's southern coast, sheer rock faces provided no easy way to climb down and reach the water. The stairs to his left lead back up the wall to the top of the cliffs high above. Cyrus was nowhere to be seen.

Ebon climbed the stairway. There was no handrail to steady him, and so he leaned against the cliff wall. Once he reached the top, he spotted them again: Cyrus in his dark grey robes trimmed with gold, and Adara in blue. He began to run, for they had built quite a lead. They made for a break in the cliffs far ahead, which opened like a rent cut by some great axe.

He began to close the gap, but not quickly enough, for they reached the lip long before him. But just as they reached it, Adara happened to glance back over her shoulder. She froze in shock, her mouth falling open in a perfect circle.

"Ebon!" she cried.

He stopped short, now ten paces away. The dean turned in surprise. When he saw Ebon, he gave a small smile. But then Adara broke away from him and ran for Ebon, and Cyrus' lips twisted in a scowl. He reached forth a hand, eyes glowing, and unseen bonds snatched Adara where she stood. She turned her head back to him with a frown.

"What is the meaning of this? Release me at once."

Cyrus shrugged and obeyed her. But she did not run for Ebon again, and the dean looked at him with a sneer.

"Why have you followed me, boy? Should you not be with the rest of your sheep?"

"What are you doing with Adara?" said Ebon. He tried to keep his voice steady, as well as the sword in his hand. "Leave her be."

"Leave her . . .?" Cyrus threw back his head and laughed. "You foolish boy. She is coming with me, away from this place. I have hired her."

Ebon could not put meaning to the words for a moment. When he finally looked at Adara, he saw she wore a sad smile. "Is this true?"

"I am a lover, Ebon," she said. "I told you once not to dwell on the others I spend my time with."

"But with *him?*" cried Ebon. "You do not know what a monster he is."

He took a few cautious steps forwards. Now he and Cyrus were only a few paces away from each other, and Adara to the side between them both.

Cyrus waved a hand. "Save your whimpering. I know now that I struck at you in error. Our family has abandoned you here to your death, as they have done with me. But you should count yourself fortunate to have found me. I will let you come along if you wish, for I could use a servant as I travel."

"Servant? For you?" Ebon's hands shook, not with fear now, but with rage. "Do you think I would lift so much as a finger to help you? You nearly killed me."

Adara turned to Cyrus, fixing him with a steely gaze.

"I thought you were in league with our clan," Cyrus snapped. "But they have outwitted us both, and used us as pawns. Now we have only one chance: to flee to the outland kingdoms where no one will find us. I have paid for Adara's entertainment, but I can take you as well. You will need my protection."

"I need *nothing* from you!" cried Ebon, taking another step forwards. He still held his sword, and was almost angry enough to use it. "I would not accept any gift from you, no matter how freely given. I would take my chances against all the wildlands between Idris and Calentin before I took one step by your side."

Cyrus sneered. "How dramatic. Very well. Come, Adara. We will leave this simpleminded fool to his own devices."

"No," said Adara. She folded her arms. "I will not go with you."

Something evil flashed in the dean's eye. "What?"

"You heard my words. If you attacked him, then you and I are no friends. You will go on your way without my companionship."

"Friends?" Cyrus jeered. *"Friends?* You are a lover. I have paid you already. Now come. Your guild's rules are very strict, after all."

"Take your coin and be damned, you bleating steer." From her dress Adara pulled a handful of coins and flung them at his feet. "The King's harshest law is strict as well, and very clear. I will not take one step by your side more than I wish to."

Slowly Cyrus' face twisted into a mask of fury. A glow crept into his eyes. "You are mine until I say otherwise," he hissed. A hand leaped forwards, shaped like a claw, and Adara cried out as she was hoisted in the air. "Always you whine about your wish to see me cast some spell. Well, here is your spell, woman. Do you like it?"

"Stop it!" Ebon raised his sword and attacked. But the dean stretched out the other hand and caught him, too, with magic. Though only a pace away, Ebon was frozen still, unable to move a muscle.

"What do you hope to do with that, boy?" said the dean, chuckling. "Your gift is an utter waste. Look at how you squander it, batting at me with steel. You have not even begun to glimpse the power of magic, and you never will. Your father was right to hold you from the Academy."

While still holding Adara suspended, he pushed with his power, and Ebon was thrown upon his back. The sword flew from his hand across the dirt. Then Ebon flew upwards again and came crashing down on his face. The pain of the last beating redoubled, and he cried out.

"Whimper and whine, little pup. You refuse my hospitality? Very well. I will not bother to kill you, for you will die here regardless. And what would the family think if I slaughtered one of our own?" Then he gave a cruel smile. "Although mayhap your father would reward me if I rid him of his worthless son."

The dean loomed over him now. The glow in his eyes brightened, until Ebon could not look into it for fear of being blinded. The force holding him against the ground increased, pressing him down, down into the dirt, crushing the breath from his body. He fought for even a death gasp.

His head twisted as it was shoved into the ground, until his eyes fixed on Adara. There she hung, watching him die, weeping in fear. No, not fear, he saw, for her eyes never left his. She wept in grief. Grief for him.

Something rose within him, like the whisper of a familiar voice he could not place. The world grew brighter, though he knew not why. Was this what it was like to die? A bright light seeping into the world, banishing the shadows and turning the sky to a blinding fire?

No, came the whispering voice. *It is your magic. Your eyes are glowing.*

Ebon looked at his hand. It twisted where it was crushed against the dirt. He could feel the power emanating from it, the strength of his will turned to wizardry.

With a cry he reached out despite the crushing force. His fingers clutched at Cyrus' ankles.

Ebon felt the cloth beneath his fingers, and the flesh beneath the cloth. Through his fingers he *saw* them—saw them as they appeared, and then saw them as they truly were, all the fibers and tissues and specks of dirt. Their essence was laid bare before him, awaiting his command.

Change it.

His eyes flashed brighter, and Cyrus' feet turned to stone.

The force pressing Ebon into the dirt ceased. He looked up. Cyrus' face was frozen in a mask of horror. Then he screamed, a horrible, screeching wail that cut through the air and turned Ebon's stomach. Frantically the dean tried to take a step backwards, but now his feet were weights he could not hope to move. He wavered.

Ebon heard quick footsteps running towards them. Adara came from nowhere, and with both hands she shoved Cyrus in the chest.

The dean tumbled backwards, struck the edge of the cliff, and slid off it.

Ebon scrambled forwards to look over the edge. Cyrus plunged, still screeching, into the water of the Great Bay. He vanished into the waves.

A long moment passed while they sat there, looking at the spot where Cyrus had vanished. The water churned, with not so much as a ripple to mark his passing.

Then, Adara reached down and took Ebon's arm. She helped him up, clutching him tighter as he nearly fell back to his knees.

"Are you all right?" she said quietly.

"I am hurt," he said. "He attacked me once already. This time it was worse."

"I will help you walk," she said. "But first, this."

She seized his face and pulled him in for a deep kiss. Ebon melted into her, and it was as though a great weight rose from his shoulders. When she was done she pulled back, leaning her forehead against his, and he joined her in closing his eyes.

"I am sorry," she said. "I did not know."

"You could not have," he said. "But come. We must flee. The Seat is lost."

She helped him hobble to the edge. There he saw a staircase leading down, and far below a cove was waiting. In the wall of the cliffs was a cave, wide and dark, and a crude wooden dock had been built into its edge. Tied to the dock were three small rowboats.

"The final mark on the map," said Ebon.

"Hm?"

"Nothing."

With Adara's help he lay in the bottom of one of the boats. Then she cast off the dock tie and began to row, and slowly they pulled away from the island.

"South and west," he said. "We must make for the coast of Selvan, but not where the invaders might catch us."

She nodded. "Who are they? What do they want?"

"I do not know," he murmured. "I only wish I had discovered them sooner."

Her eyes grew distant, looking past him and above him to the island they had left behind. "I doubt you could have prevented it," she said quietly.

Though it was a great effort, Ebon lifted his head. Behind them the Seat was burning, burning with the fury of the sun, and black smoke drifted towards them on the wind. Tears spilled freely down his cheeks, and neither of them dared to speak as they left the flames behind them.

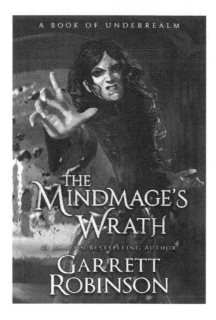

CONNECT ONLINE

FACEBOOK

Want to hang out with other fans of the Underrealm books? There's a Facebook group where you can do just that. Join the Nine Lands group on Facebook and share your favorite moments and fan theories from the books. I also post regular behind-the-scenes content, including information about the world you can't find anywhere else. Visit the link to be taken to the Facebook group:

Underrealm.net/nine-lands

YOUTUBE

Catch up with me daily (when I'm not directing a film or having a baby). You can watch my daily YouTube channel where I talk about art, science, life, my books, and the world.
But not cats.
Never cats.

GarrettBRobinson.com/yt

THE BOOKS OF UNDERREALM

THE NIGHTBLADE EPIC
NIGHTBLADE
MYSTIC
DARKFIRE
SHADEBORN
WEREMAGE
YERRIN

THE ACADEMY JOURNALS
THE ALCHEMIST'S TOUCH
THE MINDMAGE'S WRATH
THE FIREMAGE'S VENGEANCE

CHRONOLOGICAL ORDER
NIGHTBLADE
MYSTIC
DARKFIRE
SHADEBORN
THE ALCHEMIST'S TOUCH
THE MINDMAGE'S WRATH
WEREMAGE
THE FIREMAGE'S VENGEANCE
YERRIN

ABOUT THE AUTHOR

Garrett Robinson was born and raised in Los Angeles. The son of an author/painter father and a violinist/singer mother, no one was surprised when he grew up to be an artist.

After blooding himself in the independent film industry, he self-published his first book in 2012 and swiftly followed it with a stream of others, publishing more than two million words by 2014. Within months he topped numerous Amazon bestseller lists. Now he spends his time writing books and directing films.

A passionate fantasy author, his most popular books are the novels of Underrealm, including The Nightblade Epic and The Academy Journals series.

However, he has delved into many other genres. Some works are for adult audiences only, such as *Non Zombie* and *Hit Girls,* but he has also published popular books for younger readers, including The Realm Keepers series and *The Ninjabread Man*, co-authored with Z.C. Bolger.

Garrett lives in Oregon with his wife Meghan, his children Dawn, Luke, and Desmond, and his dog Chewbacca.

Garrett can be found on:

BLOG: garrettbrobinson.com/blog
EMAIL: garrett@garrettbrobinson.com
TWITTER: twitter.com/garrettauthor
FACEBOOK: facebook.com/garrettbrobinson

EPILOGUE

THE BUILDINGS THAT LINED THE STREETS WERE BLACK-
ened and ruined, for the fires had run amok across the
whole of the Seat. Ebon did not guess that more than
one building in four could be salvaged. The rest would
have to be torn down and rebuilt.

Only two structures on the Seat had withstood
the sacking: the High King's palace, bloodstained
but unbroken; and the Academy, whose thick granite
walls even the fury of the attackers could not cast
down.

The invading armies had left before the sun set on

the day of their attack. The fleet of Dulmun sailed east, returning to their kingdom. The blue-and-grey clad soldiers, who some were now calling Shades, vanished into the forests of Selvan. Rumors about the reason for their retreat abounded, and Ebon wondered if anyone would ever learn the truth.

A voice inside told him that someone already *did* know the truth, and that they were of the family Drayden.

For a week, the students and instructors of the Academy had stayed in Selvan, under the hospitality of that land's king. But when the attackers did not return, and the High King's armies marched hastily back from the war in Wellmont, they had prepared themselves to return home.

Now they stood before the Academy. Ebon stood amid the other students, and in a ring about them were the instructors. Every eye was turned skywards, where the peaks of the citadel loomed above them like an angry father—or, mayhap, like a tired old aunt, welcoming her nephews and nieces into her home, though she was weary to the point of death.

"It has not been touched," said Kalem, voice hushed in awe.

"Good," said Theren fervently. Her arm was still in a sling from her wound, though she swore every day she was going to throw the thing in a rubbish heap.

Jia stepped forth and threw open the front door. Slowly, and without a word, they all filed in.

"You!" shrieked a voice, the moment Ebon stepped inside.

He looked over in surprise. There was Mellie, sitting in her old chair by the front door as though she had never left. "You left without permission! You and your friends!"

Ebon could do nothing but smile. Jia arched an eyebrow. "Mellie, do you mean to tell me you stayed?"

The little old woman blinked up at her through watery eyes. "What is that supposed to mean? Where else would I go?"

Jia only shook her head and led them inside.

Once they had assembled in the entry hall and the doors had closed again, Ebon felt a curious peace settle over them all. Within the citadel, they could not see the destruction that had swept the Seat. The hall was unchanged, and he suspected that the dormitories and the classrooms would be the same.

"Students," said Jia. "Students, assemble. Together, please. *Quiet!*"

Her final bark threw them all to silence, and every eye turned to her.

"Now," she went on. "A terrible tragedy has befallen the High King's Seat. Thank the sky, the Academy suffered less loss than we might have. But all of Underrealm is reeling from this attack, and I will not bandy words with you: these are uncertain times. Many of you will likely be called home by your families. Try not to blame them if they do so. They seek only to ensure your safety."

Ebon felt eyes upon him. He looked to his right, and through the crowd he saw Lilith staring at him. The moment he met her gaze, she ducked her head as if ashamed, but then quickly looked back at him defiantly. He turned away.

"Now, Dean Cyrus of the family Drayden has been missing since the attack. It is presumed he fell in the fighting. We will respect and honor his noble memory."

Kalem snickered. Theren elbowed him hard. But Ebon flushed deep crimson. He had not told his friends what happened to Cyrus. Only Adara knew the truth. He wondered if that would always be the case.

"With the Academy resuming its normal operations, a new dean is required. And it is now my duty to present him to you. He is an accomplished wizard, who I am certain some of you will already have heard about. Please show him your utmost respect."

She stepped down from the stairway. A man went to take her place. He was thin and gaunt, and his black hair hung limp and stringy about his face, almost reaching his shoulders. He had a grim look, with thin lips pressed tight together and dark eyes that held neither humor nor warmth. And yet Ebon thought he felt something noble in the man, something in his bearing that commanded respect and attention, like a general returned home after a lifetime campaigning—though this man looked to be hardly older than Ebon's father.

"Well met," he said, his thick, rich voice rolling

forth to echo around the entry hall. "I am Xain, of the family Forredar, and I pledge myself to your learning, and your safety, for as long as duty may require of me."

Made in the USA
Columbia, SC
21 August 2018